THE NEAREST EXIT
MAY BE
BEHIND YOU

THE NEAREST EXIT
MAY BE
BEHIND YOU

AMULYA MALLADI

Published by And Then She Said Press

Cover Design by Carolyn King

Cover Image by Jelena Zivkovic/iStock

For Gabby, Søren and Soumitra, thank you for everything you do to help women play big in their lives and careers.

Acknowledgments

In my day job, as a marketing and communication professional, I meet many women who struggle to believe in themselves, find their voice, fight for a seat at the table, be authentic and have the confidence to play big. This novel is telling some of their stories.

I thank all the amazing women in my life who work hard every day to make the world a better place for women: Annie Ricci, Aparna Malladi, Diane Kerek, Fatima Aller, Francesca Boschet, Gabriella Gagliani Virchow, Jeanne Fredriksen, Kayla Hill, Maite Brehmer, Martha Davis, Monica Rassai, Rayhané Sanders, Romelia Persaud, Stephanie Nicol, Suvarchala Yendru, Valerie Soulier and Vennus Zand.

I also thank the men in my life, the feminists who speak up because they understand that the fight is real, important and as much theirs as it's ours: Hanumantha Rao Malladi, Isaiah Malladi Rasmussen, Matthew Winkler, Murray Masterson, Oliver Brunchmann, Rodolphe Boschet, Soren Rasmussen, Soumitra Burman and Tobias Malladi Rasmussen.

"What would you do if you weren't afraid?"

— Sheryl Sandberg, *Lean In: Women, Work, and the Will to Lead*

IN THE EVENT OF AN EMERGENCY, ASSUME THE BRACING POSITION

IN ONE'S CAREER, there are certain pivotal meetings. Those that define the future, the meetings that you tell others about for the rest of your career. Meetings where you wish you had said this instead of that.

Asmi knew this was one of *those* meetings, as she stood in front of the mirror in the restroom on the fifth floor, the executive floor of the offices of GTech.

She'd had her eyebrows and upper lip threaded the day before to prepare for the meeting. She'd gone to the salon to have her grays darkened. She'd had her nails done. She'd bought a new lipstick at Sephora, a color she'd normally not wear, *Jungle Red* by NARS. She even darkened her eyes to make them pop, which was a major deviation for her.

She was wearing a new dress that had been hanging in her closet, waiting for a special occasion. A dark green *uber* professional outfit that showed off her legs from M. M. LaFleur, a brand that emphasized that a *woman must be listened to and not looked at.* It had the right tone, but it was still feminine; an outfit that some women executives avoided because it made them less competitive against men, no matter that Marissa Mayer did a spread for *Vogue* or that Sheryl Sandberg didn't dress like a man.

Asmi had decided years ago that she was not going hide

behind a gender-neutral man suit. Her friend Cara had raised her eyebrows more than once at Asmi's dangling pearl earrings, which she wore to boost her confidence. Asmi tended to overemphasize her femininity, whether it was earrings or nail color or shoes, when she met with the top brass. It was her form of rebellion for all the women who dressed like a man because you had to, or risk being accused of just being a pretty face.

She flicked the pearls on her earrings and stepped away from the restroom counter. She looked down at her shoes and smiled. She'd chosen bright blue suede Aquazzura's sandals called *Wild Thing* with flirty fringes. As she walked out of the bathroom, her Chanel Gold Edinburgh Charm Leather Bracelet made a tinkling sound.

Before knocking on Matthew Baines' door and nodding to Celeste, his assistant, Asmi worried she had overdone the whole "I am woman, hear me roar," thing. But it wasn't every day a woman walked into the office of the CEO to find out if she was being promoted to top marketing executive of a billion-dollar global company.

There were only two candidates for the job, Asmi and her colleague, Scott—Matthew had been clear he was going to promote from within—and Asmi had spent the past nine months outmaneuvering Scott for the job. She was far more qualified for it than Scott. She was smarter than Scott. She had more integrity than Scott. And she was wearing sandals with fringes to put a spring in her step, *regardless* of how this ended. Right?

Today, was the day of reckoning.

Asmi took a deep breath, put on her game face and knocked on the door. When Matthew said, "Come in," Asmi stepped inside the CEO's penthouse corner office, her hands just slightly unsteady as she closed the door behind her.

THERE IS NO COMPENSATION FOR A FORCE MAJEURE EVENT

9 MONTHS earlier

A WOMAN with no husband or children must *at least* have a stellar career.

If a woman doesn't have a career, she should *at least* have a husband and beautiful children (the children are always beautiful, even when they're not). She *must* have one or the other—if not, she might as well jump off a cliff or get hit by a bus and no one would miss her.

There was a tacit understanding between a single woman and the entire workplace that she didn't have a life and was therefore perfect for dumping work on that no one else wanted.

However, a successful career woman who has no husband or children is looked upon as a charity case. "Well, *at least she has that*," they'll say with a tilt to their head and a pitying look. Or, as in the case of Asmi, the whispers wondered *if maybe a better candidate for the position would be someone with a family, you know...someone well-rounded and stable*. Because it went without saying, a single woman was unstable. The subtext: *no one wanted to marry or impregnate you!*

What was truly offensive, it was usually women who said

this about other women. Madeline Albright was right: *there is a special place in hell for women who turn against other women.*

The *worst* single woman was the woman who slept with a married man. Combine: single, home wrecker, and career failure all in one place—that was who Asmi felt she was.

Fueled with these negative and self-flagellating thoughts, Asmi ordered yet another Lagavulin at the Lark Creek Grill in San Francisco International Airport, when her plane was delayed due to stormy weather a day after Valentine's Day.

"Neat?" the bartender asked her.

"With one rock," she replied, and stared into the depths of her phone...reading once again the email that she felt signaled the end of her career at GTech, her company for the past six years. She had received the email from her friend in HR on the flight from CDG (Paris Charles de Gaulle Airport) to SFO (San Francisco International Airport) en route to SNA (John Wayne International Airport) and her apartment in Laguna Beach.

"It kills the taste," a man said to her.

Asmi looked up, her eyes glazed with irritation. *Really? My life is ending, and you want to hit on me?*

The man smiled at her. He was African American, in his late sixties, well suited, and not the type of man who normally hit on her. He looked downright decent.

"The ice kills the flavor," he said.

"I'm okay with that," Asmi responded, a little more curtly and despondently than she would have liked, but there were extenuating circumstances. She went back to her phone, her eyes sore and her heart heavy with despair. A part of her wanted to dramatically lean her head against her forearm and in operatic Bollywood heroine style say, "I wish I was dead."

She'd cried all the way from Paris to San Francisco. It was something she did on long flights, when they dimmed the lights and a hush fell over the plane, huddled alone and private in business class. She would sob into the side of her seat, big tears flowing, her whole body shaking. Her therapist, Shohreh, a lovely Persian psychologist seemed to understand how Asmi's head worked, thought it was cathartic that Asmi cried on flights. But the fact that she did this on nearly every long-haul flight—Asmi was on such a flight nearly every other week—concerned the psychologist. *"That's not normal,"* she said.

The Bollywood heroine would then fling her hands up in the air and cry out, *"My life is not normal."*

"I'm Allan Sanders," the man next to her said and put his hand out.

Asmi shook his hand automatically. "Asmi Vemula."

The man nodded. "Is your flight delayed as well?"

Asmi wanted to tell him to leave her alone but then something about his eyes, those kind eyes framed in square metal frames, made her answer, "Yes. I'm on my way to Santa Ana."

"I'm on my way to LAX," the man said. "Work or pleasure?"

"On my way home," Asmi said. "I live in Laguna Beach."

"That's nice," Allan said. "I lived in Newport Beach ten years ago. But then I moved to Silicon Valley and joined the rat race."

Asmi told him she'd gone to university in Irvine and had stayed in Orange County though she was born and raised in India, a country she left nearly two decades ago.

"I hear that all Indian names mean something," he said. "How about yours?"

"I am," Asmi said. "My name...I mean, my name means *I am* in Sanskrit."

Allan grinned. "No kidding. Tell me, Asmi, what sorrows are you drowning during this storm in peaty whiskey?"

There was something about airports and airplanes where you told your life story to a stranger or heard theirs. Once on a flight from LHR (London Heathrow) to JFK (John F Kennedy Airport), Asmi sat next to a woman who was returning home from Rome. She was a cellist and used to play for the New York Philharmonic. She left all that because she had fallen in love *with a married man.* Asmi had been in her mid-twenties then and fascinated because this woman had been a man's *mistress.* An old-fashioned word, but apt, the woman told her, because he had paid for her life in Rome for three years. He'd paid for her apartment, her car and driver, her clothes...*everything, even the bikini waxes.*

She'd finally left when she realized that she was thirty-five years old with no career anymore because she had left it behind for *love*. But what had she got to show for it? *Nothing.* No career. No husband. No family. No children.

He hadn't wanted her to leave, she told Asmi and she had left him before, but he'd always brought her back. They were addicted to each other, she said. But this time was different. She just knew it. This time he wouldn't come and get her. This time she wouldn't go back, even if he did. It was now time for her to either find a family or get a career...because she couldn't not have at least one or the other.

Considering that Asmi's story right now as she sat in SFO with a stranger was like the cellist's, she felt compelled to unload.

What she really wanted to do was throw herself onto the counter and dramatically declare her life was over, but she pulled herself together to speak like a rational adult. Because despite the turbulence, Asmi knew how to land on her feet.

"I'm a director of marketing at a global biotech company," she started and then shook her head, "Well...not for long because I just found out that our VP of Marketing, my boss, is retiring at the end of the year, all hush hush and they're going to choose a replacement from within. I predict that it's going to be a corporate *Hunger Games*."

"Are you in the running to become the VP of Marketing?" Allan asked.

Asmi shrugged. "I don't know. I come from R&D; I've worked in sales and now in marketing. I'm...what they call... well rounded, well, except for the fact that I'm single and have no children and that makes me, as I overheard one of my male colleagues say, *edgier* than a woman who has kids."

Allan nodded, but didn't offer comment.

"My colleague, another director of marketing, a dipshit called Scott Beauregard the Third from Baton Rouge, Louisiana, you know the type, used to be the quarterback for LSU, frat house, father of two, beautiful wife...he's the favored one," Asmi said. "Am I sounding bitter?"

Allan shook his head.

"Of course, I'm sounding bitter," Asmi said. "You know what this election taught us women? It taught us that a capable, smart, intelligent woman will lose her job out to a complete idiot just because he has a penis."

"Which puts you at a disadvantage," Allan agreed.

Asmi took a sip of her drink. "My friend, a director in HR, told me in confidence, obviously, that I probably don't have much of a chance because the CEO *and* the board don't think I'm suited."

"Why?" Allan asked.

"I'm not ready. I lack executive presence, maybe."

"Really?"

"I don't know," Asmi said honestly. "I don't feel ready. It's a *really* senior position."

"Do you think Scott thinks he's not ready?" Allan asked.

Asmi took a sip of scotch and shrugged. "It isn't about what he thinks, it's what *they* think."

"Men apply for a job when they meet about 60% of the qualifications, but women apply *only* if they meet 100% of them," Allan said.

Asmi took a deep breath. "I know that statistic. But my case is different ..." she saw Allan shake his head, "You don't think so?"

"What are they looking for in a VP of Marketing that you don't have?"

"A penis," Asmi said blandly after thinking about it for a long moment. "If Scott gets the job, I'll have to find a new job because he's an asshat and I won't work for him. And to be honest," tears filled her eyes, "I don't have it in me to start again and prove myself in a new place and fight the fight."

Allan handed her a paper napkin.

"You may not be the frontrunner, Asmi, but the race is not over," Allan said as she dabbed at her wet eyes.

Asmi looked at him. "What do you mean?"

"If your VP is retiring at the end of the year, you have until Q4 to make your case, that gives you most of Q1 and all of Q2 and Q3 to get the job," Allan said. "If you want it that is. Do you?"

Asmi eyed him carefully. *Who was this guy?*

"I want it...I think," she said. "I do. But...."

"Then go get it," Allan said, smiling broadly. "You've had your cry. You've had your whiskey. Now get that Beauregard guy and show *them* that the job should be yours."

Asmi felt a surge of strength. Yes, she thought, I'm going to get the job, damn it. As she thought it, she wondered how. *I'll figure it out*, she told herself. *I'm going to win this*. But as soon as she pictured herself with the title Vice President of Marketing, she knew it was too rich for her, the climb too steep. *Wasn't it?*

"Once when I was a director, run of the mill, one of my managers was hiring. He interviewed several people and then offered the job to a man. The man turned it down because he got another job, he liked better. He offered it to his second choice who also turned it down because his company counter offered. He then offered it to his third choice, a woman, but for some reason the salary was fifteen percent less," Allan said. "I asked him about it, and he said, 'Well, *she has less experience*.' I pointed out that she didn't. It wasn't until then that he realized what he was doing. That was nearly a decade ago. And regardless of *Lean In* and *Girl Boss* and whatnot, you still get the short end of the stick in the corporate world."

"Did you get him to increase the salary by fifteen percent when he offered the woman the job?" Asmi asked.

Allan laughed. "Yes, and she rose the ranks and is a senior executive. She was a damn good hire. The thing is, and I can speak because I'm an old codger and have seen a lot, women just don't fight hard enough."

"Oh, that's bullshit," Asmi said.

Allan shook his head. "You're thinking this Beauregard guy has the job. He's thinking the same thing. The problem is that neither of you knows who has the job because it's still not been decided. Yet, you believe it will go to him. Society has conditioned you to believe you'll lose. This is why men will apply for jobs they don't quality for and negotiate a higher salary than a female counterpart would."

"I negotiate…sometimes," Asmi said sheepishly, because the first time she negotiated was when she was promoted into her current position and that was only because she *really* wanted to buy her apartment in Laguna Beach.

"Why not do it *always*," Allan said. "Now, don't give up and hide in whiskey. Stand up and be counted."

"Hmm…," Asmi said.

"You know it struck me what you said about women with families seen as being more suitable because of stability. We used to say the same thing about men. If a man wasn't married and had no kids, he was considered flighty…or worse, gay," Allan said as he picked up a handful of peanuts.

"I had someone tell me that because I didn't have a family, I was only focused on my job and that made me aggressive," Asmi told him, swirling a little on the bar stool, the alcohol was sinking in and she was slightly tipsy.

"It's the usual, isn't it? Men are driven, and women are aggressive," Allan said. "I have a daughter, about your age. She's a lawyer, isn't sure she'll make partner because they *prefer* men. She told me, *'but that's okay, daddy'*. When I asked her why the hell she would say that, she said because she has her husband, Robert, and the girls."

"You have to have the one or the other," Asmi said, shaking her head. "A single woman needs to have a block *fucking* buster career, otherwise she's a loser. And I seriously messed up on the family account, too. I…," she looked at him and then shrugged, "I'm probably never meeting you again, so it doesn't matter. I just ended a four-year relationship with a married man. Married with two kids. I met him on a flight from Chicago to Paris. He's French."

"He wouldn't leave his wife?" Allan asked.

"I never asked," Asmi said. "I think that I wanted him because he wouldn't leave his wife or maybe I hoped he would, but I never asked. It was quite explicit that there was no future. Just the present."

"And you *just* ended the relationship?" Allan asked.

Asmi nodded and raised her glass. "Twenty-four hours ago. He took me out to dinner to celebrate—it was an anniversary of sorts and Valentine's Day—to Pierre Gagnaire. He was showing me love with Pierre Gagnaire's three Michelin stars. We ate our six-course meal. And I told him I wanted it over as we drank our *café* and ate our *petit fours,* which were gorgeous, especially this chocolate one with kirsch...anyway, I digress, I told him I didn't want to see him again. We went to my hotel and...you know... had a goodbye...," Asmi trailed away.

"And now you feel lonely?" Allan asked with no judgment in his voice.

"Yes," Asmi said. "Even though he wasn't *mine,* obviously, but *maybe* he was a little mine. And now I have no one." As a fresh batch of tears arrived, she shook them off. "I sound like a teenager."

"No," Allan said. "The heart is a mysterious thing. It beats with its own rhythm. I left my wife of fifteen years for a lover. My daughters were heartbroken. *But* I loved Jennifer and I didn't love my wife. It was tough the first year, but it worked itself out. I never knew what it meant to be truly happy until I was with Jennifer. It's been twenty-three years now and I know I sound like a cliché, but it's been the best of times, actually even the worst of times have been the best of times. The thing is, I believe, that there is a soulmate for all of us. We sometimes find them and sometimes we don't and sometimes we find them at the wrong time."

"So, I'm not a fallen woman?" she asked.

"Oh no," Allan said. *"Because love is love,* as Obama said and if we're in a world where we accept a man loving a man and a woman loving a woman, why can't we accept a man loving a woman, regardless of who he's married to?"

They contemplated getting another drink, when someone in the bar yelled, *they're resuming flights again*. Allan and Asmi sat on their barstools and finished their whiskey. Allan's phone beeped, probably a message from his airline that his plane was getting ready to board.

He rose and pulled out his wallet. Asmi waved him away. "It's on me. I owe you a drink, at least."

"Too many of us live our careers by default and not by design," Allan said as he put his wallet back in his pocket. "This step in your career will need design."

He put his computer bag on his carryon suitcase and as he was wheeling himself away, Asmi called out, "Who are you?"

"Just a guy at an airport," Allan said and walked away.

EXCERPT FROM THE BUSINESS WORKBOOK

"AND THEN SHE SAID...10 COACHING LESSONS TO HELP THE EVERYDAY WOMAN TAKE HER NEXT STEP"

IT'S best to accept a few facts.

- Gender inequality still exists…yes, in your workplace too
- It's harder for women than men to get promoted; in fact, a study shows that at all organizational levels, women are a whopping 15% less likely than men to get promoted[1]
- It's harder for women than men to negotiate because when women negotiate forcefully, they are perceived by both men and women as going against the societal norms of being an unselfish caretaker[2]
- It's harder for women than men to have role models because there aren't many women in senior leadership positions
- It's harder for women to take the next step, grow from individual contributor to manager, grow from administrator to professional, or grow from director to VP to CEO
- *Let's face it, it's just plain hard*

The above list is not exhaustive but summarizes some of the external forces that work against women. However, there are internal forces inside women that also impede us. Most women have one or two of the following thoughts every day:

- Today is the day they'll find out I don't know my head from my ass
- I just don't want to deal with this anymore, it's all too much
- I don't think I want a career, I'm fine where I am
- Did I behave myself at that meeting? Did I talk too much? Did I talk too little?
- Will I sound greedy if I ask for a promotion or that job or more money that I want and deserve?
- If I get that job that I really want, will I be a bad wife/mom/sister/daughter?
- Am I too loud, too pushy, too bossy? Am I not assertive enough? Am I a bitch? Am I wallflower?
- I'm such a screw-up

After talking to hundreds of women in various positions and places in their career journey, this workbook is for *you* if you doubt yourself and don't know how to navigate your career, take that next small or big step, or make that small or big tweak in your work-life to create a balance you can live with. This book is not for the CEOs, directors, billion-dollar entrepreneurs, though they're welcome to read it, after all, this book is for the *everyday* woman.

Who is the everyday woman?

- The woman who doubts herself
- The woman who worries about being found out

- The woman who doesn't speak up at meetings because her voice catches in her throat
- The woman who has never negotiated a fairer pay check but wants to because she knows she's worth more, she just doesn't know how to frame the words
- The woman who doesn't want to negotiate because it makes her appear greedy
- The woman who doesn't know how to take the next step
- The woman who wants to take the next step, but doesn't have the courage to apply for the job that will take her there
- The woman who has given up, because it's too hard
- The woman who has experienced harassment and isn't quite sure if it was harassment or if she was being too sensitive
- The woman who doesn't know what she wants in her career
- The woman who's juggling work, home and kids and is too exhausted to think about her career
- The woman who feels neglected in the workplace
- The woman who has become bitter, because her career hasn't moved and now, she doesn't know if she even wants it to
- The smart and high-performing woman who is passed over for mediocre men
- The woman who is not being coached by anyone
- The woman who…

YOU GET THE PICTURE.

The *everyday* woman is all of us. Every woman should read this book, do the workbook exercises, go out there, and get what she wants and deserves.

2

DISARM YOUR DOORS
AND CROSS-CHECK

"I LOVE THOSE SHOES," Cara, Asmi's friend and work confidante said about Asmi's red Mephisto Sabatina Oxford shoes.

"Singapore Airport," Asmi said as she pushed her salad away.

"Changi is the best airport for shopping," Cara said.

"Do you think for two feminists we focus too much on our attire?" Asmi asked.

"If Amal can wear couture, be married to Clooney and still be a high-powered lawyer who's saving the world...why the hell not?" Cara said and then looked around the café patio to check that there were no eavesdroppers.

Cara and Asmi tried to have lunch at work at least once a month because that was the best they could manage with their travel schedules. It was nearly two in the afternoon, and they were left with the sad prepackaged salad from the café because the warm food was gone, and the fresh salad bar was closed.

"I just found out that they're going to go through a full process to hire the VP of Marketing. They still only intend to look internally but with lots of formal and informal interviews, some test projects...you know the drill," Cara said. "Apparently, our dear CEO, Matthew Baines, wants to do a sort of ..."

"Corporate *Hunger Games*?" Asmi suggested.

Cara nodded. "I was going to say *The Apprentice* but in the current political climate that just exacerbates my ulcer."

Matthew used to be the VP of Marketing for GTech, the biotech company Asmi and Cara worked for, and for the past five years had been the CEO. The current VP of Marketing had also been promoted from within, but everyone had known that Jim was going to retire sooner than later and now it was sooner.

"You have a good working relationship with Matthew," Cara said.

Asmi shrugged. "Scott has a better one, I think."

"Scott has a good rapport with everyone, as long as *everyone* is a man who once belonged to a frat house," Cara said. "You won't believe the stuff I've had to deal with in his team. It's all borderline you know. He said, she said. Intent versus impact. That guy is a legal liability, but Max *loves* him. They play squash together."

Maximilian Hoffstätter was the VP of HR and Cara's boss. A German who had risen through the ranks via the German office of GTech, Max was no bullshit and direct for the most part but for some reason bought into Scott, hook, line and sinker.

Asmi met Scott for the first time when she was doing her "meet and greet" with her peers in marketing when she was hired six years ago at GTech as a marketing manager. Scott worked for another business unit, run by a hotshot from Harvard who had since left. "All the managers in this business unit have been handpicked for future leadership roles. I'm going to make director in six to ten months, max."

"But you started this job two months ago?" Asmi said.

Scott nodded. "Yes, it's my first people management position but I am leadership material, you know?"

"Okay," Asmi said, baffled by his lack of self-awareness and his massive confidence.

It took him four years to become a director, six months after Asmi had been promoted. She never rubbed his face in it but had immensely enjoyed the six months that she was director and he wasn't. Now, he was going to be her boss. The universe had found a way to equalize.

Scott was a leader who managed up well, was passive aggressive with his peers and shit on people below him if they weren't like him. He was a man's man and charming when he wanted to be. He was a decent marketer, Asmi gave him that— but an executive leader needed to be more than just a good marketer and Asmi didn't think Scott could elevate and become the leader that GTech needed in their new VP of Marketing.

When Asmi talked about Scott in therapy, her therapist believed that Scott was a bully in high school, not as an individual but in a group—and then joined a fraternity in university to do more of the same, then a finance company where the culture was all about machismo. Now he was succeeding at GTech without ever having any reason to evolve. He had obviously hired other men who were also like him and the result was a group of leaders who were all the same, with the same tailor who made their suits and the same hair gel they bought at the same upscale men's salon, the definition of *"group think"*.

"I better start calling headhunters," Asmi said.

Cara raised her eyebrows.

"Oh, come on! Do you *really* think there's a chance in hell they'll give me the job?" Asmi said and when Cara didn't speak, added, "*You* don't think I'm ready. I don't think I'm ready."

Cara shook her head. "No, no. Don't put this on me. I think you're an awesome marketer and leader. You turned your department and business unit around. Come on, the baking business grew from four to nine percent last year. You're on your way up. But *you* don't think you're ready. You're confident, you're sure of yourself, you're a good leader; something inside you pulls you back from thinking you can take on that big job. Something that doesn't let you play big."

"I met someone at SFO who told me to fight for the job, show Matthew that I was the right choice," Asmi said. "I want to, I really do, I don't think I'll succeed." Asmi paused and played with a sad lettuce leaf and then shrugged. "But I have nothing to lose, do I? If I don't try, I don't get the job and if I do try and don't get the job, the result is the same."

Cara eyed her friend speculatively and dropped her fork on her salad plate. "Are you telling me you're going to play *Hunger Games*?"

Asmi waited a long time and then stabbed a tomato with gusto. "You know what...*absofuckinglutely*," she said.

Cara cheered and gave Asmi a high five.

ASMI LIVED in a one-bedroom apartment in Laguna Beach with a view of the ocean. It was overpriced and uninhabited for nearly two weeks every month, but Asmi had bought it as a reward for herself when she was promoted to Director. It was sheer vanity, a way to say, *look at me, I made it.*

Regardless of why she bought the place, there was peace in coming home and sitting out in the balcony and feeling and smelling the sea breeze. But a week of the sea breeze and she was ready to travel. There were conferences. There were meetings...there were an endless number of meetings around the world. When her apartment went from cozy to claustrophobic, she happily exchanged it for the emptiness of a hotel room—and when that became too much, she had a comfortable home to come back to. The balance between traveling and being grounded was vital for Asmi's equilibrium.

A sales colleague once joked that the only time he and his wife had come close to a divorce was when the company grounded all their sales people for budget reasons. Asmi wasn't married, but she could relate.

"How can you stay in hotels all the time?" Ananya, her sister did not understand.

With ease!

Sometimes.

There really was nothing as lonely as a hotel room: its air conditioning on full blast, those white tucked sheets that Asmi hated to wrestle out from the under the mattress, the carpet that she was unsure about the cleanliness of, and the damn doors. Why were hotel room doors so heavy that it took trickery and skill to keep them open, while rolling a suitcase in? Like that wasn't bad enough, who had thought that it was a clever idea to need the guest to stick the room card into a narrow slot to turn on the lights? Maybe the sustainability people thought it was a smart way to save energy; Asmi thought it was annoying.

But there were the many positives. There were the evenings with no work dinners when Asmi could call room service and order food and wine and watch whatever was on television, even *Friends* in German while she ate in bed. Asmi always wondered if they'd come change the sheets if she spilled her red wine. She thought that was the real advantage of a room with two queen beds.

Etienne, her erstwhile lover used to joke that one bed was for sex and the other for sleep. Asmi always slept on the bed they had sex in, so she wouldn't feel quite so bereft after he left. It was pathetic. That whole relationship had been pathetic.

She said as much to Mila, her friend from UCI, when they met for lunch at Nick's in Laguna Beach.

Asmi thought that Mila had it all. She was a pediatrician with her own practice, had a husband who was a partner in an advertising agency and two lovely children, a boy and a girl. To add to that, Mila was a size two, tall, blonde and elegant.

"He made you happy…for a while, even if it was cosmetic happiness," Mila said to Asmi and grinned enthusiastically when her order of fried chicken and waffles was brought to their table.

"How can you eat that and keep that body?" Asmi asked.

"Good Scandinavian genes," Mila said and gleefully picked up her fork and knife.

Asmi ordered an omelet because she needed to manage her waistline before heading off to Macau for a regional sales meeting in a week. The problem with business travel was the rich food in restaurants, the lack of sleep, and no time to work out unless Asmi was super-diligent—business travel was a journey to going up a dress size in six months if she was not careful.

"I miss him," Asmi admitted.

"The breakup is new," Mila said. "You have to give it time."

"I keep wanting to call him," Asmi said. "He didn't want it to end but admitted that if I wanted to find a man and have a baby, *blah, blah,* then he wouldn't stand in the way."

"Do you want a man and a baby?" Mila asked.

Asmi shrugged and cut into her omelet.

"How are things at work for you?" Asmi asked to change the topic. She knew that Mila never judged, but Asmi wondered if Mila saw her as an adulteress, wondering how it might feel if Javier, her husband, had an affair.

"Oh man," Mila said and rolled her eyes.

Mila shared her practice with two other doctors, one of whom she called Dr. Nemesis.

"You won't believe what *she* did last week ...," Mila began and told Asmi all about a new adventure with the indomitable villain in her story.

~

NO, no, no, you can't be in Macau next week," Asmi's older sister Ananya yelled into the phone. "Where *is* Macau?"

"It's an island off Hong Kong. The Chinese Las Vegas," Asmi informed her.

"Whatever," Ananya said. "You have to be in Milpitas next weekend to prevent me from committing suicide or murder."

Asmi and Ananya's parents were visiting from India, which they did every year in the spring and stayed for three months so they could get to know their grandchildren. And even though they preferred Ananya to Asmi, because Ananya had an employed husband and two *beautiful* children, a boy and a girl— compared to their mother Madhuri, Ananya was simply not good enough. Not good enough as a parent, woman, wife, sister...you name it.

This time they had decided to come for six months so they could attend a friend's daughter's wedding in Livermore in early September. They'd only been with Ananya for a week and she was already losing her mind.

"Are you sneaking out of the house and smoking?" Asmi asked as she heard the click of a lighter.

"They're here for six months this time. *Six*. If I don't smoke, I'll have to find something else to do with my hands. I'm trying to keep my options legal. *Venkat* actually got me the cigarettes for mental health reasons," Ananya said.

"Man, I'm sorry."

"Asmi, you promised."

"Ananya, it's work," Asmi said. "It's not like..."

"Are you stopping by Paris? Is this a global booty call?" Ananya interrupted and Asmi could almost hear her sister's head puff up, ready to explode. Asmi had worried about what Ananya would say about her having an affair with a married man and didn't tell her for nearly a year. But then one night three years ago after their parents (who had been visiting then) had gone to bed and Ananya's husband and kids had gone to bed, Ananya and Asmi sat out in the patio drinking scotch and she spilled the beans about Etienne.

"Maybe his wife thinks, *good he's getting sex somewhere else, so I don't have to sleep with him*," Ananya said, surprising Asmi.

"Are you and Venkat okay?" Asmi asked about Ananya's marriage.

Ananya shrugged. "We are...except when *they* are here. Then we're not okay. I'm not okay and he's not okay. No one is okay. Venkat's father died when he was sixteen. His mother comes to visit us for a week here and there and then goes and visits his brother, her friends...she has a life. And then we have Madhuri and Prasad, our dysfunctional parents, who have no life except bitching about their children."

"Well, Prasad only bitches when *she* is around," Asmi said.

"And she's *always* around," Ananya said.

"Have you wondered what we'll do if he dies before her?" Asmi asked.

Ananya downed her whiskey. "Don't say things like that. The universe might hear you and make it true."

"Seriously, Ananya, you don't care I'm having an affair with a married man?" she asked.

Ananya looked at Asmi and shook her head. "Is the sex good?"

"Amazing."

"Well, that's more than I'm having," Ananya said. "You know married life is in some ways a prison. I made these stupid choices. I had a bachelor's in engineering, but I chose to have an arranged marriage, come to the United States and get pregnant. I have *nothing* to do except run a house that doesn't need running. Take care of children who're too old to be taken care of. The kids are sixteen and fourteen—they have their own lives. I have *no* life. I'm forty-four years old and my mother manages to make me feel like a loser for having the exact same life she did. Asmi, if you're having fun with this French guy, more power to you. I'd like to be sleeping with a French guy, flying around the world, staying in cool hotels and ordering room service and wearing...I love those shoes."

Asmi looked down at her green Gucci Princetown lace slippers and said, "Fiumicino."

"What?"

"Rome International Airport," Asmi said. "I do all my shopping in airports. Trust me, Ana, you don't want my life. I'm a natural fucking disaster."

Asmi assured her agitated sister over the phone that she wasn't going to Macau via Paris because the City of Lights had gone dark on her three weeks ago. Three *long* weeks ago.

"I'm sorry, sweetie," Ananya said. "*But* I really need you here —I need a break."

Asmi sighed. "Fine. I'll fly home via SFO from Hong Kong. You'll owe me."

"Like hell I will," Ananya said. "They visit me every year and I had the two grandchildren, so you owe me for keeping them off your back for the rest of your life."

AND THEN SHE SAID...I'M NOT ENOUGH

EXCERPT FROM THE BUSINESS WORKBOOK "AND THEN SHE SAID..."

THIS MAY BE A CLICHÉ, but clichés come from somewhere... usually reality.

A male individual contributor was promoted to manager, even though he wasn't entirely ready for the position. Let's call him Scott.

Scott is being promoted because the hiring manager believes he has potential. Remember, "men are often promoted based on their potential to be successful in a new role and women are often only promoted after having experience that largely mirrors the content of that role.[1]"

Scott thinks he is the cat's ass and ready to take on his next challenge. His problem is not lack of confidence.

Now, let's flip this. Instead of Scott, let's say it's Alice. The hiring manager really believes in her. Alice doesn't do what Scott did and say, "Oh sign me up." No, Alice thinks, "Oh my god, I'll have to manage all these people and be responsible for them. Can I do this? Am I really ready? Will I ever be ready?"

I see this all the time. I have done it myself. My husband and I have had this conversation with each step I have taken in my career.

Me: You really think I can do this?

Husband: Of course.

Me: Really? Are you sure?

Husband: You can absolutely do this.

Me: I'm just not sure. Maybe I'm not as good as they think; hell, maybe I'm not as good as I think.

Husband: Why do you do this to yourself?

Almost all professional women I know have had this conversation, either inside their heads or with a real person. And the question my husband asks is apt: "Why do we do this to ourselves?"

There are many reasons, mostly all revolving around self-esteem. I meet women with plenty of self-confidence, but self-esteem is sometimes lacking, and that gives rise to paralyzing self-doubt.

Self-esteem refers to how we feel about ourselves overall—how much we love yourself, while self-confidence is how we feel about our abilities based on a situation. A person can have healthy self-esteem but not be confident about juggling data in Excel sheets. A person can be very certain about their abilities and how well they do their job; but go back home every day and think they're a failure and any day now their house of cards is going to collapse.

It's just recently that I have stopped saying to myself, "Today is the day they'll figure out I'm a fraud." I meet no men who think like this and even if they do, they don't express it. Most of the men I know think and believe that they deserve where they are in their careers and they have a right to their next promotion. Most women don't have that sense of entitlement.

So, we've established the problem, and sort of established a root cause of the problem. The question is, how do we get past the "I'm not enough" internal monologue we have going?

3

PLAYING FOR HIGH
STAKES IN MACAU

GETTING to Macau required Asmi and her colleagues to take one plane, one train, one taxi, one ferry and one bus…one way.

The Asian offices of GTech had decided, despite their infinite wisdom on air travel that they would have their sales meeting in Macau, the Las Vegas of the East, which looked nothing like what Asmi had seen in that James Bond movie where Javier Bardem and Daniel Craig had a sexual moment.

"It's so exciting to go to Asia," Gustav, a manager who worked for Asmi said as they waited in a long snakelike queue at passport control in the Hong Kong International Airport. "This is so different from my usual travel, you know, which is mostly to Omaha to the R&D facility."

Gustav was a product manager and worked more with R&D than with the commercial teams around the world. He was accompanying Asmi this time because they were launching a new baking enzyme for the Asian market, which Gustav was presenting to the sales team.

"Oh, come on, you also go to the Quad Cities in Iowa on occasion," Asmi teased him.

"For my next job, boss, I'd like something less domestic and more international," Gustav said. "Then I can say cool things like

I just flew in from Buenos Aires yesterday and I'm going to Shanghai tomorrow. James Bond without the spy shit."

"Who said that?"

"Scott," Gustav said and grinned. "He's doing the whole his is bigger than everyone else's since the secret of Jim's retirement blasted out on the grapevine. I can't believe they'd give him the job. He stinks."

"Don't talk about a director like that. And speaking of stink," Asmi said, curling her nose and not wanting to discuss a peer in a poor light with her associate, "This smell is what I don't like about Asia. It's the 'The Third World' smell."

"What did you say? That's a horrible thing to say," Gustav said.

"I'm from the third world, so I can say third-world smell. It smells of urine, disinfectant and…wait for it…sweat," Asmi finished, sniffing hard. "I grew up in India and I remember this smell *very* well. All the bathrooms have them. This smell can be found in all third world countries, or whatever it is we call them now. What do we call them? Developing markets?"

"Growth markets," Gustav said, "We call them high growth markets, Asmi. What's next? You're going to call them shithole countries?"

"Of course not. India is not a shithole. I take offense to that. But I'll be honest that there is a smell and not limited to India. And that growth bet definition is bullshit because for some industries the United States is a growth market," Asmi said as she stepped forward, passport in hand to show to the passport control agent.

There were four of them from GTech who were attending the sales meeting from the United States—Asmi, Scott (Asmi's passive aggressive nemesis), Gustav, and Cécile, an R&D scientist who worked out of the R&D facility in Omaha. Cécile and Asmi had become good friends after they had worked on a product launch together two years ago.

"How was the flight?" Asmi asked Cécile whom they found waiting for her suitcase at the baggage carousel.

"I flew with Scott and it was a *very* long flight," Cécile said. "He kept complaining about how he couldn't get an upgrade. How terrible monkey class is and how he *always* flies business because of his position in the company. The guy wouldn't shut up about how important he is."

"Where is he now?" Asmi asked looking around. It always made her uncomfortable when a colleague bitched about Scott to her and she couldn't say anything back, except defend Scott or change the topic. Since it would be disingenuous and dishonest for her to defend Scott, she chose the more authentic option.

"Restroom," Cécile said and then while Gustav was focused on something else, she whispered to Asmi, "Is Scott getting Jim's job?"

"I have no idea." *Why did they ask her? How would she know?*

"Because that won't be a good thing," Cécile said. "The man is a moron, but I'm sure that won't stop him from getting the job if that's what Matthew wants."

"Matthew will put the right person in the right position," Asmi said.

Cécile sighed. "You know the one thing that this election proved is that for some reason a qualified woman will be sidelined by an incompetent monkey...as long as he has a penis."

Preaching to the choir, girlfriend.

"Who's an incompetent monkey?" Scott asked as he materialized from behind them.

"The president," Cécile said without batting as much as an eyelid.

"Oh no, are we talking politics again? We just need to go back to the time when we didn't discuss sex, religion and politics in the workplace," Scott said.

"And look where we ended up because of that," Asmi said. "Maybe if we all talked about the things that are important, we wouldn't have the great American democracy hanging by a thread today."

"You know, Asmi, for someone who isn't like American,

American, it's remarkable how passionate you are about *our* democracy," Scott said.

"She's an American citizen," Gustav said irritably, wheeling his suitcase as a wall between Asmi and Scott.

"Of course, she is," Scott said, uncomfortably. "What I meant was…hey, can we let this go? I just checked Wei Lin's email and we have a *long* journey ahead of us. First, we take the train to the central station."

Next, they had to take a taxi to the ferry, all the while with Gustav dragging Cécile's suitcase because it was too big for her. At the ferry station they had to buy tickets to Macau and go through passport control again, alongside hundreds of people from Hong Kong who were also going to Macau because it was a Friday night, and everyone wanted to go to Sin City for the weekend.

It was while they waited for the ferry, blind with jet lag and exhausted that Gustav said, "You were right about the third world smell. And Scott is a jackass."

"I don't want to hear you talk about my peers in that fashion," Asmi said and then added silently to herself, *not that I can disagree.*

"Are we *really* waking up at six tomorrow morning for that business case meeting?" Gustav asked once they were settled in the ferry.

Asmi nodded. "I'll go through the deck one more time before I go to bed."

"How can you work after a day like this?" Gustav asked. "I've never met anyone who works as much as you do."

"I don't work all the time," Asmi said and then shrugged, "This business case meeting is important. Really important."

"Why?"

Because I think it's the first contest of the Corporate Hunger Games, Asmi thought. Both she and Scott were presenting a business case for their "big win" project and how it was going to influence the annual forecast for their business units.

"Because we need to grow by ten percent this year and even

with this big cake enzyme project we will only grow by about nine percent. I don't know where to find that last one percent," Asmi said.

"Scott has the same problem, Asmi," Gustav said.

Asmi sighed. "Scott inflates his numbers. He always has."

"They'll see through that when he doesn't deliver," Gustav assured her.

But then it'll be too late. He'll already have the VP of Marketing job and she will be frantically calling recruiters...or worse, resigning without a job in hand. Maybe she should also inflate her numbers, just a little. Even the thought made her feel dirty. She was a conservative marketer, not building a business case on the best-case impractical scenario where all the stars align, but one founded on real data and foreseeable risks.

"Remember when he put that business case for the whole nine enzyme blend thing in the Middle East? That fell on its face —no one was going to buy such an expensive blend there," Gustav said. "The only reason he wasn't up shit creek without a paddle was because South America did so well last year. If Brazil had tanked, his whole business would have tanked."

"It's going to be what it's going to be," Asmi said. "I can't make up revenue numbers for which a market demand doesn't exist."

ASMI SAID as much to Matthew Baines, the CEO and Gary Baker, the Vice President of Sales for GTech as she paced her hotel room barefoot, her air pods in her ear and her phone in her hand. She had just presented her business case for the cake enzyme project and as she had predicted, the "big win" project was not winning big enough.

Scott had gone first and as Asmi had thought he would, his numbers neatly matched the company stretch expectation from the detergent business unit, which he managed. Asmi had wanted to ask several critical questions but had restrained herself to the minimum. A woman who aggressively questioned a colleague in a meeting such as this was deemed a competitive bitch.

"Have you looked at Brazil some more?" Scott asked.

"Brazil is included in the forecast already," Gary commented. "Asmi, do you think you're being too conservative?"

"I am being conservative," Asmi said. "But not unreasonably so. There are risks and I have flagged them."

"What about IndiaMART, Gustav?" Gary asked.

"We're going to start trials with them in the summer," Gustav said. "We tried to push but they said they don't have time to invest in trials right now."

"You don't think you can win that business?" Matthew asked.

This was the first time he had spoken.

"I think it's risky," Asmi said. "With trials in the summer, it's going to take a few months before…"

"Maybe you need to show more courage in your business case and believe you can close the business," Matthew said, cutting her off. "That is what we want from our leaders in GTech."

"I just don't think the IndiaMART deal is something we can count on for this year. They have always been slow at making decisions," Asmi said. "Even if we won the business, I don't think we could recognize the revenue this year or earliest, Q4…if we get *very* lucky."

"You keep saying it won't happen and even if it happens it won't happen this year…how about saying that you will make it happen for this year?" Matthew asked in that ice-cold cutting voice of his that rattled Asmi even over the phone.

"Matthew, I wouldn't add IndiaMART to the forecast either if they won't start trials until the summer," Gary said in Asmi's defense. "Asmi, Scott, Gustav thank you for dialing in so early from Macau. I'll ask Celeste to book us another meeting for next week. Maybe you can look at your numbers one more time. Scott, I want you to try to be a bit more conservative about

Brazil. We're still having trouble with collecting revenue there from our distributor. I think you're being more aggressive than needed."

"Gary, aggressive is good," Matthew said and then added, "But let's not live in fantasy land, either."

Asmi sat down on her bed after the call and threw her air pods on the mattress.

The races had begun, and she was already behind.

LATE IN THE bar on day two of what was turning out to be a very long death by PowerPoint sales meeting, Gustav told Asmi that he'd heard from the rumor mill that Scott's business case was mostly bullshit.

There were several people from GTech at the lobby bar of the hotel. Macau was just like Las Vegas but less opulent. When it came to money, however, the Macau casino strip earned more revenue than Las Vegas did. All wealthy Chinese came to spend their money on gambling, shopping and hookers in Macau. Just like Las Vegas, there were no windows and no concept of time. The food was passable, the décor a combination of Las Vegas tacky combined with Chinese kitsch.

"You should call Scott on his BS numbers," Gustav said.

"Look, I'm not going to pretend I'm the smartest person in the room when the leadership team is there. If I can see it, I'm assuming they can see it as well and if they don't want to do anything about it, then…" Asmi said exasperated.

Gustav nodded. "The others are planning to go into the old city tonight. You want to join?"

Asmi shook her head and held up her glass of scotch. "I need to get some sleep. I have a call with legal about the patent case in Germany at five in the morning."

Cécile came by and sat down with Asmi after Gustav left.

"You look down," she said.

Asmi shook her head. "Just tired. It's been a long few days."

"You know I wanted to come to Macau for two reasons. One is obviously professional. R&D never meets sales and I don't want to be *that* scientist. You know, the one who doesn't know the market or the business and is stuck with her rats in the lab. I want to meet customers and sales people," Cécile said. "But the other reason is…*delicate.*"

Asmi raised her eyebrows and waited as she held her glass of whiskey in suspense.

"I have an appointment with Master Dingbang, the famous Feng Shui fortune teller, tomorrow afternoon in Hong Kong," Cécile confessed.

"The Ding who?"

"Master Dingbang. He's famous," Cécile said. "He predicted some of the biggest global events, political and otherwise. He's truly amazing."

Asmi sipped her whiskey and then put her glass down on the bar. She swiveled on the bar stool to face Cécile. She was going to crack a joke about clairvoyants, but Cécile looked so serious that Asmi decided against it. "I don't know what to say."

"I believe in Feng Shui. My house is totally Feng Shui," Cécile said. "The difference between my life with and without it is so massive that I can't help but believe. I think you need Feng Shui in your life."

Asmi nodded and asked the bartender to pour her another drink. "I still don't know what to say," she said as she watched the liquid gold of a Yamazaki 12-year Japanese single malt fill her glass.

Cécile was in her early thirties and had recently married her longtime boyfriend, Francisco, a software programmer from Mexico whom she met at UC Berkeley. They had been married for a year and the end of the honeymoon period was marked with Cécile wanting to move back to France, and Francisco who had no desire to leave the United States, wanting to have nothing to do with her plans.

"You know the last time we talked, I told you how I worried that I couldn't have it all, be a career woman and have children,"

Cécile said, "And you're going to hate me for being so unambitious…but what if I had a baby and quit my job? Would that be so bad?"

Asmi considered how to answer that question. Women often asked themselves if they could do it all. *Can we have it all?* Men never did. A man never thought *I'm going to have a baby, I wonder how this is going to impact my career*. No, he thought, that's the wife's problem and what's worse is that the wife also thought it was her problem.

"Cécile, from what I know of you, and I won't say I know you *very* well, but it takes a certain tenacity to get a PhD from MIT, which you did. I think that if you stayed home with a baby it might drive you out of your mind," Asmi said and then added, "And it'll be a huge loss to the workforce to lose someone as competent and able as you. You can have your baby *and* a career. You don't have to give it up. I know several women who have the children, the husband and the career. Not everyone is a loser like me."

"You're not a loser," Cécile said. "But…what if I wanted to be a stay-at-home mom? Francisco makes enough. Don't you sometimes wonder why we do this…career thing?"

"No," Asmi said. "I have to work to pay for my life, Cécile. No Francisco here to pay my bills."

"Do you mind that there is no Francisco?"

"Sometimes," Asmi said. "And other times I'm glad I have my freedom to live my life the way I want. It's just me. I can make all the decisions."

"We're happy. We really are. I love him. But…he won't leave the US and I *really* want to have my baby close to my family. I just feel like a family is what I want," Cécile said.

"In France," Asmi said.

Cécile nodded. "In Lyon to be specific. I'm so confused. And that's why I made an appointment with Master Dingbang. He'll be able to guide me."

The bartender came up to them to ask if they'd like another drink as it was last call. They both declined and as they walked to the elevators to find their rooms, Asmi surprised herself by asking Cécile, "Can I come along with you to see this fortune teller?"

Cécile lit up. "That would be great. Maybe he can tell your fortune, as well."

"Let's hope he's more optimistic than I am," Asmi sighed.

~

MASTER DINGBANG'S Feng Shui Peace Palace was in the Repulse Bay Building right above the dragon hole. In Hong Kong, the skyline was planned and designed by architects in close collaboration with Feng Shui masters, Master Dingbang being one of them. The buildings were designed to be in harmony with nature and to bring good fortune to those who live in them.

Cécile and Asmi were escorted to a room where all the Feng Shui elements, Cécile told Asmi were in perfect harmony.

"Water, wood, fire, earth and metal are the five building blocks of Feng Shui," Cécile explained. "And in this room all five elements are balanced and that's why it feels so comfortable and harmonious. In a Feng Shui room you feel productive and you're more effective and therefore more successful."

"You've definitely drank the Kool-Aid," Asmi said.

"Or the cucumber water," Cécile said and pointed to a pitcher of water with fresh cucumbers for the clients in the waiting room.

The room was wafting with the light scent of jasmine. It was a pleasant room with a water feature on one side, which Asmi assumed was the water element the room needed to have in addition to the pitcher of cucumber water. The candles were fire and...there seemed to be a lot of wood, the furniture, the plants with thick woody branches and a drift wood sculpture.

"Can there be too much wood?" Asmi asked.

A quiet heavily accented voice responded, "Too much wood can result in fiery tempers and aggression."

Master Dingbang didn't look like something out of *Dr.*

Strange with flowing robes as Asmi had expected. Instead, he wore a suit and red tie and looked like a businessman. He led them into another room, which was also Feng Shui'd floor to ceiling.

"Please, sit," he said, gesturing to the green sofa that was shaped like a leaf. He sat across them in a scooped metal chair with a green cushion.

Cécile and Asmi sat down and he smiled at them pleasantly.

"Legend says that the mountains in Hong Kong are home to the dragons and in our culture, dragons bear powerful positive energy," Master Dingbang began. "The energy from the dragon blows through Hong Kong as they make their way from the mountain to the sea to bathe and sustain. This is why this building and many others along the waterline have dragon holes to give the dragon a clear path to the water, and this is why the winds of positive energy continue to flow through this great city. Hong Kong's prosperity is due to good Feng Shui."

Both Cécile and Asmi nodded dutifully.

"You are Cécile. You sent me the video of your house," he said and smiled broadly. "If there is too little fire it makes you feel low, reduces your ambition and takes happiness...the zest for life... away."

"Do I have too little fire?" Cécile asked.

"You don't have enough water," he said. "You need...an aquarium or you can bring home a sea shell. Keep it in the north corner of your home, where you have the painting of the fire. This way you temper the elements and bring balance."

Cécile nodded eagerly. "Master Dingbang, I'm confused about my future. I want to move back to France, but my husband doesn't. I feel like my job is not important enough. I don't know what to do."

Master Dingbang listened to her carefully and waited a long silent moment before he said, "Feng Shui is about positive energy and you can bring together positive energy with positive thought. You have too many negative thoughts. You need balance. Bring more water into your home and the energy will become positive."

He spoke with his hands and Asmi was reminded of a *sadhu* she had met in her grandmother's village in India. This holy man would tell people's fortunes by reading the palms of their hands in exchange for money. Asmi thought the holy man was a charlatan.

"*You* also have a lot of negative energy," Master Dingbang said as if could read Asmi's mind. She rubbed her hands on her black slacks and nodded. Yep, she was all negative right now, down to her revenue growth targets.

Maybe Master Dingbang was not a fraud and could tell her how to change her life, so it would make sense to her. She had nothing to lose.

"I have no Feng Shui," Asmi confessed.

"You have pictures of your home?" he asked.

Asmi nodded. She'd recently had pictures taken, wondering if she should sell the place and just rent. She was never home, and it was a huge financial burden. But as soon as she had it all set up with a real estate agent, she realized she couldn't part with the *only* bedroom in her life that didn't open with a keycard.

Master Dingbang looked through all the pictures on Asmi's phone and then gave her phone back to her. "Too much wood. Not enough metal. No earth. There is water with the view of the ocean. Fire is okay, but be careful."

"The real estate agent thought it would be nice to have pictures with the fireplace turned on," Asmi said.

Master Dingbang shook his head. "Too much wood. When you have too much wood, you have aggression. Are you fighting in your house?"

"I live alone," Asmi said. "I have no one to fight with."

"Too much wood," he repeated.

"What should I do? Throw the wood out?" Asmi asked.

"Spread it around the house. Add metal. Add plants for earth. Your house is out of balance. If your house has no balance, you have no balance," Master Dingbang said, a slight agitation in his non-verbal communication.

"Nobody lives in my house," Asmi said.

"You live in your house," Master Dingbang said unimpressed.

Asmi shook her head. "I live in hotel rooms," she said.

"Get your house in Feng Shui balance," he said and then as if losing interest in Asmi turned back to Cécile to talk about her Feng Shui balance for the rest of the hour they were there.

AT THE AIRPORT as they waited for their flight at the gate, Cécile was thrilled with the results of meeting Master Dingbang.

"I've already bought a Feng Shui water candle and a water element amulet," Cécile said.

"Where did you buy that?"

"On Amazon," Cécile said, "It'll be delivered by the time I get home. I think this is going to make it all work." And then because Scott and Gustav were close by, she leaned closer and said, "I bought you some stuff as well, to balance your wood."

Asmi sighed. "You didn't have to, Cécile, but—"

"Ladies, talking about fairies and unicorns?" Scott asked as he walked up to them.

"No, about Feng Shui," Cécile said irritated.

"Who on earth talks about fairies and unicorns, Scott?" Asmi asked.

"Women in fairytales?" Gustav suggested.

"I heard you met with the famous Master Dingbang," Scott said. "That's almost fluffy enough to be in fairytale unicorn territory. Asmi, I didn't take you to be one of *those* girls."

Asmi felt her back stiffen. What was it with this asshole that he couldn't make a remark without it being somehow sexist or misogynistic? And who were the *girls* he kept talking about? Asmi was nearly forty and hadn't been a girl for a very long time.

"What does that mean?" Cécile asked.

Scott shrugged. "Just...you know...girls who believe in hocus-pocus."

Cécile just shook her head and was about to say something, probably impolitic, when Asmi said, a bit too sweetly, "It was an insightful experience, Scott. Master Dingbang said I was too much wood."

"Can you translate? I don't speak Feng Shui," Scott said.

"It means I'm aggressive and spoiling for a fight," Asmi said.

FAKE IT UNTIL YOU MAKE IT!

EXCERPT FROM THE BUSINESS WORKBOOK
"AND THEN SHE SAID..."

YEP! This one goes against the whole "be yourself" ethos that I will advocate later in the book. For those of us who are struggling with the whole "I'm not ready for this" feeling every morning, "faking it" is the best way to proceed. A long time ago, they used to say, dress for the job you want and not the job you have. This follows the same premise: fake it long enough and you'll start believing it. If you believe it, then those around you will as well.

A friend of mine had been promoted from being an individual contributor to a manager. Suddenly, she was attending meetings that she never had before. In the meetings she found that she didn't know enough about the business—and she struggled with who was who when they talked about competitors.

"At one point I wasn't sure if they were talking about a specific technology or a competitor," she told me. I asked her what she did.

"I did my homework—I studied market data and strategy documents before every meeting," she said. "And I spoke only when I had a specific question, or I made a point that no one else had made. I didn't talk much at meetings. I felt like an idiot because everyone else had so much to say."

"So, what happened?" I asked.

"The thing is not to fake that you understand things or know things you don't. I faked that I was sure I would learn everything even though I was scared shitless," she said. "Since I didn't talk *all* the time in meetings, when I did speak, people listened to me. This was a bonus. And in six months, I could start faking with more confidence until I didn't have to fake it anymore. I had made it."

Faking it is not about "lying" to others—but to yourself. To say, I can do this even when you're afraid you can't. It's boosting your self-esteem and saying, "I've got this."

4

WE ARE NOW CROSSING A
ZONE OF TURBULENCE

ANANYA, Venkat, Madhuri and Prasad all sat on one side of the living room, while Asmi sat on the other, Ananya's coffee table between them.

Ananya also had too much wood, Asmi thought and not enough water, unless unshed tears of frustration counted.

Her older sister mouthed the word *sorry*. Asmi didn't have to be a clairvoyant like Master Dingbang to guess what they were doing. After all, she had sat on the other side of the living room a few times now. This wasn't her first rodeo. But now that she was nearly forty and *completely* over the hill, she didn't think, her parents gave a damn about her marital status.

"He has an MBA from Kellogg and now is a VP of something at HP. Very good job," Prasad, Asmi's father said and then nudged Venkat who was looking through his phone. He looked up distracted at Asmi and shrugged, "They want me to tell you that he's handsome."

Both Ananya and Asmi frowned.

"I told them it'd be strange but ..." Venkat said and stood up.

"Because a man would be objective," Madhuri, her mother explained. "He is very handsome."

"And how old is he?" Asmi asked.

"Forty-two," Prasad said.

"Forty-one and a half," Madhuri corrected him.

"And why is this VP from HP who's *very* handsome and an Indian still single in his early forties?" Asmi asked.

"Well...he's divorced, obviously," Madhuri said, fidgeting with the *pallu* of her sari. "Men that age aren't sitting around on trees, without a family, waiting for you."

"He has children?" Asmi asked horrified at the thought that she'd have to be a stepmother and that her parents thought that would be something she'd want.

"He only has them every other weekend. One boy and one girl. The wife has custody," Madhuri said. "This is a good thing. Your eggs are probably dried up by now, so you'll have an understanding husband who doesn't care if you can have children or not."

Asmi winced at the "dried up eggs" part and looked at Ananya in horror.

"You didn't tell us that he had kids...and her eggs are fine. Many women her age have children if they want to, that is," Ananya said, trying to mitigate the situation and went to stand beside Venkat who immediately took two steps back to indicate he wasn't part of this circus.

Asmi's niece and nephew, Anjali who was fifteen and Arjun who was thirteen, came into the living room just then. They saw the audience, felt the tension and looked at their father. He nodded, and they followed him out of the house without saying a word.

"Where are you all going?" Ananya called out after them.

"We're going out for sushi," Venkat replied and before Ananya could respond that she had dinner ready, they were out of the house.

"Way to clear the room, *Amma*," Asmi said to her mother. "In fact, I'd rather go out for sushi with them."

"You marry this guy and you can eat sushi all the time," Madhuri said, her forehead narrowed so her round *bindi* looked oblong. Asmi thought she looked like one of those Indian goddesses with the angry forehead, the bright red sari, and oiled hair coiled in a bun.

She had grown up with this woman in her house and yet they were strangers. In the past two decades, she had become a person her mother didn't recognize, and her mother was someone she didn't understand at all.

"I can afford my own sushi," Asmi said and as she heard her own words, she knew she sounded stupid. Why was it that she, a grown, independent and successful woman with a flourishing career (even if she was too much wood) turned into a defensive teenager in front of her mother?

Once when a boyfriend asked her to describe her *close* ties with her family because everyone knew that Indians had tight-knit families, she had said that her mother was a pro-single life contraceptive advertisement. Growing up, Asmi saw her parents fight, argue and manipulate their children, their parents, their siblings and everyone else in between. Asmi had decided as a child that she would *never ever* get married. There just didn't seem to be any profit in it.

"But he can buy the *best* sushi," Asmi's father said lamely because his wife nudged him.

Asmi walked up to her mother, leaned down and looked her in the eye. "Let me make this crystal clear. I will never get married to some guy you arrange my marriage with. *Never*."

"You're an ungrateful daughter making your mother sick with worry," Madhuri said, her eyes flashing.

Her mother went so quickly into fight mode, Asmi thought sadly. A decade ago, she'd been affected by her mother's moods, the acid she spouted, the inner critic she had become—but now, Asmi couldn't and didn't let her mother control her emotions. It had taken years of therapy to get here, but it was money well spent.

"Stop worrying about me," Asmi said. "My life is mine. It's a good life. It's a life I have earned and like."

"You need to get married," her mother protested.

"I don't *need* to do anything," Asmi said.

44

VENKAT POURED his wife and Asmi another good measure of scotch. The parents had gone to bed after another hour or so of fighting, and the children had hidden in their rooms since they'd come back from dinner.

Venkat, Asmi and Ananya had congregated, as they always did in the evenings when Asmi visited, on the patio with scotch and ice.

"I can't believe they still keep doing this," he said. "And seriously, can't you find a nice guy and get married and put us out of our misery?"

"Yeah, that's what I should do, marry someone for *you*," Asmi said as she stretched on the patio chair and took a sip of a new Islay Scotch whiskey she had picked up for her sister at the Hong Kong airport. The *Askaig* was harsh and peaty, not smooth like a Lagavulin and it suited the occasion.

"Anjali just told me when I went to kiss her goodnight that she wants to be just like her *Pinni* Asmi and never marry," Ananya said and then added after taking a sip of her drink, "I think it's a sensible decision. And this scotch is *really* good."

Venkat and Ananya had a semi-arranged marriage—this was the type of marriage where boy met girl under the aegis of the family, and they dated (with full guarantee that there will be a marriage). They liked each other from the start so there hadn't been any need to rebel against their parents.

Asmi also liked Venkat—he was easy going, charming and smart. He was an engineer at Google in a senior position, but he'd never been one of those guys who claimed that his work was his life. Venkat had always had a good work-life balance. He worked hard but his priority was his family, the job was just a way to pay the bills. He was good at what he did, so he was able to provide well for his family. Unlike Asmi, he didn't care about the next promotion. He cared about spending time with his children—going hiking, white water rafting, skiing…a job just paid for that.

Maybe it was because he had children, Asmi thought, maybe that's why he had this balance. Maybe the people who said that a woman of a certain age without kids gets obsessed with her job were right, because Asmi didn't have work-life balance. Hell, she didn't even have work-work balance.

Sometimes she envied Ananya. Her sister had no work pressure. She had a husband who carried the load. For Asmi there was no one else. To survive, she had to work. To keep her life worthy, she had to succeed at work. When she left India at the age of twenty-one to come to the United States to do her master's in biochemical engineering, Asmi had envisioned a career—but she had also assumed that she'd somewhere down the line get married and have children. She was never going to be like her mother or her sister, a homemaker, but she had also not imagined that she'd be a single woman who was ambivalent about marriage. In the beginning of her career, she'd had time to date but nothing serious evolved. It wasn't until she was in her early thirties that she realized that she didn't want to *live* with a man, that she didn't want to make the commitment and concessions she saw so many of her friends and acquaintances make. What she had thought was her being careful about the man she chose, she realized was a commitment phobia. In a way, Etienne, married and otherwise compromised, was the perfect man to fall in love with because there was no way he would intrude on her life. When being alone was a choice, being lonely didn't come into the picture. Asmi had mastered the art of being self-sufficient and of taking care of herself, now if she could just figure out how to keep herself in a place of contentment without the drama of work or personal life, she'd have it made.

"You *really* never want to get married?" Ananya asked.

"For now, I don't. Never is a long time."

"Come on," Venkat said, "You don't look at couples and families and wish that you had a husband and kids?"

Asmi shook her head. "No. I kept waiting for that feeling to arrive. A part of me wants to find this man and have this family because society has deemed that is how we humans must live.

46

But even as I think about it, the idea of sharing my life, giving my time to someone...I feel it'd be suffocating."

"You've dated, though," Venkat said.

"Well, the last man was married," Ananya said and when Asmi glared at her she shrugged. "He knows. He doesn't care."

Asmi sighed. "He was the perfect man in so many ways."

"Then why did you let him go?" Ananya asked.

Asmi shrugged. "Because a part of me didn't like being second best for him—I always felt like his wife was more important. She was the one who he had to take care of, and I was expendable. That feeling...well, it made me feel less."

"Would you cheat on me?" Ananya asked Venkat.

He contemplated the question as he drank his scotch and then shrugged, "I can say no, but the fact is that an opportunity has not arisen. I don't know. How about you?"

Ananya nodded. "If he's really hot and wants my *motherly* sagging tits body, sure."

"*I* want your body," Venkat said and put his arm around Ananya and kissed her.

Asmi watched the easy affection and searched for that feeling inside her, that feeling that she wished she had what her sister had. But in *that* very moment, she couldn't find it.

ASMI TOOK a Lyft to San Francisco International Airport to get on a flight to Santa Ana that next morning. Her parents had intentionally not said goodbye to her to let her know they were still *very* angry with her.

Why can't you at least meet this guy? Is too much to ask of you? We are your parents; don't we have any rights?

She knew how it looked. All these men and women around her married with children and here she was forty and single. No relationship in sight. She wasn't living with anyone. She wasn't dating anyone. She had heard the gossip about being an *ice queen*. She was a ball buster at work and maybe that's why no man put up with her, because she emasculated them. *They* didn't say it aloud, but she heard them all the same. She hated the smugness of these people with their partners. Like they had achieved something great and that she had failed. She was sick of these *happy* couples.

Asmi was waiting for the plane to board when she heard a woman call out to her. She turned to see Scott and his wife Andrea, a *happy* couple.

"I told him it was you, but we weren't sure," Andrea said and hugged Asmi. They'd met a few times and Asmi had been surprised to like Scott's wife. How could an ass like him have a woman like Andrea? There was obviously no justice in the universe. Andrea was blonde, beautiful and seemed like a nice person. A homemaker, she was bubbly and energetic and smiled a lot.

"Hey, Asmi," Scott said. "What are you doing here?"

"I came to see my sister," Asmi said. "She lives in Milpitas."

"Did you come directly from Hong Kong? Because Scott did," Andrea gushed. "It's our tenth wedding anniversary so I flew in from Santa Ana and he came from Hong Kong and we had the most amazing weekend at this gorgeous B&B in Napa."

"Oh...congratulations," Asmi said, forcing a smile.

"It's such a luxury to take a weekend off," Andrea said. "My parents have the girls...and what a pleasure to wake up late and not worry about breakfast and birthday parties and whatnot."

Scott had two girls, one was seven and the other was five. Asmi had seen photos of them in his office.

"I'm sure," Asmi said politely.

"Oh, you single women have no idea how great your lives are without kids and a husband. I sometimes I feel like I have *three* children," Andrea said, looking affectionately at her third child, Scott.

She wasn't being rude about Asmi's status; she thought she was being somehow complimentary.

"I know how great I have it," Asmi said.

"You ready for Nice?" Scott asked her.

"Yes," Asmi said. They were going to have a clinical seminar in Nice and Asmi had fought for the budget to make it happen. It was a big deal for her marketing efforts. It also had nothing to do with Scott, but his wife was with him, so she didn't respond with a polite variation of *mind your own business*.

"Lots of money going into that seminar," Scott said. "I hope you get a good return on our investment."

Asmi nodded. "You ready for Copenhagen?" she asked instead.

Scott shrugged. "I'm going to go with the company line on this one," he said. "I don't like to argue with the CEO on his decisions. Now…"

"Oh, can we stop the shop talk," Andrea said.

But before Scott could answer, they started to board those with elite status, so they all fished for their boarding passes.

Asmi managed to avoid them during the short flight and even at the airport. She'd made a concerted effort to do so. There was nothing like seeing Scott happy in his marriage to make her feel worse about herself. He had a career, a happy wife and what did she have?

THE SELF ESTEEM WORKBOOK

EXCERPT FROM THE BUSINESS WORKBOOK "AND THEN SHE SAID..."

THERE REALLY IS no easy alternative when it comes to building self-esteem, faking it only gets you so far. Here are **two things you can do** to help boost your self-esteem and stay grounded.

1. **Now is not the time to ignore your blind spots:** We all suffer from personal blind spots and none of us has reached that state of enlightenment where we're completely self-aware. To be able to believe that we can do what we want to do, we must be aware of our inner workings. Since I have low self-esteem, my blackest blind spot was the impact I have on others. I couldn't imagine that I had any impact, "Me? But I'm a nobody." When people said, "You're noticed when you walk into a room," I decided that was because I was often the only brown woman in an all-white-male meeting. I had to understand my impact so I could use it smartly and not let it hold me back. And the only way I could see this, or any other blind spot is by accepting feedback from others. Feedback tells us how we're perceived, and we can either choose to change that perception by tweaking our language, tone,

behavior, or decide that is not a change we want to make—but it's always good to know. Remember, feedback often reveals as much about the person giving the feedback as it does about you. So, be careful about who you accept feedback from.

2. **Don't be afraid to fail:** Many women I know are afraid to aim high, because to try and fail is a bigger blow than just not aiming high at all. We're in a work culture where we're not supposed to fail. We make so many careful decisions to avoid failure, but as Queen Latifah has said "Fear can be good when you're walking past an alley at night or when you need to check the locks on your doors before you go to bed, but it's not good when you have a goal and you're fearful of obstacles. We often are trapped by our fears, but anyone who has had success has failed before." *The question to ask yourself is, are you playing to win or are you playing to not lose?* I'm just as afraid of making a mistake as the next person. I don't want anyone to point a finger at me. But the thing is, when we act out of fear, we're not creative, productive or having fun, we're just covering our ass.

Self-esteem requires constant internal reinforcement and here is a trick to keep that top of mind:

o   When was I truly happy at work? _____

o   What do my colleagues love about me? _____

o   What am I proud of? _____

o   What is my #1 strength? _____

o   What makes me unique? _____

Print this out and put it on your wall where you can see it or use at as the cover image for your phone and iPad. Seriously. This is important for you to know and be aware of daily.

~

IF YOU'VE EVER SAID, "I'M NOT ENOUGH," REPEAT AFTER ME

- I will be ambitious, and I will dream
- I will get honest feedback from trusted sources and only trusted sources, because irrelevant and *mean* feedback will make me take three steps back
- I may never conquer my fear, but I will not let it paralyze me
- I will fake it until I make it

5

THE COPENHAGEN AFFAIR

IT STARTED like any other meeting, a lot of suits in a meeting room—this one was on the twentieth floor of one of the high rises in the Islands Brygge area of Copenhagen—but it ended in a *very* strange "Oh, this is so Scandinavian" way.

Matthew had invited Scott and Asmi to Copenhagen to meet with a company that GTech was interested in acquiring. Short Poppy was a small Swedish-Danish agritech company, which had recently developed a new bacteria-based technology for nitrogen fixation, a method to help crops fix nitrogen from the air so they didn't need nitrogen fertilizers, which are harmful to the planet. On paper, it seemed like a promising idea.

"You know why he's asked us both to be here, don't you?" Scott whispered to Asmi as she poured herself a cup of coffee in the meeting room of the Short Poppy offices, where they were the first to arrive.

"Because we're marketing directors and he'd like to know our opinion when he's acquiring a new company?" Asmi offered.

Scott shook his head. "You know what this is about."

Asmi let her eyelids flutter. "Do I?" she asked.

Scott narrowed his gaze. "Yes, he's picking the next VP of Marketing."

"Is he?" Asmi said as she made a production of picking up a Danish pastry and putting it on a plate.

Scott looked at the pastry pointedly and said, "Wow."

"Hmm?"

"I can't eat heavy stuff when I'm jet lagged," Scott said.

"It's a pastry, light as a feather," Asmi said and bit into the flaky Danish.

"I meant...the calories," Scott said

May the odds be ever in your favor, Asmi thought as she walked away and stopped by the floor length window and looked onto the city of Copenhagen in the near distance. Her hand shook slightly as she ate her pastry. She saw her reflection in the window and saw none of the turmoil within. If Scott thought that he could rattle her by bringing to light that Asmi wasn't skinny, which she wasn't, but neither was she fat (was she?)— then he was right. All the talk about how he works out, does cross fit, runs marathons and how he *always* works out in the hotel gym, won't even book a hotel without a gym—they were all designed, Asmi felt, to let her know that she was less than him and it worked.

I need to start working out more regularly, Asmi thought as she looked at herself in the black skirt suit she was wearing. The band of the skirt was snug, wasn't it? Maybe Scott wasn't always wrong. Maybe she shouldn't be eating a Danish pastry with a million calories. Maybe she should be waking up at six in the morning and working out. Maybe...she sighed as the *must do*s layered themselves in her mind, one flakey crust on top of another.

Asmi had walked into many rooms where she was the only woman and she had seen all the tactics men used to indicate that she didn't fit the societal stereotype: of not looking like a super-model, of not being a wife and mother, of being brown, of...*simply* not fitting in.

Once, in her junior days in a meeting she had been asked if she had been able to get someone on the phone to get some answers. Asmi had said that she had tried but she couldn't get what she needed. Her boss had commented, "I thought you Indians were good on the phones, that's why you have all those call centers, don't you?" Everyone at the meeting had laughed and Asmi had said nothing. *What could she say?* The minute she said something she'd be told that she was too sensitive and couldn't handle a joke.

Then there was that time when during a work dinner she had spilled something on a white blouse. A male colleague had taken a picture with his phone, specifically of her breast with the stain. Asmi had been horrified and told the colleague to delete the picture, which he didn't. A few weeks later when she was unable to make a meeting with that colleague, he sent her a text message with the picture, saying, "We miss you." This time Asmi told HR about it. They concluded that it was an isolated incident and the colleague was sorry about it. They suggested that Asmi should move on. Asmi did. She found another job in another company.

Sometimes it was subtle like the Danish pastry comment and sometimes overt—but always, it hit the mark. Ultimately, she left the pasty half eaten.

MATTHEW BAINES CAME into the meeting room and filled it with his larger than life presence. He wasn't a big man: about six feet tall, he was fit (in shape because he liked to run marathons *just like Scott*) and looked a little like Clint Eastwood in his late fifties. He had charisma and he knew how to use it.

Asmi turned her focus from the building she was staring into where it appeared a film crew was setting up and turned to face the big boss.

"Scott," Matthew thumped Scott on his shoulder. "They do a great run here, not long, like thirteen kilometers at the Hermitage…a deer park with a castle. I think we need to finagle a visit in October for that. What do you think?"

"Absolutely," Scott said. "And maybe squeeze in the Berlin marathon? I have high hopes of getting in this year."

"Sounds like a plan," Matthew said, and then more somberly turned to Asmi and nodded. No shoulder thumping for Asmi. "How was your flight?"

Asmi set her plate down on the table even though what she wanted to do was throw it against the glass window and scream. *Fuck your fucking boys' club!*

Asmi had spent the entire flight reading up on Short Poppy, and was concerned that she would be at odds with Matthew in her assessment. GTech was a commercial enzymes company. Agritech was an adjacent market and Asmi agreed that they should invest in some of these technologies, but Short Poppy was not incubated enough to be interesting just quite yet. In her opinion, GTech wasn't equipped to take on a nascent company like Short Poppy and grow it. She was going to keep an open mind, she promised herself. The final decision would be Matthew's and he had asked Scott and her to join him for these acquisition discussions to test them. If she went against Matthew, would she blow her changes for getting the VP of Marketing position? If she kissed his ass, would she blow her chances of respecting herself?

Welcome to the corporate conundrum—*should you be career smart or have integrity? Was this hill worth dying on?*

"It was a good flight," Asmi said and then cleared her throat as she decided how to phrase her question before the Short Poppy people arrived, "I read through the investor report for Short Poppy and I was ..."

Before Asmi could finish her question, a tall blonde woman walked into the room, followed by a tall blonde man. They introduced themselves as Elvira Ekström, CEO, and Mats Bengtsson, COO of Short Poppy. They were delighted to meet the GTech family and name dropped the chairman of the board as well as Jim, the man both Asmi and Scott were hoping to replace.

∾

IT HAD TO HAPPEN.

Even though Asmi was with GTech, she ended up sitting on the same side of the table as Elvira with the windows behind them, while Mats ended up on the *male* side of the table. Asmi had been in enough meetings to know this was a common occurrence. It was a man's world and the women were still fighting to get a seat at *their* table.

They all turned to the screen as Elvira started to present.

She wasn't bad, Asmi thought as Elvira made a case for GTech to buy and therefore invest to grow Short Poppy. Regardless of Elvira's presentation skills, Asmi continued to feel that it wasn't the right time for GTech to acquire Short Poppy and the presentation was not changing her mind. She stole a glance to look at Matthew and Scott and found all the boys on the other side of the table, watching Elvira keenly as she spoke.

Damn it, Asmi thought, they were eating everything she was serving, and she knew she would now have to play this even more carefully than before.

"So...any questions?" Elvira asked. "I just wanted to stop here for a minute before I present the R&D pipeline."

The men cleared their throats and shook their head. Even the Short Poppy guy, Mats was shuffling. Matthew Baines had no questions? And that's when Asmi realized that they had not been watching Elvira but something behind her.

Asmi turned and her eyes widened. On the balcony in the building across the one they were in, a man and woman were naked, having sex against the balcony railing. There was a cameraman, a fan blowing the woman's hair and a guy holding a light diffuser.

Obviously, they were making a porn film.

Asmi looked back at the three men who started to look elsewhere as if caught with their hands down their pants.

Elvira looked at them confused and then at Asmi who turned her head to indicate Elvira should also see what was happening behind her back.

Elvira sighed loudly. "Mats, I thought we had discussed it with the building manager that they need to stop filming these movies outdoors during business hours."

"I did but you know how it is, they do what they want," Mats said and then turned to Scott and Matthew. "We're pretty relaxed about porn in Scandinavia."

"Relaxed, yes, but we try to not film it during a professional meeting," Elvira said tightly. "Mats, why didn't you tell me that was going on as I presented? I wonder if our guests could even pay attention to the presentation."

"Of course, we could," Scott said smoothly.

"Maybe you could, but I couldn't," Matthew Baines said honestly. "I'm so sorry, Elvira but I was flummoxed and …"

Asmi stood then and closed the blinds on the tall window. She turned around and said with a flourish, "Since I was not distracted with pornography, maybe I could ask you some questions."

Scott glared at her and Asmi smiled back sweetly. Asmi: 1, Scott: 0.

ASMI HAD a soft spot for Copenhagen and mostly because of the airport, where she spent most of her time when she was in the city. She could eat a steak cooked medium rare or have sushi or caviar or a hotdog…whatever her heart desired at one of the many airport restaurants. Besides the food, there was the shopping. Asmi had discovered a Danish brand, Marlene Birger and always stopped by to see what they had on sale. Over the years she had bought shoes at Gucci, a scarf at Hermes as a present for Ananya, makeup and whiskey (obviously) at the duty-free store and had fallen in love with the spicy tuna sandwich with a Prince of Green fresh-pressed juice at the chain eatery *Joe & the Juice*.

She liked European cities, and in the past three years, she had liked them even more because she saw Etienne when she was in Europe.

The GTech team was staying at the Hotel Admiral and nostalgia smacked Asmi. She had stayed here in a corner room with a view of the Royal Opera House with Etienne. Just a year ago, they had walked over the pedestrian bridge across the water to have dinner at the famous restaurant, Noma. She'd had to stay on hold in the middle of the night in Laguna Beach to secure that table. It had been her treat. It was his birthday.

Unable to stay in her room because it stirred up too many memories, and because she had to physically stop herself from calling Etienne to simply ask, "Are you still there...for me?" she went down to the hotel restaurant and bar SALT.

She sat at the bar with a view over the water. She ordered an Ardbeg 10, decided against checking her email on her phone and silently watched the boats sail past the window. Hotel guests were starting to fill the bar and she heard a variety of languages. English, French, Italian and German. The drink orders ranged from gin and tonic to Manhattans to wine. There was laughter and discussion and Asmi felt the comfort of yet another hotel lobby bar engulf her. This was familiar.

Her phone beeped with a text message and since it was Ananya, Asmi didn't ignore it.

They're driving me mad. How's Copenhagen? Any news from Paris?

Asmi responded: *No news from Paris. Copenhagen reminds me of him. They're nuts.*

If you love him, just be with him.

Asmi shook her head thinking that Ananya should not encourage her. *It's not authentic, this life as his lover with his wife sleeping on the other side of his bed.*

Call if you want to talk.

I'm okay. Having dinner with Scott and Matthew. Oh, and when I'm back, remind me to tell you about this porn movie we saw being filmed.

What???? Tell me now.

Later.

You've left me in suspense. You'll be made to pay for this.

Asmi grinned as she put the phone away and braced herself as she saw Matthew walk into the bar. She took a deep breath and waited for him to join her. Bars were the best place to conduct corporate politics.

It was March and cold in Copenhagen and Matthew was wearing, as he usually did, a pair of jeans with a T-shirt and one of those cashmere wool coats. No one knew much about Matthew's personal life except that he was *still*, as he liked to say it, married to his first wife. He didn't share holiday details or *what I did over the weekend* stories. He was an attractive man and with his gray hair and angular features, he exuded charisma.

The charisma intensified with intrigue because Matthew wasn't accessible, he didn't make people comfortable—a problem for any leader as it prevented his staff from challenging him. The standing joke was that Matthew wanted to be the kind of leader who liked to be challenged and enjoyed a discussion, but he was *that other leader* the autocratic kind who wanted people to do what he said without question and occasionally kiss his ass to feed his ego. For many years now, Asmi had had a layer between herself and their imposing CEO—but now he was her line manager, which was a problem because she didn't kiss anyone's ass, no matter how fine it was.

"Asmi, what're you drinking?" Matthew asked.

Asmi told him and he ordered himself a Macallan 12 Year on the rocks and said, "I simply can't stand peaty whiskey...some of those are so strong I feel like I stuck my head inside a barbecue." He paused as he sipped his whiskey and then added, "But no one will accuse it of being a girlie whiskey. You know what I mean?"

No, you misogynistic son of a bitch, no, I don't know what you mean and your insinuation that I drink peaty whiskey to compensate for a dick is a dickie thing to say.

Asmi smiled. "What did you think of Short Poppy? We didn't have a chance to discuss after the meeting."

"I thought we could talk about it during dinner," Matthew said. *"But* we could talk now, as well. What do you think? Scott thinks it has potential."

It's a trap, Asmi. He wants you to bitch about Scott because he knows you disagree.

"I agree," Asmi said. "They do have potential. But seeing how nascent their technology is, I feel that the potential may take too long to realize. We're not angel investors, we usually like to acquire companies with commercially proven technologies. Also, to support this, we'll have to build a commercial organization because what we have now will not be enough."

Matthew looked keenly at Asmi. "Why not just use Short Poppy's commercial organization? They have a sales and marketing team."

The bartender asked Asmi if she'd like another drink and she shook her head. She was having dinner with Scott the Bastard and Matthew the Beast and she needed her wits. Also, getting drunk at a work thing, even getting tipsy at a work thing never worked out for anyone—you either ended up saying something stupid, which was bad, or you ended up doing something stupid, which was super bad. Asmi had done both early on in her career.

"The sales team is small, and their biggest victory has been getting the Swedish government excited about them, which I think was a slam dunk, as they won a government grant last year," Asmi said.

"They might still be a good bet," Matthew said. "A government contract is not something to frown at."

Shut up and nod. Shut up, smile and nod. Shut up…

"That deal hardly matters because just about two to three percent of their revenue comes from Scandinavia. The bulk of the revenue will have to come from the US, and they don't have the manpower to support that," Asmi said and saw Matthew's eyes darken, his body language, telling her to let this go…and yet, she persisted. If he wasn't going to give her the job then so be it, she wasn't going to sit here and pretend her opinion was any other than what it was.

She picked up a peanut from the bowl in front of her, to give her mouth something else to do instead of speaking.

"What if we buy them and run them separately? Make them a separate business unit...or operating company," Matthew suggested.

"If that's an expansion model we're looking at it, I haven't seen the strategy for it. From what I know, our strategy is to grow by acquiring smaller enzyme manufacturers in high growth markets like India and China," Asmi said even though the career smart thing would've been to smile and nod her pretty head. This was important to Matthew, that's why Scott had played it safe and said Short Poppy had potential, even though he probably could see the pitfalls as she did.

Scott was smart.

Asmi talked too much.

Matthew shrugged. "I want to do this."

Asmi nodded at the bartender then. She needed another drink.

"You're the boss," Asmi said after her drink was served and raised her glass to him. *Yes, she needed to find a new job. Damn it!!!*

"Yes, I am," Matthew said with a smile. "What's it you want, Asmi?"

She was caught off guard. "Well..." she began, trying to rein in her thoughts. She knew what she wanted. But it wasn't easy to just balls out say it. I want the big office and the big job with the big money. No, she said things like *the next step* or her favorite, *a challenging job but I don't care about titles or money*. Like hell, she didn't, but she said it anyway because ambition didn't look good on a woman. One of her colleagues a few years ago in marketing had a reputation for being *too* ambitious. That's what people said about her, not that she was a good marketer or a good leader, just ambitious and not like it was a good thing, but a greedy thing.

"Jim is retiring, and..."

Asmi was going to blubber something inane when she was saved by Scott Beauregard the Third who walked in with his Louisiana swagger.

"Y'all are already here," he said and sat down next to Matthew. "How many drinks is that, Asmi? You better be careful, I speak from experience."

He was such an asshole. Scott was known to get loaded in work parties. There was the infamous story of him in Las Vegas with his team, falling down the stairs because he was so drunk that he had to be carried to his room. Now imagine that it was a woman who had slipped up. There'd be no next step, no next challenge, no nothing.

"Not all of us are light weights," Asmi said and raised her glass to her lips, "I speak from experience."

She saw Matthew grin at that comment, and he turned to look at Asmi, as if saying, *nice one.*

"I managed to get us a table reservation at 108," Scott said instead of responding to her. "You'll like it Matthew, it's by the Noma people. Noma, Asmi, was rated one of the best restaurants in the world several…"

"I've been to Noma," Asmi said, cutting him off. Scott liked to portray himself as a big foodie who knew the all the *best* places to eat in every city around the world. He was one of those guys who liked to talk about that little restaurant in Lille or Provence or somewhere remote that had a Michelin star and served the *best* Coquilles Saint Jacques or some other local dish with a wine cellar that was to always *die for.*

"When were you at Noma?" Scott asked surprised.

"Last year."

"What were you doing in Copenhagen?" Scott asked.

I was meeting my lover, Etienne, who likes good restaurants and it was his birthday present. After dinner, we came back to the Admiral Hotel and had sex every which way we could.

"I was here for a conference and I went with friends," Asmi said casually.

"I've never been to Noma," Matthew said. "I've been to the French Laundry in Napa. Now that was impressive."

"Then you'll like 108," Scott said.

It only got worse during dinner and Asmi was exhausted with the back and forth with Scott. In the end, she just gave up and focused on the food, which was incredibly good and gave her something to do besides try to not look foolish when she was subtly sidelined by Scott in every conversation.

Asmi had told a coach once that she felt, often, in meetings that she was ignored. She was a woman, a brown woman walking into meeting rooms with mostly white men and the men made her feel unsure and uncertain. Many women Asmi knew felt like this and the coach concurred that one of the hardest things for women in middle management was getting a seat at the table.

"The problem is," the coach said, "You're waiting for someone to give you permission. No one will. You must accept your right at the table and take your place. Use your elbows if you need to. No one is going to hold the door open for you."

The only problem, she'd added, was that it was exhausting to be that woman at the table, constantly fighting for her place and many capable women gave up, feeling it wasn't worth it.

"The trick is to recharge your batteries often enough so that you don't reach the point of exhaustion," the coach warned her. "Choose your battles. You don't have to die on every hill."

A dinner conversation at a restaurant was *definitely* not the hill to die on. Asmi instead enjoyed her wine and her food and recharged her batteries.

IN THE HOTEL lobby after dinner, Asmi declined a drink at the bar, since she was already over the drinking limit, and went to her room. She should be hanging out in the bar with Matthew and Scott, lobby bars were where you networked. But her nerves were shot. Was Jim's job worth all of this? Scott could have it, for all she cared.

She knew she needed respite when she found herself wondering: *Why am I doing this? I should take it easy and stop fighting. I should find myself a nice man, make some babies and live my life.*

In the past, the fastest way to ease her stress was to reach out to Etienne. On evenings in Europe after a work dinner, he'd be waiting for her in the hotel room with a bottle of champagne, a comforting ear and high-quality orgasms.

She remembered one time in Lisbon when she'd had a tough meeting with a customer and Matthew who'd just been promoted to CEO. She'd come back to her room to find him with a bottle of Ardbeg Uigeadail that was never easy to find but he had found it for her. Usually, they fell on each other—but he could see she was still in the meeting room. So, he sat her on his lap and listened to her. He didn't try to solve her problems or give advice, he merely listened.

When she'd asked, "What do you think?"

He'd said, "I think you've had a long day. I promise, tomorrow morning, it will all look much better."

The next morning while they had breakfast and she was rested, who wouldn't be rested after such good sex, he'd talked to her about the meeting again. He gave her advice on how to handle herself. In many ways, through those years when she and Etienne had been together, he had been her business coach as well.

"Insecure men will always find a strong woman like you intimidating," Etienne said.

"But why?"

"Because you're intelligent and articulate," he said. "You have charisma and what you need to learn is how to use it, how to charm instead of intimidate."

"That sounds sexist."

Etienne kissed her then and said, "Yes. But the world, *ma chérie*, is sexist and I'm teaching you how to beat a man at his own game."

She missed him!

When Asmi reached her room, unable to help herself, she picked up her phone and sent Etienne a message.

Will I be better off leaving the corporate rat race, getting married and having babies?

He responded almost immediately.

I don't see why you can't do both. Climb the corporate ladder and have the family. Men have been doing it for centuries.

For a French banker with a mistress, Etienne was his own brand of feminist and boosted Asmi's confidence with his faith in her.

I'm struggling with Scott. He knew who Scott was.

Ignore the asshole. Focus on what you want. He's just a diversion. You're stronger and smarter. You can crush him.

Asmi lay down on her bed and looked at his messages, she was smiling as she typed a response and that was when she stopped typing because she realized what she was doing, she was sliding back into him, the comfort of him. This was easy. He knew her. She knew him. The intimacy. But he wasn't hers.

Yes, now he responded but there were times when she wanted him, maybe even needed him and he couldn't be there because he had a family. He was a lover, not a friend or a partner. He made her feel lonely even though she was used to being alone.

The back and forth of their relationship through the past four years—the I want you, the I have a family, the I can't do this, the I want this…on both their sides, the push and the pull, the *this is over* scenes…the stuff that affairs are made of—all that was bigger than the comfort he offered. In the end, he made her feel worse, not better, not good, not after a point.

Goodnight, she wrote to end the conversation. Then she put her phone face down on the bedspread and started to cry.

AND THEN SHE SAID...THIS IS ENOUGH

EXCERPT FROM THE BUSINESS WORKBOOK "AND THEN SHE SAID..."

I OFTEN MEET women who say to me, "I'm fine. This is enough. I don't want more." This is not just happening to women across the organization, even senior positions. An Executive Vice President I recently met told me that she was doing well enough—why did she have to do more?

HERE ARE three different reasons why women say, "this is enough" and knowing what these are can help mitigate the obstacle we place in front of us.

1. **Baby, baby:** This is the most common. Woman gets pregnant and woman decides that she doesn't need to have the career right now, because she's going to be oh so busy with the baby. In fact, a woman thinks about getting pregnant and starts to pull away from projects, because she won't be there to complete the projects, since she's going to be busy with the baby soon. Babies are great, but let's not use them as excuses to lean back and compromise. If you genuinely feel that you want

to be a full-time mom, then you probably shouldn't be reading this book anyway—but if you want to climb the corporate ladder, having a baby doesn't stop you from doing that.

2. **Husband, husband:** The man has a career and the woman has a job. It's such a cliché, but as I said in the first lesson, clichés come from a real place. So, the mom must pick up the kids, save vacation days to stay home with a sick child, cancel meeting to accommodate husband's schedule et cetera, et cetera, because your husband's job is more important than yours. You're the one who's juggling it all, work, lunch boxes, runny noses, the lot. Maybe it's time to let the husband be an equal partner in this whole marriage and family team set up. Maybe it's time to demand it and get it.

3. **I'm exhausted:** Sometimes the fight is so hard as a woman that you just want to give up and say, I don't need to take that next step, I'm happy where I am. Because there is just this far you can go with the fight —fighting for a seat at the table, the opportunity to speak, avoiding ripping someone's head off for cutting you off again.... It's hard to deal with performance reviews that call you abrasive, aggressive and/or emotional. It's hard to be told to be less or be more or be...someone else...anything other than who you are.

Ultimately, the root cause of all these "this is enough" feelings stem from something common, a four-lettered word that starts with F. Yes, you guessed it: FEAR.

Yoda is right, fear leads to anger and anger leads to the dark side. In the corporate world, for women, fear leads to saying things like "I'm done. I don't need more. This is enough for now."

6

IT'S NOT SO NICE IN NICE

"ISN'T NICE GREAT?" Gustav said as he passed by Asmi on the patio of their hotel where she was sitting under an umbrella and drowning in her work email inbox. He was wearing a pair of shorts, had a beach towel slung around his shoulder, a bottle of sunscreen in one hand, a paperback novel in another and a pair of sunglasses on his forehead, waiting to slide onto his nose.

Gustav had lately started to travel beyond the confines of the United States. His last trip was Macau with Asmi and now Nice; he was having the time of his life. Asmi, who remembered how it felt like in the early days when she started to travel internationally, knew that the long flights and jet lag soon took its toll and global business travel lost some of its charm. But in the early days it had been magic.

Asmi would have liked to join Gustav on the beach but it wasn't to be. Matthew had decided to continue to look at Short Poppy, no decision yet, but that meant that Asmi's workload had gone up as her marketing intelligence team was building market models to evaluate the business potential of Short Poppy. This was, Matthew said, so Asmi could investigate the agritech market to her heart's content, as she was the one with doubts. Scott had said he didn't have a problem with the acquisition, so he was off the hook.

No good ever came from of integrity and taking a stand.

"Enjoy the beach," Asmi said sourly. "I need to work on these Short Poppy numbers."

They were having a Clinical Seminar for wine enzymes in Nice and nearly everyone from GTech and the customers invited from the Americas were at the beach that Sunday evening. The meeting started the following afternoon and ran through Tuesday night. They had chosen to start late on Monday to allow the speakers for the seminars, mostly French and German wine makers, to come in on Monday morning.

"You want me to stay and help?" Gustav asked. He'd stay if she asked him to and she could use his help but why should he suffer when the pebble beaches of Nice beckoned. Also, Gustav had worked like a dog to set up the seminar and if anyone deserved an evening off, it was him.

"Go ahead, I'll wrap this up and maybe even join you for a drink on the beach," Asmi said even though there was no chance of that happening, not until way past beach closing time.

After Gustav left, Asmi decided the least she could do was make her Sunday evening slightly more pleasant with something to drink. The waiter assured her that their bartender made a very good Manhattan so Asmi ordered one.

Her phone rang then, and she almost didn't pick it up when she saw the caller was Scott.

"Asmi, do you have the presentation you did on GTech for your big distributor in Australia?" he demanded as soon as she said hello.

Well, hello to you too. How are you doing? Fine. Me too.

"Yes," Asmi said.

"Can you email it to me?" he asked. "I need it. I have to present GTech to a customer in China so...can you send it? Immediately?"

Yes, sir, Scott sir.

"Of course," Asmi said.

"Thanks," Scott said and then as if realizing that maybe he should be a little more congenial, added, "I hope everything turns out well with your seminar. That's a lot of money we're spending on it."

"Thanks, Scott," Asmi said. "I'll send the presentation."

A part of her didn't want to send anything to Scott and wanted him to panic right before his presentation, but that wasn't who she was. She wondered as she emailed the slide deck to Scott if he'd help her in the same way. She already knew he wouldn't.

If she hadn't been so absorbed with her thoughts, her computer and Scott, she would've noticed the man watching her.

It wasn't until she heard her name called out hesitantly in a French accent that she looked up, half expecting Etienne because of the French intonation and then squinted slightly.

Oh no, not Etienne's friend.

"Yes, Asmi?" he said a little more confidently and stood up, starting to walk toward her.

"*Bonjour*, Henri," Asmi said and tried not to shake her head in despair. It was bad enough being in France and now she had to deal with Etienne's friend. When would this affair die? When would she stop feeling anything for him? She had been advised by her friend Cara that the best way to get over someone was to get under someone, but Asmi didn't have the heart. The heart as such was still broken. She couldn't just jump into bed with someone else. Could she? Should she?

Henri owned a vineyard in Bordeaux and Etienne knew him from when he had apparently courted his wife who had grown up in the wine country. Henri had helped Etienne win his wife's hand and they had been friends ever since. When Etienne had introduced Asmi to Henri, she had wondered how Henri would respond since he knew Etienne's wife. She had worried for no reason. The clichés about French mistresses were rooted in reality.

If only he wasn't Etienne's friend, Asmi thought practically, he would be just the sort of guy she could get under to get over Etienne.

"It is you," Henri said in relief and did the whole cheek air kiss-kiss thing before sitting down across from her.

The waiter brought her Manhattan and Henri asked him to bring one for him as well.

"What are you doing here?" he asked.

"We're hosting a seminar on enzymes for wine production," Asmi said.

Henri crinkled his nose. "Enzymes...it's too radical for us French."

Asmi smiled. "Our number one market for white wine is New Zealand, because of the heat. Our number one market for red wine is France. Enzymes help improve the color."

"It must be those fuckers in Alsace, not us in Bordeaux," Henri said genially. "Does Etienne know you're here?"

Asmi took a sip of her Manhattan because hearing his name in her head was one thing but it was quite another to hear it from someone else, someone who knew him, knew her, knew them as a couple.

"I have no idea," Asmi said as nonchalantly as she could muster.

Henri nodded. "He told me you ended it."

"Then why did you ask?"

Henri shrugged. "I didn't know if you'd tell me, and I didn't want to embarrass you."

Never before had Asmi wanted to go back to her Excel sheets as much as she did right now. She didn't want to discuss Etienne with anyone, especially not his friend.

"You know affairs, they come with a time limit," she said and started to practice, in her head, an excuse about a conference call with California so she could go back to her room. She *really* had work to do and she *really* didn't want to cry in front of Henri who would report back to Etienne as soon as he could.

"And you're lonely now, *oui*?" he asked tenderly.

Asmi smiled to prevent her eyes from filling. "What are you doing in Nice, Henri?" she asked instead.

The waiter brought Henri's drink and he leaned back on his

chair. "I have a party invitation at Le Negresco, but they were full so I'm staying here. It's business. One of my father's friends is turning seventy and so there's a party. He has a vineyard close to my father's in Bordeaux. Would you like to join me?"

"Me?" Asmi stuttered. "No, no, I have a lot of work. But thank you for asking."

"It's just drinks and a little entertainment," Henri said and then pulled out his phone to look through it. "They have...a... cabaret...ah...*burlesque*."

Asmi raised her eyebrows. "Do they now?"

Henri grinned. "You Americans are so...a *prude*, is that the word in English?" Asmi nodded and he continued, "You know you have a president who grabs Madam Macron's arm and says she has a good figure. Though we all know what he wanted to really *grab, eh,* and you're rolling your eyes about burlesque." He looked through his phone again and then cried out, "*Viola!* It's Dita von Teese. I'm told she's a...*célèbre*...very *populaire* in America."

"Dita von Teese will be dancing at this party?" Asmi asked. Of course, she'd heard of the most famous burlesque dancer in the world.

"Yes," Henri said, "Jacques has more money than he knows what to do with."

Asmi considered his offer and then ran through her wardrobe choices. Pant suit in grey, skirt suit in blue with white stripes, sheath dress in white with blue flowers...yes, the sheath dress would do. She had packed it for a dinner. It came with a blue jacket, but it was warm in March in Nice and she didn't really need that business jacket...and ...*no, no, no*.

"Henri, I'd love to but ..."

"*Non, non*...come on, live a little," Henri said and then he leaned closer and Asmi could smell his cologne, "And you need a little lightness, don't you? And it's for a...*deux*...two hours. Just come, have a drink and see the performance. I'll have you back by ten."

Asmi eyed her computer. If she came back by ten, she could

still put in another couple of hours of work before getting to bed. The seminar started at one in the afternoon, she could sleep in a little if needed. And she deserved a little Dita von Teese, didn't she?

~

LE NEGRESCO, Henri told Asmi as he led her through the exquisite lobby to the ballroom with a view of the sparkling Bay of Angels, was a hotel as well as a museum because it hosted works by Moretti and Dali, amongst others.

"It's a French Historic Monument," he whispered as he put his hand on the small of her back, making her tense. His face was too close to hers and his body assumed an intimacy they didn't share. Asmi wanted to step away, but it was *just* Henri. It was Etienne's friend. She was just hanging out with her ex-lover's friend, nothing special, nothing to see here.

The party was *not* a casual thing but one of those exclusive affairs with nearly fifty guests in enough Dior and Hermes to drown in. This was *not* Asmi's scene. She was the corporate type. Most of the parties she went to had something to do with work where she stuck to her two-drink rule and tried to avoid any political pitfalls by talking too much.

Jacques, the birthday *boy*, was appeased that Henri was making an appearance because his father was too busy to make it to the party. It was after all a Sunday night, but Jacques wanted his party on the day of his birthday and not a day "convenient for the guests," as Henri put it.

Jacques was how Asmi thought of older French men, flirtatious, heavily accented, mostly drunk and overweight with a woman next to him who was in tip-top shape, about twenty years younger than him and had a name like Sabine or Simone or something like that.

"And you bring a beautiful woman with you," Jacques said and took Asmi's hand in his and kissed it.

Feeling out of place and extremely uncomfortable, Asmi

sidled close to Henri and when he put his arm around her, she wondered if she should shrug it off but didn't because it was nice to have a man's arm around her again. *Pathetic!*

They met several people with glasses filled with Perrier-Jouet champagne. Asmi didn't speak or understand French and found herself smiling ear to ear and trying to look less bewildered as people hugged, kissed and shook hands.

In the confusion of all these new and strange people, Asmi had managed to finish her third glass of champagne, mostly because she'd lost count. And she didn't complain about the fourth because the golden bubbly had put her at ease, almost to the point that she felt she belonged as she sat next to Henri in the slightly darkening room when the music began.

The stage was set with a large martini glass decked out with Swarovski crystals and a hush fell in the room as they waited for the legendary queen of Burlesque to walk onto the stage to Mae West's *A Guy What Takes His Time*.

Dita von Teese was as stunning in real life as she looked on the cover of magazines that Asmi had seen at doctors' offices and the supermarket checkout stand. She wore a red dress that cupped her whittled waist and stood stark against her pearly white skin. The dress matched the red flower pinned to her dark hair. Asmi had been to a burlesque show at the Crazy Horse in Paris with Etienne. It had been a memorable evening with champagne, oysters, sexy dancers and lots of sex when they got back to Asmi's hotel room, slightly tipsy and very much in love. Etienne had left in the middle of the night, from the mistress's bed to the marital one.

But that performance had been in a club with a few hundred people, this was intimate. Dita was right there, within touching distance and as she playfully stripped off her gloves, Asmi felt conscious of sitting next to Henri. He had been extremely attentive, introducing her to everyone as *ma belle amie, my beautiful friend from America*. He had plied her with foie gras and caviar hors d'oeuvres, made sure her champagne glass was always topped up—and he touched her arm, her hand, the small of her back and whispered, bringing his mouth close to her ear and made his presence felt inside and out the entire evening. They were so alike, Etienne and Henri, flamboyant, full of themselves, confident and entitled.

It wasn't until Dita was down to her bejeweled bra and panties that Asmi wondered if Henri was hitting on her. A dark figure came onto the stage with a ladder to put against the martini glass and Dita walked up to the glass and climbed up the ladder to get into the martini glass.

As she lay there, dousing herself with a large bottle of something, splashing sexily—*and* naively to seduce, Asmi turned to look at Henri who wasn't looking at the seductress in the martini glass as any able-bodied male or female should be, he was looking at her.

Asmi licked her lips. She missed sex. It had been a while hadn't it and...it would be maybe months before she was attracted to another man enough to have sex. But here was Henri, obviously available.

No, Asmi, she told herself sternly and looked away from Henri and onto the stage where Dita was evocatively bathing in the jeweled martini glass and arousal hit Asmi.

She felt Henri brush his mouth close over her ear, "I'm starving, do you want to get some dinner?" he said.

She should've said, *no, I must go back and work.* Instead, she nodded blindly, her eyes on Dita, her heart on Etienne and her Champagne-addled brain telling her, what she did with whomever she did it with was none of Etienne's business.

But Henri is Etienne's friend, she tried to warn herself and then shrugged mentally. Etienne had a wife. She owed him nothing.

～

IT WAS NEARLY ten at night when they were seated at a table by the window at Restaurant Flaveur.

"The Tourteaux brothers started this restaurant. They both

76

used to work at Le Negresco where we just were," Henri said. "They buy our wine, so I have an in."

It was a lovely restaurant decorated in that understated way that expensive restaurants these days were—and the food was, Henri promised, worthy of its one Michelin star.

"Of course, nothing like the Pierre Gagnaire but…it will hold, *oui*?" Henri said.

"How do you know about Pierre Gagnaire?" Asmi asked, suddenly cautious. What was this man up to?

Henri waived to the waiter and then smiled charmingly at Asmi. "Etienne may have mentioned it."

"He told you?" Asmi asked, surprised and slightly humiliated that Etienne had shared their last evening with Henri.

"He told me you ended it," Henri said. "But as you said, *ma chère* affairs come with time limits, *non*?"

Before Asmi could respond past the knot in her throat, they were served their first course, which was a roasted tentacle of octopus cooked in paprika and tomato confit. It was a beautifully plated dish and usually Asmi would have tasted each bite and felt its glory, but this time, she felt panicked. What was she doing here with Henri? This was stupidity.

"Good isn't it?" Henri asked.

Asmi took a deep breath and nodded with a smile. "How's your wife, Henri? Etienne told me that she's a school teacher?"

If she'd thought that talking about his wife would fluster him, it didn't and Asmi realized he was a lot like Etienne who also didn't mind talking about his wife to his mistress. *French men*!

"She teaches second grade science," Henri said and then waved his hand, "It's a little distraction, she doesn't need to work but she does. It's nice, keeps her entertained."

"Must be nice to have a job without worrying about paying the bills," Asmi said a little more bitterly than she intended.

Henri put his hand on hers, "I'm sure there are men out there who would take care of you. I'm certain Etienne would have if you wanted that."

Unbelievable, Asmi thought, she was in an Edith Wharton novel, playing Countess Olenska who needed to be saved.

"I can take care of myself," she said. If she wasn't on her fifth glass of wine of the evening, way past her bedtime and alcohol quota, Asmi would've pulled away, called an Uber and gone to her hotel. But she was tired of doing the right thing or at least *trying* to do the right thing. Mostly, she was tired of being on her own, so she let him keep his large warm hand over her cold small one.

By dessert, the awkwardness had passed and Asmi was enjoying Henri's company. The wine helped. It also helped that Henri, like Etienne, was well-read, well-traveled, intelligent and genuinely interested in Asmi.

"For a winemaker, we live and die with the weather. When I was little and we fermented the wine, my father would pace up and down the cellar, afraid that if he fell asleep it would become too warm and his wine would ferment *trop vite*...too soon," Henri told her. "Now, I pace the cellar. And in thirty years, my son will. What keeps you up at night, Asmi?"

"Revenue numbers," Asmi said without thinking and closed her eyes as the world swam around her. She had drunk too much, it was way too late and there was no way she was going to be able to look at an Excel sheet for at least six to eight hours.

"Henri, I'm exhausted, do you mind taking me back now?" Asmi asked.

"Of course," Henri said.

He paid the bill. There was no question. With an American man, Asmi could pay her half but the French were still living in pre-historic times and Asmi knew from experience that arguing didn't do any good. Also, he could afford it.

"The hotel is just a fifteen-minute walk from here," Henri said. "But I can get us a taxi."

A walk would do her good, Asmi thought. She didn't mind that he held her hand on his forearm, so she leaned on him slightly as they walked.

"When I first met you...it was in London, wasn't it? You were there for a conference and Etienne and I were there to have fun. I didn't know he was planning on having fun with you and not with me," Henri said.

Asmi smiled, remembering. They had met at a South Indian restaurant and Henri and Etienne had eaten *dosas* with *sambhar* and *chutney* with their fingers and with the same gusto as they showed for French cuisine.

"I had thought that Etienne was a lucky bastard. *Merde*, I thought, she's beautiful," Henri said and now his thumb caressed her hand slowly, small circles.

They walked onto the Promenade de Anglais, the sea air cool and crisp but without a bite.

"Do you want to go to the beach?" Henri asked.

Asmi looked at him and nodded, her mind blurry with emotion and she pretended she was surer than she was.

They took the stairs and went down to the pebbled beach, empty at midnight, devoid of the laughing children, the gossiping adults and the light of the sun.

She knew as it happened because she let it happen. It was Dita von Teese, it was the wine, the good food, the sea air, the missing Etienne, the not having a companion, the wanting to run away from work and the stress of Matthew's corporate *Hunger Games*, it was all of it. She let him push her gently against the wall and lean into her. When his mouth touched hers, Asmi closed her eyes. Did it matter, she wondered, whose lips were on hers? Did it *really* matter? In the dark, could she tell the difference? Would she be less aroused with Henri than with Etienne? He could be anyone. Hell, Etienne could have been anyone. *Anyone*.

It was when his hand came upon her breast and she heard the slamming of her heart inside the back of her closed eyelids that she opened her eyes. This wasn't Etienne. This wasn't her.

She put her hand on Henri's chest and pushed him away from her and he didn't resist.

"I have a room in your hotel for the night," he said softly.

Asmi licked her lips. He didn't taste like Etienne. He tasted foreign. Unfamiliar. Some other man and an overwhelming sadness gripped her.

"I don't want you," she said softly and let the tears fall down her face.

Henri stepped forward and wiped her tears with his thumbs. "I thought I could slip in because he was foolish to let you go."

"Flattery will not get you into my room tonight," Asmi said on a small laugh.

He didn't walk her to her room, and let her take the elevator alone.

Asmi burst into tears as soon as she closed the door behind her. Of all the stupid things to do. Her drunkenness was already fading as adrenaline pounded through. She had really done it this time.

She wished she didn't have to, but she knew she had to. She sent a message to Etienne before the embarrassment of what she had done overwhelmed her into silence.

I met Henri in Nice.

It took ten minutes for him to answer and Asmi was surprised he even answered because it was late, and she knew from experience that after eleven at night, he didn't respond to her messages.

How nice for Henri. I wish I was there, but I'm in New York. Missing you.

Asmi set the phone down and thought about it. She knew she had to tell him. It wouldn't be fair for him to hear it from Henri, who would *definitely* tell him.

I saw Dita von Teese with him and then he took me out to dinner.

It took five minutes for a response this time.

The bastard. He always wants what I have.

Asmi took a deep breath and plunged.

I was drunk, and I kissed him. It was one kiss. I thought you should know.

She waited first five and then ten minutes but there was no response. She got out of her clothes, her heart heavy, and got ready for bed. It took him thirty minutes to answer.

I don't know what to say except don't call, don't message. This time, Asmi, it's over. I don't want Henri's leftovers. I wish you a good life.

Things couldn't get worse, Asmi thought as she cried herself to sleep.

She felt as if she'd barely closed her eyes when there was a banging at her door.

The light coming in from the curtains said it was daytime and Asmi walked up to the door groggily and looked through the peephole. Gustav was standing on the other side.

She opened the door. "What happened?"

"We have a situation," Gustav said. "Most of our speakers aren't going to make it today, both Lufthansa and Air France ground crews are on strike, no planes are taking off or landing in Nice Airport."

Asmi tried to focus on what he was saying and then shook her head. "But our customers are here?"

"Yes, most of our customers came from the US and South America so they came yesterday. The speakers were supposed to come today because they were coming from Europe," Gustav said.

"So, what you're saying is that we're going to have to spend all the money, not have a seminar *and* we have wasted our customers' time?" Asmi said.

Gustav nodded.

"Matthew is going to love that I spent all this money and got nothing for it," Asmi said.

"I'm so sorry, Asmi," Gustav said. "I know you don't need this with Scott snapping at your heels."

"It's not your fault. Hell, this is no one's fault. It's *karma*. I'm going back to bed," Asmi said, "And...I'll wake up in an hour or so and deal with this."

She shut the door and crawled back into bed. As she stared at the back of her eyelids, she thought, *oh yes*, it could get worse and it had.

AND THEN SHE SAID...I'M SORRY

EXCERPT FROM THE BUSINESS WORKBOOK "AND THEN SHE SAID..."

JUST THE OTHER DAY, Asha, one of my colleagues presented a plan to move offices. Instead of a simple switcheroo between teams, the plan had become elaborate, because of the demands of one team, which required two other teams to move around. I heard the plan and simply suggested that maybe the team that was demanding so much could settle for less and make this process far less complicated.

Asha immediately apologized by saying, "Oh it's not their fault, it must be me, I've made it complicated." She was profusive in her apology. I responded by asking if I should wait until she was done beating herself up some more and that's when she realized that she was being needlessly apologetic.

Women in the workplace have an "I'm sorry" disease.

This disease bested me, because I thought it was a good way to counter the feedback I normally received: pushy, abrasive, aggressive, dominating, bossy, et cetera. I thought if I just said I'm sorry when I spoke, then it would mitigate my other sins. In meetings, instead of saying, "Can you please explain your point?" I'd say, "Maybe it's because I'm not smart enough and I'm so sorry, can you please explain your point again, slowly, so I can understand it?"

The fact is despite the many "I'm so sorry" starts to sentence, I'm still perceived as being pushy, bossy, intimidating and aggressive. Obviously, my apologies are not working.

Also, I find I'm not the only one.

Women in the workplace say, "I'm sorry" all the time. It's pervasive, this apology nightmare we women put ourselves through. And because we keep saying we're sorry, ultimately, we start to feel sorry and then we say it, because we really feel sorry. It's a vicious cycle.

How do we change this?

It's simple. Just stop saying *I'm sorry*.

But change takes time. You're not going to become disease-free from one day to another. You must accept that you will regress. But as they say, the first step is to admit you have a disease and then it becomes a lot easier.

7

YOUR VEGAS IS SHOWING

CARA WAS ETHNICALLY ITALIAN, born in Greece, and raised in Germany. She had left Munich—a place she disliked—as soon as she could. She'd had about a hundred dollars in her pocket when she landed in Las Vegas the day after she graduated from high school. She found a place to live and got into university, found odd jobs and made it to where she was on sheer will. That was nearly twenty-five years ago, and as she and Asmi waited to check into The Venetian, Cara remarked that Vegas may look different today than it did when she'd arrived over two decades ago, but the city's heartbeat was still the same, *ka-ching, ka-ching*.

Asmi was not a fan of Vegas. She didn't like to gamble, and she hated that everything was always indoors, but Vegas was a popular spot for meetings and Matthew had chosen it for the annual manager's meeting.

Asmi wasn't looking forward to seeing him again after the difficult one-on-one meeting they'd had after the Nice debacle. Of course, everyone understood that a French airline worker's strike wasn't Asmi's fault. But Scott had come back home with the biggest Chinese detergent manufacturer in his pocket, beating out a competitor as the cherry on top, while Asmi had disappointed her customers, spent an insane amount of money and didn't create the marketing impact she'd hoped for with the clinical seminar.

Scott was leading the race.

She had apologized to Etienne when she was sober, but that was nearly two weeks ago, and he had not responded, not even with a *stop writing me* message.

Her maybe future boss thought she was incompetent. Her ex-lover thought she was a slut. It was not working out on all fronts.

"Why did you choose to come to Las Vegas of all the cities in the US?" Asmi asked her.

Cara shrugged. "It was the ticket to America I could afford."

"You just upped and left?" Asmi asked, as she smiled at the hotel receptionist across the counter and handed him her credit card and driver's license.

"Yes, I did," Cara said smugly. "My parents had a heart attack."

"Would it be possible to put me on a higher floor?" Asmi asked the receptionist politely.

"Of course," he said with a broad smile and handed Asmi back her driver's license, credit card and a key for a room on the twelfth floor. "Our outdoor rooftop pool is also on the twelfth floor. Enjoy your stay."

"Should we meet for a drink?" Cara asked as she handed over her credit card and driver's license.

"Half an hour?" Asmi suggested. "I need to get some emails out."

"Let's say thirty minutes at the Bellini Bar," Cara said.

"YOU KNOW, for a while there I even considered if I should become a dancer to support myself," Cara said as she picked up her glass of Bellini. "I used to have a rock star body."

Asmi stuck to scotch, even in a Bellini bar. She was off champagne and wine, like forever. After Nice, she probably would never drink champagne again.

"Like a stripper?" Asmi asked.

Cara gave her a shocked look. "No. Nothing crude like that. Something…burlesque."

"I saw Dita von Teese," Asmi said, "In Nice. She did her martini number. It was very erotic."

"Who did you see her with? Not Gustav," Cara said.

"Of course not," Asmi said and then sighed, "I went with one of *his* friends. I met him by accident; he took me."

Cara waited a beat and then Asmi told her what happened.

"Was he a good kisser?" Cara asked.

Asmi laughed and shook her head. "I can't remember. I just feel like every time I think, this is the worst thing that can happen then something even worse happens. My personal life is a crash site, my professional career is one engine down and the pressure is rapidly dropping in the cabin."

"You've got this. You're going to land this plane just fine," Cara said.

"Yesterday, at a meeting, Scott spoke over me, and when I tried to interrupt so I could finish what I was saying, Matthew tells *me* not to interrupt Scott," Asmi said. "I felt like Kamala Harris interviewing Jeff Sessions. Men can get away with interrupting us or being ambitious, but I must be nice and conform. I feel like pulling a Maxine Waters and say, *I'm reclaiming my time.*"

Cara nodded. "Hey, tell me about it. You know we just did a global "diversity and inclusion" survey at GTech and you should see some of the comments we got. One woman said that her boss told her that *now is not the right time for you to be pregnant* and she was in her fifth month. One manager commented when his associate asked for some money in the budget for a project that she was just like his ex-wife, always asking for money. It's routine. And because it's normalized, it's hard to take a stand. What do you do? Say, hey Matthew, *he interrupted me first.*"

"And I'm in kindergarten again," Asmi agreed. "Sometimes I think I should find a man and stay home."

"You'll hate it," Cara said. "We're not the marrying kind, darling."

"You're married," Asmi said.

Cara shrugged and when the waiter came to ask if she'd like another, she said yes.

"With Oscar it was a Green card thing," Cara said. "I love him, and I'd live with him. And if he could stay in the US without us being married…we wouldn't be married."

Cara's husband Oscar was German, and she'd known him in high school in Munich. She met him again two years ago and they hit it off. They were married on a horse farm near San Diego. Oscar was good for Cara, a hospital clown by profession because professions such as that exist in Germany, he had a unique sense of humor and knew how to make serious things go *poof*. Asmi had once asked him if making light of everything just took the value away from everything. Oscar said that life was too short to take seriously, people should have fun because there's just one certainty and that is that you'll die, all that lies in between is a few laughs and a few cries, so maximize the laughs. She liked his philosophy even though she found it hard to emulate.

"How's his job going?" Asmi asked.

Oscar had been a year shy of getting a medical degree when he'd decided that was not what he wanted to do and instead had taken the hospital clown education. He used to love his job and the ability to make sick children going through difficult medical treatments smile. Since he couldn't work as a hospital clown in the United States, he'd found the next best thing and worked in Disneyland as a Children's Activity Host.

"He loves it and it helps him improve his English," Cara said. "And we have free passes to Disneyland. My niece and nephew are over the moon."

"Have you ever thought about having children?" Asmi asked.

Cara shrugged. "I'd like to. But…I don't know." She paused

and then said, "I've told no one. I mean Oscar knows and that's it. But...I've had two miscarriages in the past year."

"What? Why haven't you said anything?" Asmi asked. "Sweetheart, I'm so sorry."

Ananya had had a miscarriage between Arjun and Anjali. It had been emotionally *very* hard for Ananya. Asmi had taken a week off work then to stay with her sister.

"My doctor says it is work stress," Cara said.

"You work too hard."

"We all work too hard," Cara said. "My doctor suggests I find a new job. She thinks I'm not getting enough sleep and my blood pressure is high. I feel we're *always* short of resources. I'm a headcount down in my team and I'm doing three jobs."

"I know how that goes," Asmi said. "I haven't been able to replace George who moved to sales so I'm doing his job *and* mine. I can't even delegate because the team is working at hundred and fifty percent capacity."

"This is across the company," Cara said. "I've tried to talk to Max about it and he says, *welcome to the club*. Apparently, he's just as busy and I shouldn't complain."

"Can you slow down?"

"Every time I think that...there is something," Cara said. "I told Max I need a temp and he said that if Evan can manage things without one why should I need one. Evan has two more head counts than I do and a smaller business to support. I told Max, hey, give me one of Evan's people and he tells me I should be careful about being an empire builder, people might think I'm being too greedy. Empire? Who builds an empire with six people?"

"I have no idea how leaders like Max who have zero emotional intelligence become the VP of HR," Asmi said.

"Right? And he keeps sort of indicating that I'm not *that* good and I want to prove to him I am, so I work my ass off," Cara said. "Even though it's pretty obvious that Max prefers Evan."

"Because he's an old-fashioned douche who thinks women in

the workplace is still a trial balloon that he's testing out," Asmi said.

"Or maybe I'm not as good as I think I am," Cara said.

Asmi got up to sit next to Cara and put an arm around her.

"You're the best there is. But I do agree with your doctor that you need to reduce your work stress," Asmi said.

"I went and saw my doctor last week. My diastolic blood pressure is at 90," Cara said. "She told me that I need to go on medical leave, but I can't. I have so much work."

"Your health comes first."

"Look who's talking. You work like a dog. You're on the road half the time and the other half of the time you're working," Cara said. "I get emails from you at two in the morning and then five in the morning and then seven in the morning. You work around the clock."

"I'm competing in the *Hunger Games*, fighting for my life against Scott."

"I've got news for you, sweetheart, we're all trying to have the odds in our favor," Cara said. "I really would like to have a baby and I keep losing my pregnancies. I'm forty-one, Asmi. I'm already past the fertile time and I have ancient eggs. Maybe Oscar and I will have to settle for being the funny uncle and cool aunt."

Asmi pulled Cara close into a hug.

"It's not so bad, you know, being the cool aunt," Asmi said, "Arjun told me I'm quirky and cool."

"I think I can live with quirky instead of motherly...I don't want to, but I'm afraid I may have to," Cara said, wiping her tears and waved to the waiter to get her yet another drink.

THE MEETING ROOM was set theatre style to accommodate the thirty GTech senior leaders who had been invited for the annual meeting where Matthew liked to show off his CEO title and company strategy and ask each head of department to present how they would support the strategy. Since Jim, the VP of Marketing had already checked out of his job even though he wasn't retiring until Christmas, Matthew had asked both Asmi and Scott to prepare a presentation addressing how their businesses would support the strategy.

"I have to nail this," Asmi whispered to Cara.

"You're a great presenter," Cara said. "You'll be fine."

But Asmi was nervous. She knew that every time she met with Matthew, she was being tested and being compared to Scott. Now, when they presented right after one another, it would be a good opportunity for the company and Matthew to judge who was better.

Scott went before Asmi, which she decided was an advantage though she knew it didn't really matter. She was the better presenter, there was no doubt about that. Scott was more laid back, read as unprepared, while Asmi was thorough. Her presentations looked professional while Scott's looked like something he put together the night before on his flight, which he usually did.

So, Asmi was surprised when by the end of the day, she crashed and burned, and Scott landed smoothly.

"MATTHEW WAS SERIOUSLY AFTER YOU," Betty, a director of R&D said when she saw Asmi pound the treadmill at the hotel gym the next morning.

Asmi didn't respond but nodded. She didn't want to talk about it. She was humiliated. Matthew had grilled her in front of God and everyone and then ridiculed her when she stumbled. In her professional career, she had never experienced such a public defeat before.

Betty had got on a treadmill next to Asmi with the intent, Asmi realized, of rehashing the previous day. Betty wasn't being malicious, she was offering support but Asmi didn't want support, she wanted to crawl inside her skin and never come out. She had declined Cara's offer for a spa evening and spent the time in her hotel room, alone, ordering room service and going through the meeting scene by scene, line by line in her head, wondering how it could've all gone so wrong.

The first hiccup had been Scott, who presented better than he'd ever done before and had clearly gotten help with his presentation because it looked *professional*. And, he seemed to have prepared for his presentation instead of doing what he normally did, just show up like a Southern Cowboy and shoot random bullets across the room.

After Scott's presentation, Matthew had not asked him any questions, instead had lauded him for his splendid work recently in Shanghai, something on the lines of *if only more marketing people brought in business like sales people, then we'd grow twice as much*.

By the time Asmi got on stage to present her side of the business, she was flustered at how well Scott had done. The second hiccup came only after her professional, data-driven, graph-laden presentation. She told her story well and confidently, she cracked a couple of jokes at her expense and she'd worn high heels with her favorite black Ann Taylor dress that made her look skinny. Overall, she felt she'd scored because the audience had been engaged. After her presentation, unlike after Scott's there had been questions from the floor. Asmi had handled all of them well. And by the time Matthew asked his question, she was feeling like the winner, which proved to be premature.

Matthew asked her several questions about the forecast for the year, comparing Scott's business to the one she managed. Why was her growth in Brazil not as strong as his? Why was China not growing faster? Why was Australia static? He didn't comment on how strong the forecast for the US was compared to Scott's—he seemed to only focus on what was not working.

The icing on the cake came at the end.

"Can we go back to slide fourteen?" Matthew asked.

Asmi flipped to the slide and as soon as the slide came on the screen, she could see the problem. There were two numerical errors on the graph she had presented. One was minuscule and didn't count, but the other was a bigger one as someone had forgotten to convert Euros into dollars, which was how they presented revenue in GTech and she hadn't noticed...until now.

She immediately said, "I can see a mistake with the figures for Germany."

"The question is, Asmi, why didn't you see it before you presented it?" Matthew said.

Asmi was stunned. Scott had put out a pretty presentation with hardly any supporting data and Matthew was okay with that but was nitpicking hers?

"We'll be more careful in the future," Asmi said with a smile.

She was about to flip away from the slide and close the presentation when Matthew stood up to face the leaders of the company, Asmi now behind him on the stage, and said, "These are the small errors that can bring us down. As leaders at GTech, we are expected to do better because we must always be on our toes to win. There is no room for screw ups, big or small. We're a forward moving company and for growth, we have to work fast but without compromising on quality."

Asmi's ears roared as she heard Matthew. Was he reprimanding her in front of the entire senior leadership team for a small numerical error on a graph on slide fourteen that didn't make any difference to her brilliant presentation?

Apparently, he was.

Cara said she was horrified at how Matthew had behaved. Everyone knew that Asmi had been dressed down. Even Scott offered condolences in his inimitable style.

"Hey, when I'm your boss I'll not worry about the small mistakes in graphs," he said, putting an arm around her that Asmi shrugged off. They weren't work buddies and she had a problem with his feeling free to put his arm around her.

"Thanks, Scott," Asmi said and thought about her LinkedIn profile and if it was up to date. She really had to get that shipshape and then she needed to start calling headhunters. It was obvious to everyone that Matthew had made his choice for Jim's successor, and it wasn't Asmi.

Damn it, Asmi thought. She loved her job. She loved marketing. She loved her team and her colleagues. She was good at it. She was a good leader. She had fun with work and at work... most of the time.

But maybe this was the end of the road for her at GTech or... the end of the career road. She'd never climb up beyond director. She wasn't good enough. That was it. She was at the end of her career, of what she loved to do.

How could she have even thought she had a chance at getting Jim's job? Asmi scolded herself. No way would they make *her* a Vice President and give her a seat at the executive table. Maybe she'd never get there; maybe she didn't have it in her. She watched Scott move around the meeting room with confidence and certainty and she realized that she'd never had that confidence, she'd never felt that inner certainty that she could do whatever was put in front of her.

"I think that the work you're doing to support the business clinically is amazing," Betty said as she ran beside Asmi. "Scott is too sales and too little marketing. He's all about which customer he brought in but that's not his job, his job is marketing. He has a quarter to quarter focus like a sales guy and not a strategic one like yours."

Asmi mumbled a thank you.

"But...you know I'm from R&D so I'm all about the numbers and to be fair to Matthew, it was a rather *big* mistake," Betty said, indicating the enormous size of the mistake with her hands. "It wasn't *what* he said, it was *how* he said it."

Asmi pressed the stop button abruptly on the treadmill and went from running seven miles an hour to standstill. She took several long deep breaths and then started to empty her water bottle into her throat to avoid saying something rude, albeit honest, to Betty.

When she felt she was calmer, she said, "Thanks, Betty. But it's just business and it's going to be okay."

"Of course," Betty said brightly. "Life is so much more than work, isn't it?"

As Asmi walked to the elevators to go up to her room, she wondered about what Betty had said and felt a pinch she'd never felt before. Her work was her life because she didn't have a family and at that moment while she waited for her elevator, she wished she had one. She wished she had a man to call now and lean on children who'd love her unconditionally even though she felt like a failure. A family would take the sting away from a career that was in the crapper.

The elevator opened, and Matthew walked out in his workout gear. He looked at Asmi, caught by surprise and smiled. "Good workout?" he asked.

"Excellent," Asmi said and then stepped into the elevator. She wanted to tell him he'd been an asshat. She wanted to tell him to stop being a jerk and just give the job to Scott, so she could start looking for a new job. She wanted to tell him to stop screwing with her. But she didn't. She let the elevator doors close over Matthew's smiling face.

THAT EVENING, Matthew took the team to dinner at the Foundation Room at the top of the Mandalay Bay resort. They were having drinks on the patio because it was a pleasant April evening and Asmi was nursing a smoked old fashion now that smoked cocktails were all the rage.

She looked at the glittering city below them and didn't feel what she normally felt on evenings like this. She used to feel lucky.

Once she had been in Sydney and after a long and grueling day meeting with customers, she and her then boss, Marcy Brandt were sitting at the Harbour Lounge on the Circular Quay with a view of the Sydney Opera House on one side and the Sydney Harbour bridge on the other with a glass of champagne.

Marcy raised her glass of champagne and said, "We're so lucky, Asmi. They pay us to sit here and have a drink."

Since then Asmi had always been grateful for having a job that allowed her to see the world. The days may be long, the flights endless and the jet lag a way of life, but she had seen the sun set behind the pyramids in Cairo, she had seen the Onion Domes in St. Petersburg at dawn on a snowy morning, she had had dinner in the pyramid at the Louvre and seen the Mona Lisa during a private tour, she had gone scuba diving in Pemuteran when she had been there for a meeting in Bali, she had eaten at some amazing restaurants around the world, and had amassed millions of airline points so when she went on vacation, she didn't have to pay a dime. She was enormously lucky.

But not this evening.

This evening she felt like they didn't pay her enough for this shit. She was sipping her drink, leaning against the balustrade when Isadora Fonseca, their Vice President of Operations, came up to Asmi and said, "I've always been fascinated with Las Vegas."

Isadora was from Spain and had come to GTech two years ago and was known to have mostly black and gray Hugo Boss-style severe pantsuits. Sometimes in the summer, she would wear a linen pantsuit but only on casual Fridays. Her hair was cut short and her petite frame made her look like a tight ball of contained energy. As VP of Operations of GTech, she was regarded as a strong, no-nonsense leader who knew what she wanted and how to get it. She was considered a good manager who took care of her people. But there was rumored to be friction between Isadora and some of her peers as she was the only woman on the executive team.

Case in point was Max, Cara's boss, saying to Asmi in passing, "Isadora is too stubborn for a woman."

"I don't gamble so I've never liked Vegas," Asmi said as she and Isadora watched Scott and two directors of sales joke about how much Scott had already lost on the craps tables.

Isadora put her white wine glass on the balustrade and said,

"Most women I know don't like to gamble because we don't like to take chances. I'm generalizing but it's true. To succeed we have to take risks. Are you willing to take a risk, Asmi?"

Asmi squinted her internal eye, trying to understand what Isadora was talking about and then when she couldn't, she said honestly, "I'm not sure what you mean."

"Getting to the C-suite is an accomplishment and a tough ride up," Isadora said. "You don't get there without taking chances, without slipping up, without making mistakes. But you have to be careful about the mistakes you make because we women have a higher bar than our male counterparts."

Right then Scott and his friends laughed aloud, and it was obvious they were drunk and in a good mood.

"They can do that, they can drink and talk loudly and be all fraternity boys club, but you and I can't," Isadora said. "You know that, yes?"

"Yes," Asmi said.

"Do you like marketing?" Isadora asked.

"I'm a marketer," Asmi said. "This is what I love to do."

"What do you love about it?"

"Most everything," Asmi said. "I like the strategic nature of it, the storytelling of it, and the data-driven creativity of it. I like leading teams, finding and growing talent, and…" she took a deep breath, "…I like to win."

"You didn't win today," Isadora said. "Matthew can be unreasonable sometimes. But that's not the point, the question you need to ask yourself is can you have more days like this and keep your chin up? As the VP of Marketing, your ass will be kicked a lot more and just like it was today, so, Asmi, find out if you think it's worth it."

"Is it worth it for you?" Asmi asked.

"How does it matter what it means to me? You are not me," Isadora said and picked up her wine glass again. "You need to look inside yourself and ask if you want to climb further or stay where you are. Neither option is right, and neither is wrong in space. One of those options may be wrong *for you* and you need to be certain about what you want before you go chasing after it."

After Isadora left to mingle with others, Asmi wondered if Isadora had been discouraging her from pursuing Jim's job and if she was, why would she do that? As the only woman on the executive management team, she would want to have another woman there, wouldn't she? Or was she one of those women who liked to be the only one in the room, because she felt that there were limited seats for women at the high-stake tables. But like Isadora said, her motives or how she felt was not the point, the point was, did Asmi want to struggle like this every day, feel like this more often than not—because the big leagues were a step away and she wasn't sure she was ready even if they'd have her.

THE HOW TO BE
FEARLESS WORKBOOK

EXCERPT FROM THE BUSINESS WORKBOOK
"AND THEN SHE SAID..."

THE BEST WAY TO deal with fear is to let it play out, all the way to the end in your mind. For example, say you're worried about sounding stupid at a meeting. Here is how you take it to a spiraling end:

YOU: I'm going to say something really dumb.

WISE YOU: And then what'll happen?

YOU: They'll think I'm stupid.

WISE YOU: So?

YOU: They won't promote me.

WISE YOU: And then?

YOU: I will stagnate.

WISE YOU: And then?

YOU: I'll have to leave the company.

WISE YOU: Okay. And so, what?

YOU: Nothing. I'll find another job in another company. That's all.

WISE YOU: So, it won't be so bad.

YOU: No.

WISE YOU: Now what is the likelihood that this will happen because you sound stupid in a meeting?

YOU: Not very likely.

WISE YOU: Okay. Now get on with it.

Here is a matrix that might be useful in mitigating your fear by understanding it as well as developing counter measures that you can put into action if the need arises. Below is an example from my life.

OBJECT OF FEAR	CONSEQUENCE	PROBABILITY (High, Med, Low)	WHAT CAN YOU DO?
My boss hates me	I can get fired	L I'm a top performer, but my boss still hates me	Start looking for a new job
I get fired	I can't pay my bills	L I can sell the house and move in with my sister	I put my house on the market
I can't pay my bills	I lose my house	L I can always borrow money from family and friends + I also have savings	Dip into savings; and if need be, borrow money OR get a job anywhere doing anything

Use the empty matrix below when you feel the world is closing in around you and you're afraid. There is nothing like taking the fear to its extreme end to determine its likelihood and ease the mind.

OBJECT OF FEAR	CONSEQUENCE	PROBABILITY (High, Med, Low)	WHAT CAN YOU DO?

IF YOU'VE EVER SAID, "THIS IS ENOUGH FOR ME," REPEAT AFTER ME

- I will take a deep breath…and then, because it feels so good, I will take another
- I will not lead with fear; I will lead with confidence
- If I'm afraid, I will take my fear to the end of its life and crush it
- I will aim for the next step on the ladder even if I'm… pregnant or have a husband who doesn't help raise kids or am a single mom or am tired of the misogyny in the workplace or…
- I love my children or husband or myself…but I also love my career and there is nothing wrong with loving my career and wanting more

8

TAKE A MOMENT TO
REVIEW THE SAFETY
DATA CARD

"I'M DONE," Asmi told Ananya over the phone while she put on her makeup. "I actually don't care anymore. I made up my mind. Isadora asked me to carefully think about whether I wanted this or not, and I've decided that I don't want it."

"Maybe this was Matthew's way of testing you, seeing how tough you are," Ananya said.

"Why do I need to be tough? I'm good at what I do and that should be enough. This whole don't be a bitch, be tough, be an extrovert, don't talk too much, be congenial, don't be too aggressive...it's too much," Asmi said and looked at her red lipstick critically.

After Vegas, she had regrouped. She had booked a global marketing team meeting in New Orleans for the end of the month where they would share regional marketing plans and focus on what she knew she was good at and what she loved to do, which was to be creative and strategic in how they marketed products. Thanks to this whole contest with Scott, Asmi felt she had neglected her team and now she needed to get back to why she liked her job in the first place: to build high performance teams that delivered. She knew she sounded like a business self-help book but sometimes you needed to pep yourself up.

Everyone in the office had heard about the beating Asmi had

taken in Vegas and there were those who probably thought it was high time she was brought down a peg or two while others in Asmi's team were furious and scared at the idea that they may have to work under Scott's leadership.

"When you leave, take me with you," Gustav told Asmi.

The consensus was that the Corporate *Hunger Games* had ended with Scott as the victor and Asmi now had to find a new job.

"Are you at least looking for a new job?" Ananya asked.

"Nope," Asmi said and smiled at her reflection. They were having a gorgeous California April day and she was wearing a happy white summer dress with her favorite white sandals with yellow flowers and red lipstick. *Oh yeah, baby*, Asmi was ready to rock and roll.

"So, who's this guy you're meeting?" Ananya asked after sighing dramatically, the subtext clear: *Asmi is in that mood and there's no talking to her when she's in that mood.*

"His name is Warren and he's a documentary filmmaker who lives in Venice Beach," Asmi said. He was thirty-eight years old, had swiped right on Bumble and she had caught him. "We're going to meet at his place in Venice, well not *his* place but I'm going to park there and then go eat gourmet bites at The Tasting Kitchen and then for live blues at the Del Monte Speakeasy."

"And then sex?" Ananya asked.

"It's a first date," Asmi said and finished her makeup with a stroke of eyeliner on her waterline.

"But if he lives there, don't you think that's in his plans?"

Asmi picked up the phone and walked to her living room to pack her purse. "I have no problems having sex with him if it feels right. I'm not okay having sex with him if it doesn't feel right...to me."

"I can't give any advice, I never really dated. I met Venkat, we married and made babies," Ananya said. "Sometimes I wish I had your life, your freedom."

"And sometimes I wish I had yours," Asmi said softly. "If

only we could walk in each other's shoes for just a day, we'd maybe appreciate our lives better."

"The greener grass on the other side, you mean?" Ananya said.

"Ana, you have a good life. I also have a good life and I'm going to start living it instead of worrying about work," Asmi said. "It's cruise and autopilot at work and full throttle in my personal life."

"You're going to cruise at work?" Ananya didn't sound like she believed that could happen.

"Watch me," Asmi said and gritted her teeth, "What I learned in Vegas is that it's not worth it. None of this is. I love being a marketer. I love my team. But I am not paid for fighting the good fight and having integrity. I don't get the VP of Marketing job... so what? I don't need it."

"I wonder if Scott thinks like that about the job," Ananya muttered.

"I don't give a shit about what Scott thinks," Asmi said angrily. "Drop it, Ana."

"You're doing that thing women do...giving up because the going is getting tough," Ananya mocked.

"How would you know, Mrs. Housewife?" Asmi screeched.

"Because I've watched enough Oprah," Ananya yelled and hung up on Asmi.

Regardless of what Ananya thought, Asmi was confident that she had made the right decision.

Enough was enough. She had until Christmas to find a new job as that was when Jim would officially retire. She'd start looking in July...August...around that time. Someone would hire her. If nothing else, she could sell the apartment and go live in Ananya's guestroom. They'd feed and clothe her for a while, even a long while. Who knows, Warren may be a *grade-A hunka burnin' love* and she'd marry him and live happily ever after in Venice Beach.

She hadn't dated in ages, she realized. In her twenties, it had been easy, someone asked her out somewhere and it was all in good fun. In her thirties, she'd been too busy. Then there had been Etienne for the past four years. And now it was this Bumble, Tinder world, swipe left and right to find the man of your dreams.

When she told her friend Mila, she'd been surprised to say the least. "You? You're going to find a husband and sit at home?"

"Yes," Asmi told her. "I don't need this corporate shit. I'm tired of it."

"You're not tired of it, you love it. You just had a setback and that doesn't mean you give up and run with your tail between your legs," Mila said.

"I don't understand why everyone wants *me* to work harder and be stronger," Asmi said aggressively. "I just want to have some fun and I've earned it."

That silenced Mila.

Cara had also been asked to take her advice to someone who gave a shit when they met for their monthly lunch after the Vegas meeting.

"He hasn't offered Scott the job, which means it's still open," Cara said. "I spoke to Max and he said…"

"And what does Max know?"

"He's the Vice President of Human Resources, I think he knows," Cara said. "Come on, Asmi, you know Matthew, he pulls stunts like this. But he thinks highly of you, so don't give up."

"Cara, I downloaded Bumble last night and I have a profile up and a picture of me wearing Jimmy Choo shoes and a Max Mara dress. I have one goal this week, to have a date for Friday night—fighting for Jim's job is not on the agenda," Asmi said. "I'm going to take care of my team, do my job and enjoy my life."

"So, you're going to look for a new job?"

"Why should I?"

"Asmi, I love you, darling, you can't work for Scott, you know that, right?" Cara said.

"I'll be fine," Asmi said. "I don't have the energy to look for a new job right now because I'm investing my energy in finding true love."

"On Bumble?"

"Data says that thirty percent of people who use apps like Bumble and Tinder find their soulmates, get married and live happily ever after," Asmi said.

"Who are you and where is the *real* Asmi? Look, I think it's healthy that you're dating again, because that affair you had going with Etienne was as unhealthy as smoking. But you don't have to give up your job because you're looking for a man," Cara said.

"I'm nearly forty and maybe I want to have a baby," Asmi said. "Having Jim's job will be too much for me. I think this is the right choice. Cara, I deserve happiness."

"Happiness and career are not mutually exclusive."

"I think for a woman they are," Asmi said. "It's too hard and too much of a fight. I don't want to do it. Look at you, having miscarriages because of work stress. Matthew can give the job to Scott, he can give all the jobs to Scott, I don't care and if you don't mind, I don't want to discuss it anymore."

Cara didn't discuss it anymore and the past two weeks in the office had been peaceful, pleasant and without any stress for Asmi. She ignored the fact that it had also been boring as hell, but she'd had time to Bumble and set up this date. She'd had time to plan her meeting in New Orleans. She'd had time to take her direct reports out to lunch. She'd had time to run in the mornings, go for walks in the evenings and meet up with friends for drinks and dinner. This was how she wanted to work, Asmi decided. Take it easy and stop fighting destiny because Scott was fated to have that job and Asmi was fated to…what? She didn't know but she was sure she'd find it on Bumble.

∾

WARREN LIVED on the beach on Oceanfront Walk. His one-bedroom apartment had a wall of glass with views of the

Pacific. It was one of those sexy bachelor pads. The plan wasn't to go to his apartment this early in the relationship, but traffic had been light, and she'd ended up in Venice Beach about forty-five minutes before their reservations at The Tasting Kitchen. Warren suggested that Asmi park her car in his apartment complex as his car was away for service and she could use his parking spot. Once there, he suggested a drink at his place.

"It's just a drink, a quick one because the restaurant is a fifteen-minute walk so we should leave soon," he said to her.

He was cute. Not very tall, maybe five foot-eight, -nine inches and with dirty blonde hair that he cut short. He was wearing a pair of jeans and a T-shirt that said in a combination of big and small font size, *this is what a filmmaker looks like.*

Asmi agreed to the drink.

He didn't have scotch.

She said, yes, a chardonnay would be fine even though of all the wines she liked chardonnay the least. She was going to be on her best behavior. This was her first date in forever and she was determined it wouldn't be a disaster though looking at Warren's messy apartment she wasn't sure. He was in his late thirties, but his apartment looked like it belonged to a twenty-year-old.

"This is a wonderful place," Asmi said, walking out to the balcony instead where he had two plastic chairs. "What's the rent like here?" It didn't hurt to know his financial status.

He shrugged. "I actually don't know. My father owns the building."

Oh no, one of those spoilt men with rich parents.

"Tell me about making films," Asmi said, wanting to end the date now. He was not her type. She liked men with *real* jobs, fiscal demands and responsibilities.

"I'm also a photographer," Warren said and sat down on a chair next to Asmi. "If we have time…or maybe some other day we should go to MOCA, they have some my photos there."

Asmi reconsidered. "The Museum of Contemporary Art?"

"Yeah," Warren said. "I do okay work."

"That's *really* impressive," Asmi said, thinking that maybe Warren wasn't a complete loss.

She sat resolutely on one of the plastic chairs because if she stood, she worried that he'd come near her. As it was, he had pulled his chair close to her and was looking pointedly at her legs as the short sundress allowed for liberal viewing.

"You're a marketing director," Warren said. "That's super cool."

"Not really," Asmi said. "It's just a job."

Warren nodded. "I could never do the nine to five, you know. It's just not who I am."

"And since you live rent free, you never have to find out," Asmi said.

Warren grinned. "True that," he said. "Hey, you're from India, right? I just watched this great documentary; it won a lot of awards. It's called *India's Daughter*, have you seen it? It's on Netflix."

"I haven't seen it," Asmi said. "It sounded too harrowing to me."

"It's totally worth it. You should watch it," Warren said. "I'm surprised you haven't seen it."

"Why are you surprised?"

"Because you're Indian," Warren said.

"I don't understand," Asmi said.

"Just that you'd want to connect with your roots...but, hey, if you don't that's cool, too," Warren said and then uncomfortably added, "We should leave soon...if you need to tinkle or something...."

Tinkle?

They walked to the restaurant and their table wasn't ready when they got there, so they went to the bar. Warren was *okay* company. He talked about documentary filmmaking and didn't ask too many questions about Asmi's line of work.

Asmi had wanted to come to The Tasting Kitchen for a while now because it was touted to be a trendy place where it was difficult to get reservations. It was famous for its Italian charcuterie and when Asmi had suggested it and Warren had effortlessly been able to get a table, he had seemed like quite a catch.

It was at the bar that Asmi started to think of Warren as the *Invisible Warren*. The first sign was the bartender, a woman who approached Asmi and then ignored Warren who was sitting right next to her.

"He'd like a drink, too," Asmi said when the bartender placed a Lagavulin 8 Year with one large rock in front of her.

The bartender looked at Warren like he'd just shown up and then nodded at a man standing behind him, waving. That man asked for a vodka martini and the bartender went away.

"That was odd," she said. "She didn't take your order."

"Oh, this happens to me all the time," Warren said. "Bartenders are not the sharpest pencils in the box, you know?"

It took yet another try before the bartender noticed Warren and by the time she got him his IPA, Asmi had finished her drink and their table was ready.

"Do you date a lot?" Warren asked after they ordered dinner and Asmi refrained from another drink because she had to drive and stuck with water.

"You're my first in about…four years," Asmi said.

"Wow! Were you in a long-term relationship?" Warren asked.

"Something like that," Asmi said. "How about you?"

"I date a lot," Warren said. "Lots of first dates, you know and a few second and third but nothing that has lasted. I ended a three-year relationship two years ago and since then it's been sort of this and that. You know, sometimes you just want to… you know…so I Tinder."

"Right," Asmi said who had never Tindered and was almost too afraid to, not that there was anything to be afraid about. Everyone did it. It was the booty call app. Maybe, Asmi wondered, she should just do the booty call and none of this dinner and music nonsense because it appeared it was going to be tedious.

The conversation had gone from being *okay* to mundane and was now almost boring. This was not a connection made in heaven; it was almost like being at a business dinner when you were forced to sit next to someone you didn't know, and you made small talk to get through the evening.

Is this what dating was like? Dinner with Etienne had been fun and fed her intellectually. They'd talk about everything and nothing, their conversations were animated and then there was the explosive sex. The time she spent with Etienne was always a high that could sustain her for weeks after. This dinner paled in comparison. Warren was a lackluster conversationalist who didn't know how to listen and droned on about completely boring technical shit like angles on the camera.

"You know I made this documentary in Tibet," he said when their coffees were served post dessert and Asmi was looking forward to the Blues.

"Yes," Asmi said and realized Warren's repertoire was small because he'd already told her the Tibet documentary story and they'd spent less than three hours together.

The waiter left the bill with Asmi as if she'd eaten dinner alone. The servers had ignored Warren all dinner. They didn't fill his water glass when they filled hers. They didn't ask him if he'd like a refill of his beer when they asked her if she'd like to drink something besides water.

They shared the bill. Asmi had brought along cash just for this purpose and dropped the requisite dollars on the table.

Asmi had enjoyed the food, so it wasn't a total debacle. Things got worse at the Del Monte Speakeasy. The famous Blues musician Big Jimmy Taylor from Chicago was playing and Asmi who had always loved the Blues was delighted.

The speakeasy was a cozy place. After going through the same drill at the bar where the bartender asked Asmi what she wanted and didn't see *Invisible Warren* until she was made to, they waited at the bar for their drinks. Across the bar on the other side was a bored looking woman with a man and she caught Asmi's eyes at the same time and mouthed, *help me*.

Asmi mouthed back, *me too*.

The woman was blonde, about the same age as Asmi and

looked like she'd rather be anywhere than here with her date who looked like one of those slick consultant types with hair gel and a cross-fit body.

The music began, and they stood in front of the stage. The whole setting was intimate, perfect for a night of blues. Warren stood behind Asmi as they swayed to the music and somewhere down the line, Warren put his arms around her waist and Asmi didn't mind. The vibe was good. The mood was easy. It was just a little familiarity and nothing more. And it was nice, wasn't it, to have a man's arms around her waist again, she thought.

During a break, she talked to Big Jimmy Taylor and told him she loved his music. Big Jimmy thanked her and made a comment about how beautiful Asmi was. His drummer, a young Big Jimmy, agreed.

At the end of the evening when Warren was in the restroom, the drummer came up to Asmi and asked her if she'd like to join him for a drink as they were heading to the Seven Grand in downtown LA. Asmi loved the Seven Grand because it had one of the largest whiskey collections in the world, but she was technically on a date with someone.

"I'm here with someone," Asmi said.

"Who?" the drummer asked.

"The guy…you know…who was standing behind me…?" Asmi said.

The drummer shrugged as if he had no clue what she was talking about.

Warren came back then and stood next to Asmi.

"So…maybe see you at the Seven Grand after the set?" the drummer asked again, completely ignoring Warren.

"Was he hitting on you?" Warren asked after the drummer left and when Asmi nodded, said, "That's so cool."

Asmi was flabbergasted. "No, Warren, it's kind of rude because I'm here with you."

Warren waved a hand. "It happens all the time. Someone is always hitting on my date. I think it's because I have such good taste in women."

No, Warren, it's because you're invisible.

Her first date in four years and even though she'd had a good evening with excellent food and good music, the fact was that it was a complete bust because Warren had evoked no response in Asmi and apparently was invisible to everyone else.

He tried again to get her to come up to his apartment when they walked back to Asmi's car and Asmi declined by being honest, "I'm not going to sleep with you, Warren."

"But I thought we had a good time," Warren said, looking surprised as if he had thought this was a sure thing.

"I'm sorry," Asmi said. "I don't think it's going to work between us, but, yes, it was a really good evening and thank you for that."

"I don't understand," Warren said. "This keeps happening to me. Women have a good time and then don't want to see me again. Why is that? What am I doing wrong?"

It'd be too cruel to tell him, so Asmi shrugged, "I don't know about the others, but I don't think you and I have chemistry. You seem like a fun guy so I'm sure you'll meet someone soon."

She didn't wait for his response and got into her car and drove away.

ASMI SAT on her balcony after she came home and watched the white waves of the Pacific crash against the dark sand. Ananya sent her a text asking her to report back.

Asmi responded: *He was invisible.*

She poured herself a drink and contemplated her life as one did at two in the morning after a bad date. What if she never met anyone? What if the world was populated with single Invisible Warrens and married Etiennes? And did she *really* want to meet someone? Or was she just looking for a crutch to make it acceptable to fail at her career? She understood in her head, her rational brain, what Ananya, Mila and Cara told her. But she was exhausted. She didn't think she had it in her to push anymore.

Why wasn't it enough to just do a good job? Why did she have to do all the rest? She deserved the job just based on qualifications and she should get it without the many games and politics.

Her phone came alive in the dark then, it was Etienne, after nearly four weeks of silence.

It's none of my business what you do. Can you just not do it with Henri?

Asmi grabbed her phone and responded as fast as she could.

I'm not interested in Henri. It was just a weird evening.

He wrote back.

He called me and told me. I pretended I didn't care.

Asmi took a deep breath.

I miss you. I went on a date tonight and it was boring.

He replied immediately. *Me too. The world is gray since you left. Come back. Come here.*

Asmi put the phone down. She'd been here before, several times. But Etienne came and went as he wished. He got in touch when he felt like it and not when she did. He was with her when he could, not when she wanted him to.

Also…he was married!

Her therapist had said that Asmi received conditional love from Etienne—some days she deserved the love and other days she didn't, which was like her childhood. Some days, Madhuri, her mother was nice to her and others she wasn't. The relationship with Etienne had similar undertones and she knew the relationship was not good for her.

I can't, she wrote to him.

Why not?

It's all always on your terms.

What are your terms? Tell me.

Asmi typed with what came first, without planning it and decided to be honest with him and herself. *I want to be more important to you than your wife.*

It took Etienne a while to respond to that.

I have children.

And that's why I can't.

Goodnight, my sweet Asmi.

She put the phone down and wondered about the wreck her life had become. Damn it, she thought, if only they'd give her the stupid job, then she wouldn't have to find a man, she could be an acceptable successful single career woman instead of the loser single woman with no career and no husband.

She picked up her phone and wrote to Etienne, *Nothing is easy. Damn you!!!*

He responded, *I know.*

CAREER VS. FAMILY...
WHO'S WINNING?

EXCERPT FROM THE BUSINESS WORKBOOK
"AND THEN SHE SAID..."

ANGELA WAS a high performer with high potential and I really wanted to help her get to her next step. She was also pregnant and wasn't sure if this was the time that the company would promote her. I told her that it didn't matter and that she should work on a project with me; and then apply for the position as soon as it hit the job site.

Angela went on maternity leave, promising me that she would apply for the job. She never got in touch with me after that. She resigned via email and I never heard from her. A colleague, a woman, told me that Angela didn't know how it would feel to hold the baby in her arms and thought that when she did, she probably didn't want to come back to work.

I wasn't pressuring Angela, I just wanted to make sure that she could come back and that, I would make sure, she had a flexible schedule and a new managerial position to come back to. She chose to be a stay-at-home mom, which is her prerogative, and I am supportive of her decision.

However, so many women out there feel they don't have options and don't come back to work. Mothers focus so much on "flexible" work hours that they forget that men also take advantage of flexible work hours, they just don't ask for permission as women do and make it an issue. Of course, there are jobs where flexibility is not possible and that requires a different discussion, but for professional positions, women literally hammer their chances into the ground by focusing only on the flexibility part and nothing else.

A colleague of mine, Martha, a sales rep, was getting the opportunity to interview for a sales manager position. She started the conversation with, "But you know, I can't travel as much as the previous guy." This is after I told her many times that she would do this job *her* way. She had to first understand the position and if she even wanted it, liked the hiring manager and wanted to work for him—and then let the hiring manager evaluate if she was the right person for the position (regardless of motherhood) and then…after they had gotten that part out of the way, they could discuss the package and schedule; and she could then discuss flexibility and how she might approach the job differently than the previous guy. Her opening with the disclaimer, tells the hiring manager, she doesn't really care about the job, all she cares about is flexibility and it reinforces the stereotype that mothers try to work less (though research shows that mothers are some of the most productive employees[1]).

Women are also afraid of telling their bosses they're pregnant, because they worry, they may not have a job to come back to; or that during their pregnancy they will start to be made redundant with their projects being given to others.

For example, Sandy who has a kick-ass woman boss was still afraid to tell her she was pregnant until she was starting to show —and not telling was becoming redundant. Once, during a meeting Sandy had such intense nausea and she was too afraid to eat crackers in front of everyone, she faked a phone call, went into her office and locked the door. She put her head on her desk for 20 minutes before she went back to the meeting.

And from here stems the ubiquitous question: can women have it all? Can we have a career *and* a family?

I'm not going to get into this debate, because it really doesn't matter what the consensus is; what matters is what you want. If you want a career and a family, you can make that happen for yourself; and if you decide that you want to be a stay-at-home mom, then you make that happen for yourself as well. There is no judgment here.

9

LONDON IS A ROOST FOR EVERY BIRD

ASMI DECIDED that the rest of May was going to be a dry month. No more alcohol. She made the decision on the second weekend of May after she woke up with a headache because she'd consumed half a bottle of scotch with Cara the evening before.

But by Sunday afternoon on a twelve-hour direct flight to LHR (London Heathrow) from LAX (Los Angeles International Airport), Asmi said yes to champagne when the nice stewardess in business class asked if she'd like a glass.

"I decided to have a dry month but it's a long flight," Asmi said to the stewardess.

Asmi was sitting in 4A. The man sitting in 4B across the aisle from her toasted Asmi with his glass of champagne and said, "I'm always trying to have a dry month, but it never seems to pan out."

His name was Levi Coleman and he was from Memphis. He was a writer and on his way to London where he was doing a book reading at Stanfords, a book store in Covent Garden. He wrote thrillers and his claim to fame was a female private investigator called Joy Luck who was half Chinese, half American and used to be a CIA operative. His books were all titled *The Joy of Something* and even though Asmi had never heard of him, he was a bestselling writer, which Asmi found out from his Wikipedia page.

"How hard is it to become a bestselling author?" Asmi asked because she'd never ever met a writer before.

"My first two books were duds. But then my first book in the Joy Luck series did well, and so it began. A black man writing about a Chinese American woman—who knew, that would the winning formula. An author once told me how it took fifteen years for her to become an overnight success, it took me eight," Levi said.

It wasn't the first time Asmi had met a stranger on a plane and had a conversation. Hell, she'd met Etienne on a flight. But she'd never met a writer before. She didn't want to be a cliché and she'd read enough articles about authors to know they hated the question: *Where do you get your ideas from*, but really, where did they get their ideas from?

So, she instead asked, "I hear that the most annoying question writers get is where they get their ideas from, is that true?"

Levi laughed, and it was a good happy laugh. The man had a lovely smile. He was about six feet three-four inches tall and his jeans hung on his ass quite nicely (Asmi had checked him out when he'd put his suitcase into the overhead bin). He had short curly hair and dimples.

"With Joy Luck it's easy to explain. I lived in Shanghai for eight years, until I was fifteen," Levi explained. "We were there with my father's job, he used to work for the state department... not an operative, but I used to meet people at the embassy and always wonder if they were operatives."

"Wow! You've actually met a CIA agent."

"Most probably."

"In comparison, my life is boring," Asmi declared.

"Tell me about your boring life," Levi said. "Where are you from?"

"That's the most annoying question I get asked," Asmi said as they took off.

During lunch she told him about her childhood in India and

that she had a bachelor's degree in chemical engineering from Osmania University. She had come to the United States to do her master's in biomedical engineering at UC Irvine.

"I loved California and never left," Asmi said. "Do you like living in Memphis?"

"It's okay," Levi said. "I have family and friends there. How about you? You have family in the States?"

"My sister lives in the Bay Area. We're close literally and emotionally. My parents live in India...and we're not close geographically or otherwise," she said. "I have lots of friends in Orange County. I travel a lot with work and sometimes I feel my life is airports, airplanes, hotels and meeting rooms."

"Do you like the travel?"

Asmi nodded. "I love it," she said. "Maybe because I don't have a husband and kids waiting at home for me. There's an excitement about getting out in the world. Obviously, I get tired and then stay home for a few weeks but then I get antsy. This time I was in the office for two weeks and I got a lot of work done, but by the time this meeting in London was booked, I was going a little stir crazy."

As strangers on a plane sometimes do, after lunch, they sat drinking their cognac and started to get personal. There was something special about airplanes because it brought people close for a brief period where they told each other things they'd never tell anyone else—and then *poof,* after they landed, the world shifted, and they were back in their own reality.

When Asmi used to fly economy, which was not that long ago, and she still did for flights under seven hours of flying time, she had more such conversations, simply because you sat close to other people. The time she met Etienne had been one of the first few times she was flying business. Then she'd bought the upgrade with points because only senior directors and above flew business at GTech.

"I've had privilege. In Memphis, I have friends who grew up in Orange Mound and they have it much harder. We went to university together but...it's not easy," Levi said. "I'm working on a novel, mainstream, not a thriller where I want to tell our stories. People see a black man and immediately assume a history that may or may not be true. All black men are not *one* thing."

Asmi told him about being a brown woman in a white man's corporate world, the number of meetings she walked into where not only was she the only woman but the only brown person. It happened in California as well, she assured Levi, even if it probably happened a lot more in other places in the country.

"The hard part is the obvious discrimination," Asmi said. "I can make fewer mistakes than my male colleagues. It's almost like they're waiting. It's not overt but it's there, an underlying threat. The number of times I've been told I'm too emotional, too passionate, aggressive…difficult. I know that people think, oh Asmi, super confident, must be ambitious. The thing is, I am confident, but I go home every day feeling like a failure."

Levi said he understood exactly what she meant because he also struggled with the difference between self-confidence and self-esteem.

He revealed he was single, having ended a three-year relationship just a few months before. He was still raw because his fiancée had fallen in love with someone else. Asmi told him about Etienne and how she had always been conflicted about his marital status.

By the time the plane landed in Heathrow, they made plans to meet for drinks that evening at *The Luggage Room*, one of Asmi's favorite whiskey bars in London where the roaring twenties were still kicking. It was also convenient for her because she was staying at the Marriott where the bar was located. Levi was not too far, as he was staying at the London Marriott Hotel Park Lane. Levi's book reading was around five in the evening the following day and Asmi said she'd try her best to make it, though she would be spending the day in a meeting room with Matthew and Scott from GTech, and Elvira and Mats from Short Poppy.

This time, Asmi had not bothered to kill herself preparing for the meeting. Scott had said yes to the acquisition of Short Poppy and Matthew really wanted this. Asmi didn't think she had much of a role to play but had brought along a presentation with the data her team had put together as Matthew had instructed. She promised herself she'd look at it before the meeting. There was no rush and no point in over preparing.

～

IT HAD BEEN love at first sight for Asmi with *The Luggage Room*.

An authentic speakeasy, it had a secret entrance, which you had to know about to find. Inside, the bar was all burnished dark wood and mood lighting. The cocktails were amazing, their whiskey selection superb and included some very good Japanese whiskey that Asmi liked. The bonus was that she always met someone interesting at the bar. Last time, which was a year ago, she'd met an executive from Chicago who worked for an Artificial Intelligence company. They'd talked and connected on LinkedIn. They kept in touch and once when one of Asmi's friends who lived in Chicago was looking for a job, Asmi had connected her with the AI executive and she worked for her company now.

Levi was already at the bar when Asmi arrived. It had taken a little time for her to get ready because she'd wanted to look good without looking desperate. It appeared that Levi had probably had the same internal debate as they both had ended up wearing jeans with dress shirts, both white.

"We're matching," Levi said as she sat down on one of the large black leather chairs across from Levi who had found seating in one of the half booths.

"So, we are," Asmi said. "How's your hotel?"

"It's a hotel," Levi said. "Aren't they all the same?"

"Most of the time," Asmi said. "I stay at Marriott. I have the loyalty card."

"I found out about the loyalty card business when I watched *Up in the Air*. This is a big deal for business people?" he asked.

Asmi grinned sheepishly. "It creeps up on you. I fly Star Alliance, usually Lufthansa and SAS in Europe and I fly United domestically. This way I collect points for all my flights. I've thousands of miles and I've given points to my sister and her family, so they could fly free to Hawaii. I'll pay for my hotels with points if I'm staying an extra day at some place...get an upgrade, things like that."

"And like Clooney, you won't stay in a place where you don't get points?"

"Not that extreme," Asmi said, "And I'm also not trying to get to ten million points or whatever it is he was. It's just convenience. I have elite status, so I get on the plane first. I get upgraded without paying for it on domestic flights...things like that."

"I couldn't do it," Levi said. "The nine to five thing."

"I just met a filmmaker who said the same thing," Asmi said, thinking about *Invisible Warren*.

Their waiter came and Asmi ordered the Rob Roy, a cocktail that was made with an Ardbeg 10, while Levi decided to try the Guggenheimer because he was curious about Fernet Branca.

After drinks, they found dinner at Maze, a sushi restaurant nearby where they sat at the bar.

It had been a long time, Asmi thought since she'd met someone with whom the conversation flowed. And he was *certainly* easy on the eyes.

It was as they were walking back to the hotel that Asmi could feel the tension between them. He was probably thinking what she was thinking. Should they? Why shouldn't they? They were single, unattached and...why not? Then there was the rational brain that said that she didn't know who this man was and jumping into bed right now with a stranger for a one-night stand may not be the mental health choice she should make.

"You should take an Uber back to your hotel," Asmi said when they reached her hotel's lobby. "It's a bit of a walk."

"I don't mind," Levi said. "It helps with the jet lag."

They stood outside the lobby, a security guard eyeing them

suspiciously and finally Asmi asked him. "How old are you, Levi?"

"I'm thirty-two," he said.

"I'm nearly forty," Asmi said, feeling much, much older than that.

"Okay," Levi said, smiling broadly and then added after a beat, "I'd still like to come up to your room."

$$\sim$$

HE LEFT EARLY because he had a breakfast meeting with his UK editor while Asmi lay naked in bed, wondering if she should have more one-night stands. It had been a while since she had had one and this one had been *awesome*. They had good chemistry. She had, *thank goodness*, waxed just a few days ago so she was trimmed in the right places, not that he'd have noticed.

It had been good sex.

They had laughed.

They had pillow talk.

It had been easy. He didn't leave in the middle of the night to be with his wife and children. She didn't push him away because *things were getting too serious*. It was *fun*, and more importantly, it was *simple*. Sex had been intense with Etienne, but it hadn't been fun, not like this, frivolous, like eating cotton candy without the calories.

Cara sent her a text message then: *I think I need to find a new job. Max is driving me nuts.*

Asmi texted back: *What happened?*

Her phone rang then. Cara was flustered. "Oscar says I'm being crazy, but something is going on and they won't tell me what it is. Apparently, it's all top level and I'm too far down the pyramid to know anything."

"Explain," Asmi said and looked at the clock on the television. She had two hours to make their meeting in a meeting room at the Marriott. Plenty of time to talk to Cara, take a shower and maybe indulge in a little fantasizing about the night before.

Asmi was in a good mood.

"Apparently, we…as in GTech HQ HR has hired a consultant, some guy from Mercer, this consulting firm we've used in the past," Cara said. "And they're doing an investigation. As HR director, I think I should know what's going on. If they don't trust me, they should fire me."

"An investigation about what?"

"I don't know," Cara said. "And Max is saying that I don't need to worry about it. My focus should be D and I."

"D and I?"

"Diversity and Inclusion…remember that survey we did? Anyway, I'm supposed to roll that program out and that's fine, but I feel like I'm not part of the team," Cara said. "Evan knows. Vincent the legal counsel knows. I don't know."

"Maybe Max has good reason to keep it quiet…maybe it's a compliance issue," Asmi suggested. "Especially if Legal is involved."

"I investigate compliance issues," Cara said. "Between you and me, when we fired Shane Hewitt in Sales, well, that was because we investigated and found out he's a psychopath who screams at his employees and scares the shit out of them. I investigated that. I don't understand what they're doing that is so secret, unless it's something in HR they're investigating and don't want me to know."

"Cara, Oscar is right, you're overreacting. Corporations work like this. Come on, Jim used to have all those secret meetings when we acquired CoEnzyme two years ago, but that didn't mean he didn't trust me, just that I wasn't part of the process," Asmi said.

"Maybe you're right," Cara mumbled. "How's London?"

"Great," Asmi said and told her about Levi.

"I know those books," Cara screeched. "I've read one of them. You met the writer? That's so cool. Are you going to see him again?"

"I don't know. He asked me to come to his book reading so if we get done with the meeting with Short Poppy early enough, maybe I can make the reading," Asmi said. "But really, I leave tomorrow for Zurich for a meeting with this big bakery company and…he lives in Memphis. It's just an airplane fling, Cara."

"But you said the sex was good. He's smart. He's nice looking. Why not pursue it?" Cara asked.

"I'm eight years older than him and he's *really* nice looking, way better looking, and better than I deserve," Asmi said. "It's a casual thing. I can't imagine him wanting to hang around with a hag like me."

"You know, a man would never think like that," Cara said. "A man would think, yeah, baby, I have a swinging dick and that's why young women want me. We women, we think about waxing and shaving and does he like the smell of my pussy… come on, *lean in*, Asmi."

"I'm pretty sure Sheryl Sandberg didn't mean 'Lean In' in terms of sex," Asmi said. "Hey, I'll go for his reading if I can and we'll see what happens."

"I'd sleep with him again if I were you, at least one more time," Cara said and then called out, *"No, Oscar, not me, it's Asmi, she met someone on a plane."*

MATTHEW ASKED Asmi to start the meeting with her presentation. She knew he would do that. She was in his crosshairs and for some reason he wanted to give her a tough time, every time. Some of the time, she didn't mind the constant testing, but *all the time* was too much. It was a good thing she was blasé about it now because the job was gone, the worst had happened. She had nothing to prove. She was going to wait it out and find a new job when she had the emotional resources to do so.

As Asmi set her presentation up in the meeting room, she decided to not care what Matthew had to say. She was here to make a point and ensure that there was a good discussion around the viability of Short Poppy as an acquisition for GTech and beyond that, they could do whatever they wanted. It was their business. She was just a soldier.

The presentation went well, and Matthew didn't nitpick, instead he was complimentary, so much so that Asmi wondered if someone had had a chat with him about what he did in Vegas. Elvira and Mats engaged in some good discussions, while Scott spent most of his time outside the meeting room on an *important* phone call about a big customer account.

After the meeting with Short Poppy, which ended sooner than expected, Matthew, Scott and Asmi regrouped for lunch at the hotel restaurant.

"I liked that they were transparent about where they're at and what they see as the vision of the company," Matthew said. "I like these people."

"They seem very capable," Asmi agreed.

"But you still don't think they're right for us," Matthew said.

Asmi knew she should fall in with the company line, but she'd already decided she needed to find a new job in the summer, so why compromise on her integrity now?

"Their customers are different from ours; they're still not commercial, not full scale. They need a second round of funding and we like to acquire slightly more mature companies. After looking at the market data, I actually don't think they're right for us even if they were mature...the business is too far..."

"Asmi, they're commercial enough for us and we can always build a commercial organization to support the new customer base if needed," Scott interrupted her. "Sometimes companies have to take a chance and I think they're a good chance to take."

"Why do you think they're a good chance to take?" Asmi asked him.

Scott shrugged. "I think they have a cool product and the data your team put together does show market potential."

"This is an adjacency we're not looking at, Scott, not strategically at GTech," Asmi said. "If we really want to go into agritech, we need to maybe look at some mid-sized established companies with a solid pipeline like AGRO or FarmTech or...there are a few that I think would help us build a base for that business. Short Poppy is just too...short."

"I think you're overly critical," Scott said. "Matthew, you want to acquire Short Poppy, don't you?"

"I like them," Matthew said, nodding. "But I see the merits of Asmi's point. Asmi, I'd like you to think about how you can make this work rather than saying no to it—that would give you a different perspective, as well."

"That's what I presented today. To make it work we'll need critical mass, and sales in the US of around forty million to start with and Short Poppy hardly has a quarter of that in Europe and no commercial organization," Asmi said. "We'll have to build it and I think we should buy it only if we're serious about agritech and ready to spend the money to fund it, both developmentally and commercially."

"I think Matthew is serious about Short Poppy and not necessarily agritech," Scott said lazily, leaning back in his chair, his stance and demeanor that of being someone above Asmi, someone who had the CEO's ear and confidence. Someone who had the VP of Marketing job.

"There's some truth to that," Matthew said. "I appreciate the work you've done, Asmi but I feel you're biased and coming from a negative place. I'd like to see a little more...I don't know...positivity from you on Short Poppy."

"I think they have a very interesting and viable technology platform but that doesn't detract from their deficiencies and strategically, we have to think about ...."

Scott interrupted Asmi again and said, "You keep harping on about strategy. Strategies can change. Matthew wants to take the company in another direction. Why not support him, huh?"

"I am supporting the business," Asmi said as calmly as she could.

"Well, this constant Short Poppy bashing doesn't feel like support," Scott said, and Matthew didn't correct him.

Lunch arrived then. Asmi ate about half her spinach ravioli

but Scott and Matthew ate their steak and even ordered a cheese-cake for dessert. Asmi had coffee. They had another meeting in the GTech London offices in the afternoon and Asmi wanted to say she was sick and just go back to her room. Why bring her along if her opinion didn't matter? And that's when it hit her, she was slowly being displaced, not replaced but displaced with maybe the hope that she'd leave on her own if she was humiliated enough. It happened all the time in companies, though she'd not seen it at GTech. Matthew had his quirks, but he was a fair leader and believed in a strong corporate culture rooted in respect for employees. If they had to performance manage some-one, they did that—and if they wanted her gone, she assumed they'd tell her they wanted her gone, give her an exit package and send her on her way. She didn't expect them to humiliate her out of the company. But maybe she had been naïve.

∞

Asmi had never lied and said she was sick to miss work. Maybe she'd offered some white lies when she had job inter-views, but she was always conscientious and even came to meet-ings when she was *actually* ill.

"Matthew, I'm not feeling all that well," she said after lunch as they headed to their rooms before taking a taxi to the GTech offices. "Since it's just a courtesy call at London GTech, I'm going to stay in my room. I hope this is okay."

"Of course," Matthew said, immediately concerned and not doubting Asmi because she had a reputation for being as honest and hardworking as a stupid donkey.

Asmi went to her room, changed out of her business clothes and put on a pair of jeans, her sneakers and a sweatshirt because May was still cool in London.

She'd been in London many times but always for business. She'd never played tourist. She decided it was time.

She waited until she was sure that Matthew and Scott had left the hotel, and then sneaked out to the lobby. After a conversation with the concierge, she bought a *Hop On Hop Off* bus ticket and took a taxi to Leicester Square Station where she could get on one of those red buses with no roofs.

Work had always come first and Asmi had never skipped work for play, but this time as she got on the bus and sat on top, looking at London in all its glory on a beautiful and sunny May afternoon, Asmi felt absolutely and remarkably guilt-free.

Her first stop was Madame Tussauds, which was as kitsch as it got, but on a day such as this, Asmi felt she had to do the extraordinary.

She did it all. She asked another tourist to take a picture of her while she sat in the Oval Office and in front of 10 Downing Street. She took selfies with Obama and Hillary, as well as with Shahrukh and Aishwarya. She checked out if Hrithik Roshan's weird sixth finger was there in wax. It was, so she took a picture of it.

She'd gone on a few vacations alone but that felt like many years ago. There was a long weekend in New York and one in Brussels, but she'd never *actually* gone on a proper vacation by herself. She had done a Caribbean cruise with Ananya, Venkat, the kids *and* their parents, which had been a disaster. Etienne and she had had some holidays together. Usually, he'd come to where she was for a meeting and she'd extend her stay by a couple of days, always in Europe, and always on weekdays because weekends were family time. They'd pretty much hit all the major European cities: Amsterdam, London, Brussels, Berlin, Lisbon, Barcelona, Rome and Vienna. She'd always remember seeing the Vatican and the Coliseum with Etienne, seeing a sex show in Amsterdam with him, taking a tram in Lisbon...her past four years were entwined with him and she had to accept that. There was no wiping it away because if she did that, she'd also have to forget watching *Aida* in Vienna and eating the original Sacher torte at Café Sacher. She'd have to blank out *Wicked* in London, walking by the River Spree in Berlin, seeing the Gaudi-designed Sagrada Família in Barcelona, and eating a hot dog on a Copenhagen street. No, she couldn't eliminate those memories, but she had to come to terms with the fact that it was over. For real. She had moved on. She'd had sex with Levi. She'd kissed Henri. Right now, as she rode through the city of London, she didn't miss Etienne, didn't wish he was with her. He probably felt as she did, relieved it was over, and even though he missed her, he was probably enjoying guilt-free family time as she was enjoying her freedom.

For the past four years, she had been on vacation with someone else, with Etienne or Ananya and the family, but this time, this afternoon, she was free to do whatever she wanted, no obligations, no responsibilities and no consequences.

After Madam Tussauds', Asmi went to the Tower of London because she was a fan of Ann Boleyn and Elizabeth the First.

She joined a small group of tourists, all lucky to have Moira Cameron, the first female Beefeater tell them about the gory history of the Tower. Asmi had read enough Tudor fiction and non-fiction to know that Elizabeth the First feared the Tower because it was where traitors were tortured and executed.

Moira, who had an enthusiastic sense of humor, told the story of the Tower Hill, "and it was called the Tower Hill because…it's on a hill. All the public executions took place there. But contrary to popular belief, the Tower of London was never a prison but a palace and a fortress…although officially, thirty-five hundred prisoners went through here."

Everyone laughed at that and again, when she added, "They didn't execute all their prisoners, only three hundred and sixty-three of them; one in ten, just like currently in Texas."

Asmi saw the grave where they believed Anne Boleyn was buried and felt sadness for the woman whose daughter, Elizabeth was one of the female leaders in history who had Leaned In, had had no master, no man and no children—but had been a veritable powerhouse.

THIRSTY AFTER LISTENING to the gory details of the Tower, Asmi stopped for a drink at Shakespeare's Head, which had a bust of the famous playwright, watching the street from a window. She went into the pub even though she wasn't a beer person. Paintings of Shakespeare or his plays covered the walls of the establishment. She sat at the bar by a painting from Act V, Scene II of Othello, painted by a J Graham and engraved by a W Leney. The names meant nothing to her. The painting showed a dark Othello, holding a knife while a lily-white Desdemona lay on white sheets with one tit showing.

The text under the painting read: *It is the cause, it is the cause, my soul.*

"I don't drink beer," Asmi told the bartender, an older gentleman with a Scottish accent. "What do you recommend for me?"

"Water," the bartender said.

Asmi grinned. "It's been a long year. I'm going to need alcohol." And since he was Scottish, she added, "I drink scotch…but I want to give beer a chance. What can you suggest for a newbie like me?"

The bartended nodded. "Where are you from?"

"California."

"I just got this great new IPA from Brooklyn. Bengali Six Point. It's a biting hop but has a nice malt finish," he said.

"Okay," Asmi said. She had no idea what any of that meant. She understood whiskey; she didn't understand hops and malt in beer.

He served the beer in a chilled glass and while he was doing that, Asmi looked through the menu and thought that since she was in London, she had to have fish and chips.

"How's the beer?" the bartender asked her after he took her food order.

Asmi shrugged. "I don't know. I think it's…crisp…okay."

"It's not converting you to beer then?"

Asmi shook her head. "I doubt it, but the beer is nice."

Since it was three in the afternoon on a weekday, the pub wasn't crowded and there wasn't much people-watching to do.

It was one of Asmi's favorite things when she traveled, to sit alone at a restaurant and look around at people, overhear conversations and chat up the bartender.

"Charles Dickens used to come here," the bartender, who introduced himself as Gordon, told her.

"This place is *really* old," Asmi said.

"You don't have places like this in America," he said.

Asmi smiled. Europeans thought they were superior to Americans because they had history.

"I was in New Orleans last year and had an excellent jambalaya at a restaurant that used to be Tennessee Williams favorite haunt," she said.

"Never liked that bugger," Gordon said and winked at her. "How comes it's a long year when it's only May, we are not even half way to December?"

"I broke up with my married lover. I think I'm going to be out of a job because the asshole I work with will soon become my manager. I'm turning forty in a few months. I have no career, no husband or kids...so I'm approaching big loser territory," Asmi said.

Gordon placed her fish and chips and said, "Well, breaking up with the married lover was probably a good thing."

Asmi loaded a forkful of pureed peas and nodded. "Yes, that was definitely a good thing."

"How come you're forty and single? You're a good-looking girl."

Asmi thought about it for a moment as she chewed on a fry and then said what she knew to be the truth, "I like being single."

"Then what're you complaining about?" he asked genially.

Asmi laughed. "You're right. I should stop complaining..."

"And start living," Gordon suggested.

Asmi took Gordon's advice and ordered an Uber to go to Stanfords for Levi's reading. She enjoyed the book reading, had dinner and another playful night with Levi.

The next day as a car drove Matthew, Scott and Asmi to Heathrow, she was humming softly to herself.

"You look like you're feeling better," Matthew said.

"Yes, an afternoon of rest was just what I needed," Asmi said with a broad smile.

AND THEN SHE SAID...HE DIDN'T MEAN IT, I'M JUST BEING SENSITIVE

EXCERPT FROM THE BUSINESS WORKBOOK "AND THEN SHE SAID..."

I COULD WRITE pages and pages and pages of things that men have said to women in the workplace that are outrageous. In the #MeToo era, how can this still be happening? The #MeToo movement is new and we're still figuring our way around the problem.

HERE ARE **four** things we can do when faced with misogyny and harassment in the workplace at any level.

1. **Find your allies**. This is important. Network around the company with associates and leaders at different levels and make friends. These are the people whom you can then rely on when you need help in dealing with harassment. Make a deal with an ally (male and/or female) that you will support each other. Just like in the Obama White House[1], where women reinforced each other's opinions in meetings to not let them be talked over or have their ideas stolen from them. You don't have to fight it alone.

2. **There is no dignity in being silent.** Don't be quiet about it. Talk to your manager and try to make him or her understand what you see as harassment and bad behavior. If nothing changes, as it unfortunately often doesn't: talk to HR, talk to your mentor in the company and talk to your colleagues. This notion that when women face harassment, they must handle it with dignity is bullshit. There is no dignity in being abused by a superior in any form at the workplace.

3. **Document. Document. Document.** If someone harasses you and it's a pattern, send them an email to tell them how you feel. If you don't tell them in writing, there is no documentation and then when HR says, give me an example, you're left feeling like you're not believed, because you don't have proof. Do this immediately after the incident. Take contemporaneous notes of a meeting that makes you uncomfortable, then send it to your manager, and forward that email to HR. The more you document, the better you are protected and the more pressure you can put on HR to do something about the situation.

4. **Start looking for another job.** I'm afraid, you may have to do this. Research shows that a bully doesn't often change his (or her) stripes. A study found that many workplace bullies receive positive evaluations from their supervisors and achieve high levels of career success, despite organizational efforts to curtail bullying[2].

10

PINCH THE TAIL AND SUCK THE HEAD

"IS HE NOW YOUR BOYFRIEND?" Ananya asked as they talked over the phone while Asmi packed for her trip to New Orleans.

"I slept with him twice two weeks ago and we've exchanged a few text messages," Asmi said. "I don't think what we have elevated past booty call."

"I Googled him and he's *really* good looking. You should go see him in Memphis, it's what, a six-hour drive or something from NOLA?" Ananya suggested.

"And then maybe I can boil his bunny too?"

"Oh, come on, driving to Memphis won't make you a Glenn Close-like stalker. You could manufacture a business reason for being there," Ananya said, "And then you just say, *oops*, I was in town, so I thought I'd drop by."

"It was fun and that's all it was," Asmi said. "I needed a little fun. With Matthew chewing my ass out every time I speak, Scott treating me like a cross between an imbecile and a subordinate, I needed to feel my life and in London, I finally felt my life."

"How did it feel?"

"Not as empty as I thought it would," Asmi said as she zipped her suitcase. She set it on the floor of her bedroom and sat down on the bed. "I felt like it was full of opportunity and hope."

"Really?"

"Really. A bartender told me to stop complaining and start living," Asmi said. "I need to stop working too much and cruise a little at work. I need to go on business trips and do things like I did in London. Maybe I should find a job that is not this demanding. Who knows, I may find the love of my life, my soulmate...and then I'll marry and live happily ever after."

"Then how does the fairytale go? The evil witch gives you an apple or the prince kisses you?" Ananya said. "You're not *feeling* your life; you're *avoiding* your life. Your life is more than your career, but it includes your job, which you've always loved."

"It seems like a long time ago that I loved my job," Asmi said.

"This whole thing started when your boss decided to retire... before that you were having fun," Ananya said. "You were enjoying growing your team. You were so happy when Gustav was promoted. You were so proud of your revenue numbers for last year because your team worked so hard. Where did all that go?"

"I don't know."

"What do you mean by that? Stop being such a defeatist— stand up and be counted, damn it," Ananya said angrily.

"No, no, no, you don't get to judge me," Asmi yelled back. "You don't get to tell me I have to fight all the fights because you decided to stay home. I deserve a life."

"Yes, you do. But an authentic one, not this *I'm cruising over a cloud* bullshit," Ananya said.

"Maybe we're not supposed to have it all," Asmi said. "I saw this TED Talk where a woman said that nature designed us to procreate not to be happy. I'm not procreating so why not defy nature and be happy? My job doesn't make me happy anymore. I hate going to the office."

"That's because it's a challenging time," Ananya said. "Let me ask you, say you got the VP of Marketing job, would you still feel this way?"

"I'm never going to get that job."

"You don't know that."

Asmi sighed deeply. "I'm done, Ana. I just want a job now, not a career, not something that's driving me crazy. I don't need that much money. I'll sell this place and rent an apartment in Orange or something and have a life for nearly half of what I'm making now."

"This is not about money, Asmi," Ananya said. "This is about who you are. You can be both, happy and a career woman. You can be a mother, a wife and a career woman. But you have to believe in it."

"You didn't believe in it," Asmi said.

"And look where it got me? I'm bored out of my skull. I'm either turning into a Scotch whiskey aficionado or an alcoholic—the line is blurry. Venkat and I have gotten into the habit of smoking a cigarette every evening because our parents are driving us nuts, so we don't even have our health anymore," Ananya said. "You're not me. You're you. And you're amazing."

"I don't feel amazing," Asmi said, "I feel tired."

JUNE IN NEW ORLEANS was as pleasant as it could be—not too hot like it would be in a month and not cool like it was a month ago.

Asmi's team was booked into the Hotel Monteleone in the heart of the French Quarter.

Asmi had invited GTech's heads of marketing from around the world for the two-day meeting. They had planned workshops, presentations and team building activities. There were ten of them: including Asmi, Gustav and Marisol from headquarters; two marketing managers from Latin America, Leticia who managed Brazil and Mateo the rest; a new Head of Marketing, Raymond from the United Kingdom who was responsible for Central Europe; and Vasile from Romania who was responsible for the Eastern European team. Billy was from Australia; Jon from China; and Shruti from India who managed marketing for all of South-East Asia. The marketing heads from the countries didn't directly report to Asmi but had dotted lines to both Scott and her as they took care of both their businesses in their respective regions.

"I read that this hotel is haunted," Shruti said to Jon and Asmi as they met at the hotel's famous bar for a drink. New Orleans' only revolving bar, the Carousel Bar, was like an amusement park carousel, a circus-clad Merry-Go-Round where you could enjoy a Sazerac and you didn't have to get off until you were done.

"I don't believe in ghosts," Jon said seriously.

"How is it haunted?" Asmi asked carefully. She didn't want her team to know that the last time she stayed in an allegedly haunted hotel in Savannah she'd kept Ananya on the phone until she fell asleep. That hotel had a life-size doll of a woman leaning against a window and it completely freaked Asmi out. In addition, guests had added to a diary that was on the bedside table with one spooky story after the other.

"It's not there anymore but there used to be a door in the kitchen of the hotel that kept opening even though it was locked. Sometimes, the elevator takes you to the wrong floor and as you walk the hallway it gets chilly and you see the ghosts of children," Shruti said. "I read it on TripAdvisor."

"Well, if it's on the Internet then it's true," Jon said.

Gustav got onto the empty bar stool next to Asmi and said, "What are we talking about?"

"Shruti thinks there are ghosts in the hotel," Jon said.

Gustav nodded. "Sure, there are."

When the bartender came up to him, Gustav ordered a Sazerac and asked him about the ghosts.

"There was a little boy called Maurice Begere who died in the hotel in the late 1800s. He died on the fourteenth floor," the bartender said as he mixed a Sazerac.

He rinsed a chilled glass with absinthe. He stirred rye whiskey, syrup and three dashes of Peychaud's bitters into another glass with ice. He strained the ingredients into the glass rinsed with absinthe and added a lemon peel to it before setting it in front of Asmi.

"What happened to Maurice?" Jon asked the bartender.

"He just died, no foul play or anything," the bartender said and started on Gustav's drink. "His parents used to come back every year, mourning their son and one time, good little Maurice actually went up to his mother and told her to not cry because he was fine."

"Oh, come on, there are no ghosts," Asmi said and took a sip of her Sazerac.

"*Sugah*, this is New Orleans, we have a haunted house on every corner of the French Quarter. You can't shake a crawfish tail without hitting a spirit," the bartender said with a smile and then winked at her.

He was *cute*. His name badge said Remy and Asmi had a vision of a young Dennis Quaid, also called Remy in *The Big Easy*. This Remy was in his late twenties and looked like someone who would say in his N'Awlins accent, *"This is the Big Easy, sugah, folks have a certain way o' doin' things down here."*

Asmi leaned closer to the bar and said, "Well, I'm staying on the eleventh floor, so I should be safe, right?"

"Well, you could meet Red there, he wanders around," the bartender said, pushing Gustav's Sazerac in front of him, but he was looking at Asmi. "William "Red" Wildemere used to work at the hotel and died of natural causes. He's harmless."

"I'd love to see a ghost," Shruti said. "It would be so exciting."

"*There are no ghosts*," Jon said patiently. "We're in marketing and we should be able to see a marketing stunt for what it is. Come on, Shruti you can't be that gullible."

"I'm not gullible," Shruti explained, "I'm open to new opportunities for adventure."

EVERYONE IN ASMI'S team arrived in New Orleans at various

times of the day so Asmi went for dinner with Jon, Shruti and Gustav as the rest would come later or had already checked-in and had left to do some sightseeing.

"Tennessee Williams used to eat here," Shruti told the others as they settled into their chairs at the Chartres House, a Cajun-Creole restaurant, a homey place that served the New Orleans essentials, which Asmi always went to when she was in town.

"You're full of historical facts," Jon remarked.

"This one I know, as well," Asmi said. "Actually, it's written outside the restaurant in big bold letters."

"It's my first time in New Orleans and I've always wanted to come here, ever since I watched *Interview with a Vampire* and listened to *Moon over Bourbon Street* by Sting," Shruti said. "I'm going to spend two extra days and I want to see and taste everything."

Shruti was Indian and in her late thirties. She was married and had a son who was eight years old and lived in Hyderabad where GTech's Indian office was. She was tall for an Indian and had straight black hair that swished around her shoulders. She was always well put together Asmi thought, always dressed elegantly with her makeup applied perfectly and lipstick in place. Asmi wondered if people saw her like she saw Shruti. Cara had mentioned that Asmi radiated serious professionalism with a feminine toughness that sometimes came off as arrogant, something people who knew her would never think.

As they talked around quickly emptying bowls of gumbo, red beans and rice, jambalaya and shrimp étouffée, Asmi, on impulse, sent a text message to Levi: *I'm in New Orleans, how far am I from Memphis?*

He responded immediately: *About 5 hours. But I'm in Baton Rouge right now, visiting a friend so I'm only an hour away. Where are you staying?*

Asmi almost dropped her phone as if it was on fire. He could just come by tonight, that's what he was saying, wasn't he? He could drive down and be with her in the haunted hotel. At least she wouldn't have to be afraid of a ghost in her bedroom.

Her phone beeped again. *If I leave now, I can buy you a sazerac at the Sazerac Bar at the Waldorf Astoria in an hour and a half.*

How about at the Carousel Bar instead at the Monteleone? I'm on the eleventh floor, which may or may not be haunted.

I'm on my way. Don't go anywhere.

"Is everything okay?" Gustav asked. "You've gone pale."

Asmi drank some water and smiled, "I'm fine, just spooked…it must be all the ghost stories."

After dinner, they walked back to the hotel with Gustav and Jon ahead of Shruti and Asmi. It was a short walk and it was about eight in the evening. The streets were coming alive with light, people and music. There was a special energy in New Orleans, Asmi always felt when she visited, something in the air that made you feel light-headed and seduced. Or maybe it was just the smell of urine, hurricanes and stale beer on Bourbon Street.

"I want to ask you something, if you feel it's improper you don't have to answer," Shruti said as they came to stand outside the Monteleone. They were alone as Gustav had said he'd meet them at the bar and Jon went to bed because he'd flown in from Shanghai that morning and was tired.

"If I can't answer, I'll say I can't answer," Asmi said, "But that shouldn't stop you from asking."

"Good," Shruti said and licked her lips. She was nervous. "I know that things are weird with Jim retiring and we're all getting a bit nervous that Scott will become the VP of Marketing."

Asmi nodded. "Hey, whatever happens, you'll be fine, you're a top performer, you don't have anything to worry about."

"Yes, I do," Shruti said. "Look, I manage the entire marketing team in South Asia and I'm close to my people. Meena works with Scott and I work with you, but that doesn't mean I don't know what's happening in the detergent team. Scott has a boys' club. The things that happen in their meetings, the name calling, the way they treat each other, it's not professional and…I think it's not okay."

Asmi took a deep breath because she knew she had to step carefully. "What do you mean by name calling?"

"I haven't said anything so far because I didn't know for sure. I've only heard rumors. Last week, Meena told me after we heard a rumor that Scott would become the VP of Marketing. You know they promoted David as a junior strategic manager in Scott's team in California. Do you know that they call him *jism* in front of everyone?" Shruti said and when Asmi looked confused, added, "It's an acronym for Junior Strategic Manager."

"What?" Asmi was horrified.

"Oh, it gets worse," Shruti said. "Beth Baker was talking about how someone got her name wrong and called her Bugs Bath. Suddenly, they're all calling her Bugs and Buggy and Bugsy. Finally, Pam who is Beth's manager says to Henry, who is Scott's favorite, to not call her that and he says he won't stop until Beth tells him to and that it's not Pam's business. It's worse than kindergarten."

"They were calling Beth a name and her boss asked them to stop and they didn't?" Asmi asked.

"They did," Shruti said. "But after Pam all but yelled at Henry. They were at a restaurant."

"And HR is aware of this?"

"Remember Jackson? He left because he was being bullied in meetings," Shruti said. "He told HR all about it in his exit interview. Scott is awful. Riley had invited a few of the team to her wedding and they served cigars after dinner. Scott has a picture of him and Ellie, who's like twenty-three, an assistant, and he sends it to several people in his team with the caption, *Ellie said she won't swallow.*"

Asmi's eyes bugged out. She'd heard that Scott was casual with his team, which had a bit of a *bro* culture. She'd never wondered about the impact of his leadership on the women in his team. She should have, she realized.

"Has anyone, Ellie, Beth, Pam, Meena, anyone, talked to HR?"

Shruti shrugged. "I know about Jackson because we're

friends, we went through leadership training together. He told me before he left that he had spilled all to HR. To Evan."

"I didn't know about any of this," Asmi said. "I'm so glad you told me because this is *not normal,* and this behavior, if true, is unacceptable."

"You know when Scott was in India...what, three weeks ago? He met with all of us and he says to me in front of my team, *you should work with detergent, we like women like you who're good at doing laundry,*" Shruti said and she was visibly upset as she spoke. "It was humiliating."

"Did *you* tell HR about this?" Asmi asked.

"Why would I? What will they do? Everyone knows what Scott's team is like, but no one has done anything about it. Look, I can handle a joker like Scott, because I must handle men like that in India all the time. But if he gets that promotion, I'll have to find another job. I won't work for him," Shruti said.

Asmi nodded. "Look, no decision has been made so hold your horses, okay? Let me look into this and I promise as soon as I know anything, I'll let you know. If things really go wrong, I'll help you find another position in GTech. You could work in strategic communications or employer branding. There's a lot you could do. Is there something you have in mind for your next challenge?"

"I want to move to GTech HQ in marketing," Shruti said. "I've talked to my family and this would be something we'd really like."

Asmi nodded. "I'll keep that in mind and also let Cara know...so if there's an opening we'll reach out to you."

"I trust you, so I'm going to hang in there," Shruti said. "I want to be led by you and not Scott. You're the reason I'm growing as I am. I learn from you. I have nothing to learn from Scott except how to scratch my balls, excuse my language, and my balls are fine without the scratching."

"I understand," Asmi said, laughing a little. "Look, I'm an officer of the company so I have to tell HR what you've told me. That's the rule. Are you okay with that?"

Shruti thought about it for a moment and then sighed, "Just make sure Scott doesn't find out that this came from Meena or me. If he becomes the VP, I don't need him to make my life miserable until I leave. I trust you. I'm counting on you to make this right."

Well then, no pressure, Asmi thought.

≈

"I CAN'T BELIEVE you're here," Asmi said, as Levi stepped into her hotel room and set his backpack on the floor.

"I drove as fast as I could, didn't even care about getting a ticket," Levi said but didn't come close to her as if he too was gauging the situation.

"You deserve a drink," Asmi said nervously and added, "We should go to the bar downstairs." She *definitely* had butterflies in her stomach.

"Yes, I do deserve a drink," Levi said and held his ground and looked into Asmi's eyes, a big smile on his face.

Asmi had no choice but to respond to the smile and took the steps needed to be toe-to-toe with him. She stretched up and right before she placed her mouth over his said, "Let's get this out of the way and *after* we can get a drink."

After, they got their drinks from the minibar, a little bottle of Jack Daniels for Levi and a glass of some California Sauvignon Blanc for Asmi, as they lay naked on the white sheets, leaning against the backrest.

"What were you doing in Baton Rouge?" Asmi asked, staring at the art on the wall, a framed photograph of a Ziegfeld Follies showgirl, wearing a transparent black outfit. It reminded her of Dita von Teese.

"I'm with some friends, there's a book festival at LSU," he said. "They invited me to sit on a thriller fiction panel."

"You're famous," Asmi said, turning to look at him, "My sister Googled you. She thinks you're hot. You're *actually*

145

Google-able. Google me and all you'll get is my LinkedIn profile."

Levi laughed. "I'm *okay*. Not everyone knows me or anything. I'm not Dan Brown or John Grisham, you know? I'm small time."

"And so humble," Asmi said. "I can't believe you came just to spend the night."

"Yes. I'll have to leave early tomorrow morning to make my panel," Levi said.

Asmi set her glass aside and turned to him. "Then I think we should make the best of the night."

Levi downed the last of the bourbon in his glass and put it on the bedside table. "You're absolutely right."

∾

LOOSE WITH A NIGHT OF SEX, Asmi stepped into the hotel's restaurant Criollo for breakfast.

"You look all bright and shiny," Gustav said as she joined him at his table where he was sitting alone, waiting for her.

Asmi nodded at his comment and said hello to Marisol and Raymond who were at the table next to Gustav; she waved to some others from the team who were at the far end of the restaurant.

Gustav leaned closer and said, "Shruti talked to me last night at the bar and told me what she told you. What's going on?"

Asmi shrugged. "It's a lesson in what not to do as a leader."

"Seriously, what are you going to do?" Gustav asked.

"I'm going to call Cara during lunch and tell her everything, and then we'll take it from there," Asmi said. "I'm not responsible for Scott's team, he is, but I'll make sure it's addressed. Now, let's focus on our meeting. Can you walk me through the workshop you've planned this afternoon, while I get a quick breakfast?"

∾

CARA WAS SHOCKED to hear what Asmi said to her about Scott's team.

"Has anyone done a Speak Up?" Cara asked.

"I'm doing one now, with you. But I can't be involved because it's going to look like I have a personal issue with Scott," Asmi said. "And we need to keep *Hunger Games*, which has probably ended separate from this."

"I'm not Scott's HR partner, Asmi, so I didn't do the exit interview with Jackson. Evan is his HR partner and the way Max manages us...we're in silos and don't interact," Cara said. "*But* let me poke around and see what I find out. This is awful by the way. Just awful. I'm going to check in with some of the women in Scott's team and see if anyone spills."

"That's all well and good, but you have to tell Max," Asmi said. "If you don't tell him I will have to tell him. We must make this official. You know the rule. Never be the senior-most person with a secret."

"I have a one-on-one with him later in the afternoon, I'll bring it up then," Cara said. "Do you think they'll fire Scott?"

"I don't think so," Asmi said. "I've seen so many like him and they never get fired."

"HR departments in corporate America can be entirely gutless," Cara agreed. "Can you send me in writing what you said to me?"

Asmi took a deep breath. Sending it in writing would mean that *she* was the one making it official. "I will."

"I won't let anyone know it came from you," Cara said.

"I understand," Asmi said. "But if push comes to shove, you don't have to keep me anonymous. We need to protect the associates first, not ourselves."

"Aye, aye," Cara said.

That evening while they were taking the Haunted French Quarter tour as a team building activity and listening to the gory details of Delphine LauLaurie in front of the LauLaurie mansion, Asmi received a text message from Cara: *Max asked me to stay out of this when I told him. I asked Evan and he said it was a detergent business issue and nothing to do with me.*

Asmi looked at the message and realized she wasn't exactly surprised. *Did you tell him this was from me?*

Cara responded: *No. I just said I had heard.*

"That was so cool," Shruti said as they went for a drink at Muriel's in Jackson Square where the haunted house tour ended.

"This restaurant is haunted too," Marisol said. "I believe in spirits...and not just the drinking kind. I've seen my grandfather's spirit in my grandmother's house in Oaxaca. I tell you, there are ghosts and spirits and we must treat them with respect."

"You've watched that Disney movie *Coco* too many times. This is all marketing," Leticia who was from Brail said.

"That's what I keep saying," Jon said.

They all got into a heated discussion about ghosts when their waiter arrived who was more than happy to join their conversation and add to it with stories about Pierre Antoine Lepardi Jourdan, the resident ghost for whom a table was always set at the restaurant. Jourdan had lost the building that housed Muriel's in a poker game. He was an inveterate gambler and had been heartbroken about losing the house when he died. (Side note, Jourdan was also the man who introduced America to the game of craps, now popular in Casinos worldwide.)

Asmi couldn't focus because her mind was still on work. She wrote back to Cara, *what do you think is going on?*

Cara responded. *I wish I knew. Max said, don't discuss this. We have it under control.*

And that's code for, he's our boy and we're okay with this? Asmi wrote

Could be. But if that's the case, GTech is not a company I want to work for. When you leave, take me with you.

Asmi sighed when she read the message. She wasn't even looking for a job and director positions didn't grow on trees like *low-hanging fruits* to pluck off.

Gustav said the same thing. I don't even have feelers out.

Will I'll see you in Tokyo in two weeks? I'm in China next week and straight to Tokyo from there, Cara wrote.

I'm in Brussels next week, directly from there to Tokyo. Endless flight.

Cara and Asmi were going as a team to interview various candidates for the head of marketing position in Tokyo and they would be there for two days of interviews and meetings. They'd be flying for more time than they'd be on land.

Asmi didn't want to get involved. But she looked at Shruti talking excitedly about a marketing campaign that her team was running in India and knew she had to do it. These people worked hard for GTech and they were her responsibility.

She wrote a text to Cara. *I'm going to call Max first thing tomorrow. You okay if he knows you and I talked?*

If he has a problem with it, he can kiss my big beautiful Italian ass. You're doing the right thing, Cara wrote back.

THAT NIGHT as Asmi prepared for the meeting the next day, she got a message from Levi. *Hi, I wish I could come by tonight.*

Asmi looked at the message and wondered if she was walking into a relationship with Levi. Or was it just fun and games? They were from different generations; she was nearly forty and he was thirty-two, a veritable baby. Asmi had always thought she liked older men. Etienne was fifty-two, a good twelve years older than her. Besides him none of her relationships had crossed the *few dates* stage so she couldn't say if Etienne was her type or if she'd not found her type yet.

Me too, she wrote back.

What are you doing tomorrow?

We're going to some place where they do a fake Peel & Eat Crawfish Eating Contest. It's our team building.

You know, you're in the Big Easy, sugah, so do like the locals, pinch the tail and suck the head.

Asmi laughed aloud when she read his message. *That sounds kinky.*

I'm telling you, that's how you eat crawfish in the south and I know all about it because I'm a good ol' Southern Boy.

What else are you good at? Asmi wrote.

After sexting a little with Levi, Asmi worked for a while and dozed off on the big armchair she was sitting in. She woke up because it was getting cold and she thought she'd left the air conditioning at a low temperature. She opened her eyes and shimmering in front of her was a woman, wearing white. She had long hair and looked just like how Asmi had imagined Delphine LauLaurie from the haunted house tour. Her heart in her throat, Asmi stood up, her laptop falling onto the carpeted floor with a thud. Asmi looked down at the laptop and when she turned to look up there was nothing in front of her. The chill in the air gave her goosebumps.

Asmi called Ananya and made her stay on the line with her until she fell asleep with every light turned on in the room.

AND THEN SHE SAID...IS THERE A BOYS' CLUB WHERE I WORK?

EXCERPT FROM THE BUSINESS WORKBOOK "AND THEN SHE SAID..."

NOT EVERY ORGANIZATION HAS A BOYS' club...but from my conversations with friends, both male and female, they have encountered such a club at some point or the other in their careers.

The narrow definition of a boys' club is an old boy's network that usually includes men who are all from the same socioeconomic status and backgrounds. In the corporate world, the boy's club definition can be expanded to like-minded colleagues and though usually male, they can include women. Like a clique. Like in high school where one person fits in and another one doesn't. The person who doesn't fit in doesn't have a career, struggles to be heard in meetings and ultimately disengages and is then put on a PIP (performance improvement plan) or becomes that associate who flies under the radar.

HERE ARE **six** signs that an organization is suffering from a cancerous boy's club:

1. **Play together.** If you hear things like, "Yes, those guys

are close" or "they play golf together" or "they gamble together" or ... "no, I didn't know that meeting took place at the bar that evening"—then there is a good chance you have a boys' club in your organization. In my experience, the existence of the club is common knowledge even if it's not acknowledged and leadership condones it.

2. **Promote the loved ones**. Is the system of promotions and raises transparent in your organization? Or are you often confused and wonder, "How did that guy get promoted?" And then someone tells you, "Because he plays tennis with the boss or boss's friend." Or someone says, "The job was always going to be his," and it had nothing to do with performance or merit.

3. **The bar is a meeting place**. Do more than a few informal meetings where *decisions* are made take place in bars or restaurants or some social event? Do you often hear, "We discussed it last night at the bar and we decided..." or "We talked about it last week when we were in Vegas and..." or ... you know, the meetings where you weren't present even though you should've been?

4. **Get along or get fired**. Are there some male leaders you know you **must** get along well with to have a future in the company? If you don't fit into the boys' club, then you must either lay low and not create waves or leave? I had a colleague who said to me that he didn't fit into the club, because he didn't go out drinking every evening when he was on the road with colleagues and that meant he had to find a new job. Drinking was not part of his job description.

5. **Calling names**. Is there name-calling and excessive teasing—the notion that to have fun you must make fun of someone? Usually, the person being made fun of may think it's A-Okay, but it really isn't, because what if someone else isn't okay and feels excluded

because of it? At a company I know, the boys of the club call the junior sales manager, JISM in meetings and in the open. When this issue was brought up with HR, the junior sales manager couldn't understand what the ruckus was about, because he didn't mind the name—the problem was that someone else was called another name and that someone else wasn't okay about it and when that someone made it an issue, she became a target. She was not a team player. She didn't like her nickname.

6. **Be seen, not heard.** Associates who are not in the club are not allowed to express their opinion in meetings because being outside the club equals being less smart. The minute he or she speaks, they're shut out, sometimes rudely until the person stops speaking entirely and becomes disengaged.

If you marked yes to any two of the above, you have a boy's club in your organization—not just an informal power base, which many organizations have, but an honest-to-god boys' club that is hurting the business with their philosophy of exclusivity.

A boy's club can make the work culture toxic with bullying and sexism; a hostile work environment that prevents the organization from growing and thriving.

11

TOKYO DRIFT

CARA AND ASMI arranged to meet at Haneda, the Tokyo international airport so they could take the airport bus together to Ginza. The bus dropped them off at the train station from where they could take a taxi to the hotel.

"They always stick us into the Millennium something hotel and it's decent enough and close to the office, why did your assistant put us in some other place?" Cara asked.

Asmi checked her phone as they stood outside the Ginza Station, each with their carryon suitcase in one hand and phone in the other. "The hotel was full, so I asked Dominic to find something close to the office."

"What's the name of this hotel?

"I can't pronounce it but let's find a taxi and let them find the address," Asmi said.

It was always interesting to come to Japan because most people did not speak English and besides being able to bend and say *arigato gozaimasu*, Asmi spoke no Japanese. Even when she did her expenses, she would write down on the receipt immediately what it was for because the receipt would be entirely in Japanese and she would not remember what was what when she got home.

The taxi driver who did speak some English asked them twice if they had the right address.

"You sure, this is the hotel?" he asked.

"Yes," Cara said.

They assumed he was checking to be certain of the address but realized when they got to the hotel that he was *actually* checking if they wanted to go to *this particular* hotel, which was a by-the-hour hotel in the seediest part of Ginza.

They stood at reception where the man with a name plate on the desk that had Japanese characters under which it said: HOTEL MANAGER confirmed they did have a booking and then asked them how many hours they'd stay.

"All night," Asmi said confused.

"All...full night?" the hotel manager asked.

Asmi and Cara nodded.

"And you stay in separate rooms?" the hotel manager asked.

Asmi and Cara nodded again.

The reception was something out of a Hollywood movie it was such a cliché. It was small and there were stairs leading up to somewhere with a flickering red light going on and off, bringing the stairs to light and then into darkness.

"Cara, I think this is a *hook up* hotel," Asmi whispered to Cara when they saw an older Japanese man enter the reception area with a rather young Japanese woman dressed in Hello Kitty attire that was about at least one size too small for her.

"Hook up? As in hookers?" Cara asked, looking at the Japanese man and woman nuzzling one another.

Asmi nodded.

Their suspicions were further confirmed when a man came down the stairs as he was zipping up his pants and a woman was running behind him, screaming at him. She was in her bra and panties. Cara and Asmi stared open mouthed. The man yelled back at the woman. They screamed at each other for a minute in Japanese and then the man turned around and threw some yen notes at the woman and strode out of the hotel.

"One-night, full night, two separate rooms and we will leave at seven in the morning," Asmi told the hotel manager.

They climbed up the stairs to their rooms on the fifth floor that were next to one another—there was no functioning elevator; they were still fixing it the hotel manager said to them.

Not all business travel was glamorous.

"What will we do tomorrow night?" Cara asked as she stood at her door with a keycard.

"We'll go to the office tomorrow and find a new place. If nothing else, we can sleep in a meeting room in the office," Asmi said.

"I think this might be the worst hotel I have stayed in," Cara said when she opened the door and looked inside. "Do you think it's safe to sleep on those sheets?"

"I'd wear clothes to bed," Asmi said and added, "And hope to not get herpes. I did worse in Melbourne. Stayed at a motel with a blanket with holes in it and a bathroom with no lights, which they never fixed even though I complained the three days I was there. This is an improvement."

They decided to meet for dinner in thirty minutes, giving them time to unpack and take a shower after their respective long flights.

They went to a sushi place that the hotel manager recommended because they had both traveled enough to know that if you eat where the locals do, you win. He sent them to a hole in the wall, a basement restaurant, where they had to bend low to get in and sit on the floor to eat.

They ordered a variety of sushi and started the meal off with miso soup and cold sake.

"I love the food in Tokyo," Asmi said as she sipped her sake. "Tomorrow night, Hiroji-san will take us to my favorite restaurant where they serve *dashi*, Japanese soup. You add vegetables, noodles, and fish balls to the soup, sort of like fondue."

"I called Oscar and told him about the hotel, and he thinks it's the funniest thing ever," Cara said, picking up her chopsticks and mixing wasabi into the soy sauce in the small dish in front of her. "After talking to him I think it's funny as well."

"I sent an email to Dominic…maybe I need a new EA," Asmi said and peeked at the platter of sushi to pick one that looked most interesting. She chose the eel nigiri and dipped it into the soy sauce.

"He's not working out?"

Asmi shrugged. "He lacks drive. He talks the talk but cannot walk the walk. I hate to PIP people out. Why do we even do a Performance Improvement Plan when we do it only when we intend to fire them? Why not just fire them?"

"That's the law, baby," Cara said. "It's not always like that. I've seen PIPs that resulted in the associate doing better work."

"Do you think they're going to put Scott on a PIP to improve his leadership skills?" Asmi asked.

"What did happen with Max? He talked to me before I left Shanghai, and he was furious. He asked if I'd talked to you and I said no, I was in China and then I added that I *would* talk to you once I saw you here. He shut up very quickly after that," Cara said.

"I didn't tell him anything about you and me talking. You know how they are about you and me being friends," Asmi said.

"I know," Cara said. "Isn't it a good thing that the business has a good relationship with HR? I mean, most human resources business partners are seen as villains who are not to be trusted. You think Scott trusts Evan?"

"Does anyone trust Evan?" Asmi asked. She didn't like Evan because once, a long time ago in a meeting he asked her, the only woman in the meeting, if she could take the minutes. Asmi had declined by saying as professionally and politely as she could, that she was trying to avoid stereotypical behavior that required women to be note-takers and asked him to take his own notes for the meeting.

"Yes, Max trusts him…even though none of his peers or associates do."

"Max is an ass," Asmi said, and set her chopsticks down.

"You know what he said to me after I told him what Shruti said? He said that it was unprofessional of me to make unsubstantiated accusations about Scott."

"What's wrong with this guy?" Cara wondered as she refilled their cups with sake.

"So many things," Asmi said. "I said they *were* unsubstantiated accusations and that's why I was reporting it to him, so he could investigate further. After that, I may have said something about being legally responsible for telling him about such complaints."

"What did you say, exactly?"

"Just that legally I'm required to not be the senior-most person with a secret," Asmi said. "I think I said those exact words. Then I told him we're transparent in GTech. I may have said something along the lines of, *I expect an investigation and I expect someone to get in touch with Shruti and her team to interview them.* He appreciated my interest but added that I should be careful about what I say."

"What?"

"Hmm...he said that he had heard that I use the *f word*," Asmi said.

Cara raised her eyebrows. "Everyone uses the fucking *f word* at GTech."

"Not Max."

"No, he just promotes gender inequality," Cara said angrily.

"I told him that he could talk to me about my use of the *f word* in a separate conversation, because I didn't want to conflate my language with my Speak Up," Asmi said.

"Speak Up?"

"Yes," Asmi said. "I made it an official Speak Up. I sent him an email with subject line SPEAK UP, so he has no choice but to investigate and ensure that there is no retaliation against Shruti."

"When did this happen?" Cara asked.

"Last week? The day after I left New Orleans."

"I talked to him yesterday and he didn't mention this," Cara said. "I even asked if there was any progress on what I told him about Scott's team, and he stuck to his *'you stay out of this'* lane and that's when he asked if you and I talked."

"I did what I could, and I told Shruti that if Evan didn't call her within three business days, she should send him an email with Max and me on cc," Asmi said. "Unfortunately, Shruti said she would not do that. She would, however, let me know so I could do that."

"She doesn't want to stand up and speak?" Cara asked.

"Do you blame her?"

"No," Cara said, shaking her head. "The one who speaks up gets beat up."

Asmi sighed. "I'm ready to take the hit but I'm not ready to allow unprofessional behavior of this kind, especially against women."

"This place is stressing me out," Cara said. "I need a palate cleanser. Enough shop talk, tell me about your author friend."

"We've been texting regularly since New Orleans," Asmi said with a broad smile. "I had phone sex with him...two nights ago in Brussels, and he's making plans to come to LA."

"What?" Cara screeched. "Really? This is like a *real* relationship!"

Asmi picked up some salmon sashimi with her chopsticks. She didn't know what to say. She and Levi were having fun. But it wasn't a relationship. According to Ananya, Asmi didn't know what a relationship was because she'd never really been in one and what she'd had with Etienne didn't count because it was entirely dysfunctional.

"You like him?"

"Sure," Asmi said. "But Cara, I'm not the marrying kind or even the long-term type. My therapist thinks that the reason Etienne lasted for four years was because I knew there would be no *real* commitment."

"I got divorced after being married for two years when I was twenty-six and then I was single for a decade and a half. When I met Oscar, I never thought this would be it, but it is...it's the relationship that I've always wanted," Cara said. "You never know where true love will come from."

~

ASMI LAY in bed in the dark with light streaming into her tiny hotel room from the outside. The walls of the hotel were not world class, so she could hear beds creak and sounds of sex: women moaning, men grunting, and the thump, thump of the spring mattress.

She could see herself lying on the bed because the room came with a mirror on the ceiling, which was appropriate for a booty call motel. The room came with a bed that vibrated but instead of using coins as Asmi had seen in some movies, here, in capitalistic style, you could use your credit card.

She decided to give it a shot and lay down to contemplate her life while the bed jostled her gently for five minutes. Asmi didn't mind the hotel room. As a bonus, the bathroom came with that fancy Japanese toilet. With business travel, it wasn't all five-star hotels. The budget was always an issue and sometimes she'd stayed in some ridiculous hotels, especially in big cities like New York during peak tourist season when hotel occupancy was high.

She was excited that Levi was coming to LA in a couple of weeks, right after the July Fourth weekend. He had an event at UCLA and Asmi had offered him lodging and her driving services to and from LAX and UCLA. They could go to LACMA, she suggested, because they both loved museums; and then Small World Books in Venice, which had been around since 1976 and was very cool with its resident cat, Conan the Librarian. She also told she'd take the day off and they could spend time hiking in Crystal Cove or just take a walk on the beach.

Levi had said it all sounded fabulous and he couldn't wait to see her again. He seemed genuinely interested in her, and not just the sex. She'd told him about the *Hunger Games* between Scott and her, and how she knew she needed to find a new job.

He'd told her how he wanted to write *serious literary* fiction and win a legitimate literary award someday, but he felt he didn't have the skill to write that kind of novel. He told her about his family, and she told him about hers. So far, it was how relationships evolved. Based on lust and then on mutual interests and then...and then what? What was the end game? Marriage and children? *Oh, please!*

And what to do with this heaviness inside her, this love for Etienne that still tugged and pulled. The familiarity of it, the corrosive emotional ride, the intensity...the good and the bad. The stark truth that she missed him, every *fucking* day.

What time was it in Paris? She looked at her phone. It was four in the evening in Europe.

She sent Etienne a message: *I met someone.*

Ten minutes later he responded: *I knew you would. I hoped you wouldn't.*

I could have a relationship with him. But I miss u.

Her phone rang then, and she picked it up. It had been nearly five months since she'd heard Etienne's voice.

"Where are you?" he asked.

"Tokyo."

"Who did you meet?"

"A writer on a plane to London," Asmi said.

"You should travel less, so you stop meeting men on airplanes," Etienne said.

"I met you on an airplane," Asmi said. "We have to end this. This 'you and me' is not healthy. You only want me when I want to leave. The minute you feel you have me, you'll pull away, you always do."

"I know," Etienne said. "I'm a hypocrite. But I love you and I don't want to lose you."

"But I'm not yours and you're not mine. Come on, Etienne, when I come to Paris you leave in the middle of the night to go sleep with your wife," Asmi said.

"You have no reason to be jealous of her," Etienne said.

"I'm not jealous of your wife, Etienne, I just don't want to live like this," Asmi said. "What if I fall sick? You're not there to care for me."

"Is that what you're looking for? A caretaker?" Etienne asked.

"Why is that wrong? What if I'm having a lousy day and I want to talk to you; will you be available?"

"No, you're right, I can't promise that I will be available," Etienne said. "I have a family and responsibilities; my time isn't always mine but whatever time I have is yours. Can't you see how important you're to me?"

"No," Asmi said. "I'm convenient."

He blew up then. "Convenient? *Merde*. This is not convenient. You live in California, six time zones away, and travel two hundred days a year. I see you maybe once a month if we're lucky. I have a wife and two children. Don't fucking tell me that you're *convenient*."

"Fine, so you love me," Asmi said, a part of her soaking in the warmth of his heated outburst. "But you're not available to me."

"I can't divorce my wife," Etienne said.

"I'm not asking you to," Asmi said, "I'm...why are we talking again? This argument is old. We go around and round and round. I...goodbye, Etienne. I won't text you again."

"Asmi, sweetheart..." he began but she hung up on him.

He texted her immediately: *Don't shut me out. We can make this work.*

Asmi responded: *Goodbye* and hoped that this time it would stick. This time it would end because this heartache was painful and her melancholy pitiful. She fell asleep on a pillow wet with her tears.

HIROJI-SAN WAS KIND ENOUGH to find them a hotel in a more respectable part of Ginza, one that didn't ask them to pay by the hour.

"That mirror on the ceiling was wicked," Cara whispered to Asmi. "I'd love to...you know...try it out."

They settled into the meeting room and went through six interviews, the short list from the Japanese HR team. Each one lasting between forty-five minutes to an hour and three of them requiring a translator. At the end of the day, they were both exhausted, but they both liked one candidate who they felt could go to the next level so there was at least that. There had been times when they'd interview candidate after candidate and go home empty-handed.

Asmi had gone through her day in a daze. After talking to Etienne the night before, a gloom had descended upon her, and she worried that she'd always love him and want him. The fact was that she did want him to leave his wife for her. There, she'd admitted it. Why shouldn't she wish for that? She was his best friend. He turned to her when he needed emotional anything. He came to her for sex. She knew him better than his wife did. But why did his wife still come first? Was this the status of a mistress? Wanted but not needed, desired but not dignified?

With Levi it was easy. They could walk anywhere hand in hand. He could spend the night. She was free. He was free.

She was free.

She didn't have to be tied down to Etienne. But at the back of her head, she knew she'd had this conversation with herself many times and somehow the relationship always got back from off-again to on-again and they were back on their cruel and unfulfilling merry-go-round. Each time she promised herself this would be it, this time was different, it always ended in bed with him.

This was the first time that the breakup had lasted these many months. She'd been in London, and in Brussels and she'd not seen him, instead she'd met Levi. That was the other thing—this time, she was seeing someone else. She was having a fling with a good looking, smart, famous writer—she was a cougar, hear her roar.

"What's up with you?" Cara asked when Hiroji-san excused himself from the table.

They were at dinner at Asmi's favorite Japanese restaurant where they served four types of *dashi*, two spicy and two plain Japanese clear soups but each with a distinct flavor of its own.

"I'm just...you know, in a mood," Asmi said, not wanting to go into the whole Etienne discussion because if she was sick of thinking about it, Cara probably was sick of hearing about it.

"This is about Etienne, isn't it?" Cara said and when Asmi nodded, she put her hand on Asmi's, "This too shall pass."

"I know. Thank you," Asmi said.

"Oh, and I think I found out something today about the Scott situation," Cara said but before she could explain more, Hiroji-san returned, and they went back to their dinner.

Afterward, Hiroji-san went home and Cara and Asmi walked back to their *new* hotel and sat at the small bar at the hotel where a few straggling business travelers had parked their weary bodies in front of alcoholic drinks.

"Remember, I told you that they hired a consultant from Mercer?" Cara asked, after they'd ordered espresso martinis as a nightcap. "Well, that guy is working with Scott and his team to improve the *situation*."

"What situation?"

"I think they're doing *trust* exercises, things like that," Cara said. "I don't know what that means but the team is broken and needs to be fixed...*blah blah blah*."

"How come we didn't know about this?" Asmi asked.

"Well it was hush-hush until you stepped into it and made it official with your complaint to Max. Now they must interview everyone and their mother, which is a good thing," Cara said. "Evan sent me an email and said he'll read me in. They had a D&I...diversity and inclusion workshop where Scott's leadership team went through their personality types. After that, the team opened up about the issues within. I don't have a full report out on that meeting, but Max isn't happy with how Scott didn't seem to take his cultural issues seriously and said something like, *'I'll take people out to lunch to make them feel included'*."

"What?"

Cara nodded. "Evan said he heard Scott say that there was nothing wrong with having a boys' club. They just needed to include more people into the club."

"I'm sick of managers like Scott," Asmi said. "How do men like this rise so high and women, who are ten times better leaders with emotional intelligence, cannot?"

"We don't want it as much," Cara said and lifted her espresso martini to Asmi. "Take yourself, you've given up and want to have sex with Levi and become a housewife."

"That's not fair, Cara," Asmi said. "Maybe I'm not ready to be this big marketing hotshot."

"Scott is *definitely* not ready or able but he's not saying he's not, you are," Cara said.

"Look, if I'm out of the race then they stop beating up on me and I can go back to doing my job," Asmi said. "I was humiliated in Vegas."

"Oh, poor baby," Cara said sarcastically. "Get over it."

"I'm taking time until summer, when I'll start looking for a new job. Then hopefully, by Christmas, and before Jim officially leaves, I'll have a new position somewhere else," Asmi said. "That's the best I can do, and only because my mortgage is *really* high."

"I see so many women who're top performers give up because of some douchebag like Scott," Cara said and drained her drink. "I'm going to bed now because I'm very annoyed with you for being such a...such a...snowflake. And please, try and control your usage of the *fucking* f word because apparently I'm supposed to write you up for it."

"What?"

"Yes," Cara said. "I'm going to have to write an official behavioral thing, telling you to not use the *f word*."

"Are you writing up the whole management team?"

"No, just you. Then Evan will write up Scott's team, his whole team, for a lot more than the *f word*," Cara said.

"Just so that you know, I'm not going to be signing any such document," Asmi said.

Cara sighed. "You have so much integrity about these things. You'll pick a fight to protect Shruti and your people. But you'll give up on your own fights."

"I'm not signing any document admonishing me for using the *f word*, which everyone uses," Asmi said, her voice raised. "Am I being punished for making this Speak Up official?"

Cara stood up and shrugged. "What do you care? You're running away, remember?"

"Oh, *fuck* off," Asmi said. "And you can stick your *fucking* judgment where the *fucking* sun doesn't shine."

Cara gave her the finger as she walked away.

THEY MADE up the next morning after their respective meetings when they went to the Rakusuien Gardens while there was still light. A colleague had recommended the gardens, which he called a hidden gem that tourists didn't frequent.

"This is something else," Cara said as they walked through the traditional Japanese garden toward the teahouse. Roses and irises decorated the path they walked on, and a sense of calm settled inside them. A clay wall, *Hakatabei*, made with burnt rocks and roof tiles surrounded the garden, which was in the middle of bustling Tokyo. It was peaceful, almost like an oasis of quiet amidst the craziness of the rushed city. Only when they looked up and saw the skyscrapers could they feel they were still in Tokyo.

"I want to come here when it's cherry blossom season," Asmi said. "It must look amazing."

The teahouse was in the middle of the garden next to a pond. They watched children on a bridge over the pond clap their hands so that orange glowing carp fish would come to the sound. The pond had a small waterfall, a miniature piece of heaven with the sound of flowing water, soothing their nerves.

The tea room was simple with sliding doors, kept open in the summer to let the air in and the visitors could see the green garden as they drank their tea.

A woman in full geisha attire served *matcha* tea. Asmi and Cara sat *Seiza*, placing their knees on the tatami floor and resting their buttocks on the top of their feet, holding the warm cup with both hands.

"We're so lucky," Asmi said as she sipped the tea. "They're paying us to be here."

Cara nodded. "I forget sometimes how we get to see the world in a way most people don't. You're right, we are lucky."

With the tea, they were served *daifuku*, a rice cake filled with sweetened red bean paste made with *azuki* beans. Cara took a bite and shook her head. Asmi helped her out because she loved Japanese sweets of all kinds, especially the ones with red bean paste.

After the quiet of the garden, as if to contrast, they headed to Shibuya, the busiest pedestrian crossing in the world. They sat at the L'Occitane café with cups of latte, from where they had an excellent view of the famous crossing. As the light turned from green to red, hundreds of pedestrians crossed from one side to another and it looked like a symphony of movement—of the flow of color and humanity against neon signs.

"I have to come back and spend more time here," Cara said. "Like on vacation."

"Why don't you? You could do with a break."

"Tell me about it. But not for a while," Cara said. "You're not the only one with an expensive mortgage."

Cara and Oscar lived in Anaheim Hills and had a lovely house with terrific views of Orange County, and on a good day they could see all the way to Catalina. They had wanted the house and bought it with the full realization that there may be no vacations for a few years.

"Right," Asmi said. "Do you feel it's worth it?"

"Yes," Cara said.

"Why?"

"Because the house makes Oscar and me happy," Cara said.

Asmi grinned. "I'm just going through a thing. Aren't you supposed to go through a thing when you turn forty?"

"You turn forty in October, right?" Cara said. "Any plans?"

"Nope," Asmi said. "I've promised myself I'm not going to travel. Maybe, I'll sit on my balcony, drink scotch and consider the rags of my life."

"It's a big birthday, you should celebrate," Cara said.

Asmi shook her head. "Nope. Not interested. I just want to be alone."

"That's the problem isn't it, after being single for this long… you *want* to be alone," Cara said softly as the light once again turned green and the Shibuya crossing was a haze of movement.

"You say it like it's a dreadful thing," Asmi said. "I think it's the perfect place to be."

But as she said it, she knew she was lying. She was not in a perfect place, she was in turmoil and she was pretending she wasn't. This wasn't about being single or being in a quasi-relationship with Levi. It was about being at a crossroads, being able to see the crossroads and the consequences and needing to make a choice. She was living in limbo right now, not going one way or the other. Waffling about love, work and life in general. It wasn't going to last long, something would have to give eventually.

HOW DO I KNOW WHAT I WANT?

EXCERPT FROM THE BUSINESS WORKBOOK
"AND THEN SHE SAID..."

THE ANSWER to this question is subjective. A tool that has helped me determine my path forward is "The Wheel[1]," which I recommend to everyone.

The Wheel is simple to use:

1. Use the wheel below and add the parameters most important to you today: family, romance, finances, geography, career, et cetera. Add as many parameters as is relevant for you

2. Score each slice of the circle based on your current situation and connect the dots to see your spider web

3. Title this circle the "today" circle

4. Use a brand-new circle with the same parameters as before and score each slide based on where you want to be in the future

5. Overlay the "today" circle on the "future" circle and you will be able to see where your gaps are and what you want to work on and with what intensity for the near or distant future

This easy exercise helps to open the mind and understand what is *important to you*. If you find that career is important to you, maybe the best thing for you is to go back to work after the baby. If you find your circle is in better balance if career takes a back step and family comes to the forefront, then you can decide how to make that happen. You may find that even though career was a seven in the "today" circle, it's a 1 in the future circle—this is when you should change that parameter for the future.

12

LA STORY

ASMI ITCHED to get out of work because Levi's plane was going to land in three hours, and she wanted to be in LAX to pick him up. Considering the traffic on the 405, it would take just about that long to get there. But she had a one-on-one meeting with Matthew first, and she was dreading it.

Will he tell me now that he's giving the job to Scott? Or will he tell me about all the things that I do wrong? Is he going to bring up my liberal usage of the f word? Or …

She waited outside Matthew's office because his previous meeting was running late.

"How's it going?" Celeste, Matthew's executive assistant asked her. Asmi knew Celeste well because Celeste had been Jim's assistant before she was promoted to become the CEO's executive assistant a year ago.

"It's good," Asmi said and then added, because Celeste was always interested in her love life, "I think I have a boyfriend."

"Really?"

"Yep," Asmi said impishly. "He lives in Memphis and he's coming here in…," she looked at her watch, "about three hours."

"Tell me everything," Celeste said.

"He's a writer. You can Google him," Asmi said and then giggled. "I have a Google-able boyfriend."

Celeste looked him up and said, "Girl, he's a keeper."

"I don't know if it's real or not, but I'm taking tomorrow off and we're going to make a long weekend out of it," Asmi said just as the door to Matthew's office opened and Scott walked out.

He looked so smug. *She hated him.*

"Hey, how's it going?" he asked Asmi. "Heard that you and Cara had an adventure in Tokyo."

The news of the hotel Dominic, her EA had booked for them had traveled the company.

Asmi just smiled at him and walked into Matthew's office, groaning inwardly as soon as she saw him because he didn't look like he was in a good mood. *How come he was in a trashy mood and Scott was still smiling from ear to ear?*

"Okay, can you give me an update on your open headcount in Japan," Matthew started curtly as soon as Asmi sat down.

Asmi told him about the candidate they were going to hire after he went through leadership testing that all leaders had to go through at GTech. He then wanted to know about the launch plan for a product coming out the following year and the follow up on the failed clinical seminar in Nice.

At the end of the meeting, Matthew said, "You're doing a good job. I want you to know that."

"Thanks," Asmi said, a little surprised.

"I also want to talk to you about the future. What do you see for yourself?" Matthew asked.

Asmi was completely unprepared for the question. She paused for a moment and said, "Well, I don't know…ah…. I know that Jim is retiring and…," it stuck in her throat to say it because she didn't believe she could take that step, be this senior executive, "Ah…if you think I'm ready, I think that could be a next step."

She felt like an idiot. The man had asked her what she wanted, and she'd danced around like an insecure fool.

Matthew nodded. "Well, Asmi, when *you* think you're ready,

you let me know and we'll talk about what your next step should be."

Well, that was that. Matthew was not one for coddling.

"Thank you," Asmi said and bit her tongue because she'd almost added *Sir* in the end.

∽

SHE CALLED CARA, who was in Dallas for a meeting, from the car as she drove to LAX and told her what happened.

"I ruined it, right?" Asmi said. "See, this is it. I'm not ready. If I was ready, I'd say I'm ready."

"Hey, he didn't say it's over, he said you should think about it and come back to him," Cara said. "That's the silver lining of the story."

"How do you think Scott answered that question?"

"He probably said he was born to have Jim's job and that he'd rock it," Cara said. "Look...we're like this and by we, I mean women. I see this so much, from where I'm sitting. Do you know that when they made me director, instead of asking for more money I asked Max why he was promoting me? Only women do that. Men have a sense of entitlement."

"Matthew makes me uneasy," Asmi said, "Not like I'm afraid of him...but he's intimidating."

"He is," Cara agreed. "Look, forget about it. Just enjoy your long weekend. You have your boy toy over, have fun and don't think about this."

"I'm such a screwup," Asmi said. "How can a woman like me, who is so confident, be such a screwup?"

"Don't beat yourself up," Cara said. "We've all committed our shares of screw ups."

By the time she got to LAX, Asmi managed to not be too flustered. It was going to be okay. She'd already decided to find a new job so why even worry about this meeting with Matthew. It wasn't important. Scott could have the job with her blessing.

She'd been at GTech for six years now and it was time to move on. It was. Really.

～

"I HAVE tickets to Herbie Hancock and Kamasi Washington at the Hollywood Bowl for Saturday night," Asmi said as she drove them to Laguna Beach, slowly, because it was five o'clock on a Thursday evening and five o'clock on a weekday was the worst time to get on any freeway in or out of LA.

Levi had told her how he'd heard a lot about the Hollywood Bowl but had never been there. He had mentioned it in passing, just a little by-the-by and even Asmi thought it was cute she'd remembered and made plans.

He leaned over and kissed her on the cheek. "Thanks. That's nice of you," he said. "You sure you don't mind driving me up and down to LA."

"Of course not," Asmi said. "I took tomorrow off so we can do the museum thing before your reading at UCLA. And then we can have dinner at Miro where they have a lovely whiskey bar in the basement."

"I'm being spoilt," Levi said and smiled, "I've never been spoilt."

"Maybe because all the women you dated before were not as old as me," Asmi said without thinking and then bit her lower lip as she heard what she just said. "That sounded terrible."

"You're eight years older than me, which is not a lot," Levi said. "Technically you must be over forty to be a cougar."

～

ASMI FELT like she was cheating on Etienne.

A part of her had thought that Levi would come, they'd spend a long weekend together and they'd realize this isn't going to work. The longest relationship she'd had before Etienne lasted two weekends. She couldn't help but wonder, as she and

Levi sat on her balcony, scooping up the last of the Louisiana barbecue shrimp sauce with the baguette she'd bought at Zinque that evening, if this was the relationship that would last.

"It's almost as good as what my mama makes," Levi said and then added, deepening his southern accent, "But you understand it can't be better, right, *sugah*?"

"I understand," Asmi said.

Afterward, he sat comfortably in his chair, a glass of wine in his hand, his feet resting on Asmi's lap. It was domestic. *Oh, so domestic.*

Asmi stood up and let his feet fall. "Coffee?"

Levi shook his head. "Sit down," he said and pulled her down. She sat at the edge of her chair. "Something is wrong. Do you want me to find a hotel?"

Asmi shook her head and then let her face drop in her hands. She looked up at him. "It's…a bit too…domestic."

Levi nodded and then shook his head. "I don't understand. Most women I know want domestic."

"As you probably already know, I'm not most women," Asmi said.

"It's just a weekend. My sister, Toni said to me that I shouldn't hang my hopes on this trip and be prepared for the fact that we'd bore the hell out of each other," Levi said. "That's the hard part, isn't it? To find out if there's more to it than just sex."

"*Just* sex is *just* fine," Asmi said and sat back, feeling mollified that he understood her predicament, maybe because it was also his. *Oh, weren't they perfect for each other?* Intimacy, good sex and a mutual understanding of emotional shortcomings.

That night after some *just* awesome sex when Levi was sleeping, Asmi went to the balcony, feeling a weight around her chest. She texted Ananya who called her immediately.

"Are you smoking at two in the morning?" Asmi asked.

"Venkat ran away, okay?"

"*What?*"

"Yeah, he managed to get invited to some meeting in Dublin

175

and he's gone for a whole week. Arjun is at a basketball camp and he's staying there so I can't even drop him off and pick him up. Anjali is with a friend and doesn't want to come home," Ananya said.

"Ah," Asmi said.

"No, you don't say *'ah'*. You say, *'I'm sorry, Ana, I'm a bad daughter and a bad sister'*," Ananya said. "They're here *all* the time. And they want me to take them here and there. They don't like it that I wear jeans and shorts; and why can't I wear a *salwar kameez* and then they...."

"You know I have to go to Stockholm and some place in the ass end of Sweden in two weeks or so, why don't you come along. We can..." Asmi suggested.

"Are you bribing me with a trip to Europe?" Ananya asked.

"Yes."

"Thank god," Ananya said. "Because I really need a break from the parents. It's bad enough when they come for three months. This time it's *six long months*. Why can't they come for a week or two and then be gone? I tried to get them to go see Nayantara in Chicago, but they said they don't like her. How can anyone *not like* Nayantara?"

Nayantara was their cousin, their father's brother's daughter. She lived in Chicago and was a lawyer at ACLU. She was married to another do-gooder, Eshan who was director of something at *Save the Children*. They had no children, but they were good people who had dedicated their lives to helping others.

"I think Nayantara ticked the parents off when she said she was making a conscious choice of not having children," Asmi said.

"How come you're not in bed, burning a hole through it with awesome sex? How's the boy toy?"

"He's not a boy toy," Asmi said and then looked into the apartment to make sure Levi wasn't awake and eavesdropping on her conversation with her sister. "He is hot, though, and so easy to be with."

"So, obviously, you're thinking up of various ways to fuck this up," Ananya said.

Asmi sighed. "You know me so well. It's scary how nice it is. But I'm like Nayantara, I'm not planning on having children and he's in his early thirties and probably wants children and—"

"Whoa, your eggs haven't hatched and you're counting your chickens and their eggs," Ananya interrupted her. "It's just a weekend, not a walk down the aisle looking like whipped cream. Stop trying to sabotage this and try instead to enjoy yourself."

And how do I do that? Asmi wanted to ask.

When she looked back at her life, she didn't know how to have fun or what made her truly happy outside of good food and good scotch. She'd just told Ananya how it was easy with Levi and it was, like it had never been with Etienne. With him, it had always been a rush of emotion, guilt on his side, demands on hers, a relationship based on push and pull instead of harmony. But for some reason that had felt more real, more intense than what she had with Levi, even in these early days.

MILA and her husband Mason had introduced Asmi to the Hollywood Bowl. They went at least four to six times in between July and September with an assortment of friends. Mason, who was always late for everything, was *never* late for Hollywood Bowl. He and Mila got there early, around four thirty, even though the concert started at seven in the evening and they would go all the way to the top, the highest they could go and spread out a picnic. If Asmi wasn't traveling, she'd join Mila, Mason and their friends: some artists, some photographers, and some corporate schmucks like Asmi.

As a historic monument that was designed by some of the greatest American architects, the Hollywood Bowl was an iconic venue where everyone who was anyone had performed. The sound was amazing, the mood easy and as Mason said, "Everyone is so civilized and well behaved."

Last time Asmi had been in town she'd joined them to see *Belle and Sebastian* and had met with Stevie, a musician who had brought with him some good *sativa* that had chilled all of them out.

"I promise I won't embarrass you," Levi said to Asmi as they took the last escalator at the Hollywood Bowl to go up to the picnic area where Mila and company were. Mila had texted to hurry up because they were already on their second bottle of rosé.

"Of course you won't," Asmi said.

"It's just that you look tense," Levi said with a smile. "It's cute."

"I've never taken a...*date*...a *man*...to meet any of my friends," Asmi confessed.

They got off the escalator and could see Mila and Mason from their perch waving wildly at them.

"Ever?"

"Nope," Asmi said. "I never had a relationship last beyond a couple of weekends. And...well, Etienne was married so I couldn't bring him anywhere."

"I'm honored," Levi said and kissed her softly, shifting the picnic basket he held from one hand to the other. "It's just a little fun, Asmi."

Asmi nodded tightly. *What was she doing with someone almost a decade younger than her? Not a decade, Asmi, eight years. Eight years was two years short of a decade.*

Mila and Mason had prepped for Levi. Mason had even read one of his books. Asmi was touched. Mila and Mason's friends Stevie and Barbara were there as were Jean and George, two French transplants who moved to Laguna two decades ago.

"He's cute," Mila whispered while she poured Asmi a glass of wine. "And we're feeling rather...*honored* that you brought him here."

"He said the same thing," Asmi said.

He fit with her friends, Asmi thought, as Etienne never would. He was too serious and too married. But easygoing Levi talked about writing and where he got his ideas from. He talked to Mason about his marketing agency and cracked jokes about social media and how hard it was for him to navigate it. He was charming and funny, and Mason winked at Asmi as if saying, *good catch, darling*.

After they had gorged on picnic food from Zeytoon, a Mediterranean restaurant in Laguna Beach, they headed to the smoker's area to share in the bourgeois California part-time indulgence of weed.

"Stevie and Barbara wake and bake," Mila whispered to Levi.

"Every day?"

Mila nodded and smiled.

"No wonder they're so chill," Levi said.

By the time, they found their seats in the open-air auditorium Asmi and Levi were both high on *Lambs Bread* and were feeling calm and reflective. Levi held her hand as they listened to music. Asmi's stress had fallen away after the first two hits and she was in a happy place. She didn't mind that she even leaned against Levi, her head on his shoulder and his arm around her. It was cozy. It was *normal*.

Levi drove them home even though they both were sober after the three-hour concert, but he thought Asmi looked tired and he owed her for all the driving she'd done.

"I like your friends," Levi said.

"They're good people," Asmi agreed. "Mila and I went to UCI together and we've been friends ever since. She met Mason at a party. He was at UCLA then. I moved to Laguna to be close to them, so I'd be close to my tribe. But I travel so much that I maybe see them once a month. The Hollywood Bowl is a ritual and…you must think I'm a lonely hag."

"I don't think you're lonely or a hag, but I do think you like being alone," Levi said. "There is nothing wrong with that."

"My therapist thinks that after seeing my parents and their marriage, I don't want to partake," Asmi said. "It's not like I'm turning down marriage proposals every day or anything. Dating is unreliable and with my travel schedule it's hard to maintain any kind of connection."

"But you did with this married man," Levi said as he took the Laguna Canyon Road exit from California State Route 73.

"Because he was married," Asmi confessed. "The thing was that I wanted more time with him, but I also didn't want him in my life, interrupting its rhythm. It was confusing."

"But he's gone now," Levi said...or asked, Asmi wasn't sure.

"Oh, yes," Asmi said.

"So, I don't have to worry about you going back to him on one of your many European travels," he said, and he sounded like he was joking but Asmi wasn't sure.

"No, there's no chance of that," Asmi said and wondered if she was speaking the truth.

She *was* in Fontainebleau near Paris and then in Stockholm in a couple of weeks. There were some memorable times in the Swedish capital: a cruise around the archipelago, romantic dinners, and picnics in the park in the midnight sun in the summer. But she wasn't going to tell Etienne she was in Stockholm or Fontainebleau. She wasn't.

∿

IT WAS A PERFECT WEEKEND.

They made love. They ate well. They drank good scotch. They walked hand in hand in LACMA and discussed their love for Bauhaus and Kandinsky. Levi showed her pictures of the original Joan Miro he purchased at some forgotten gallery in San Sebastian.

They had fun. There was no other way of describing the weekend.

Levi's book reading at Merrill Auditorium in UCLA was packed and the panel discussion later about race and writing was engaging. For Asmi this was a completely different world, far, far away from her corporate bullshit. A weekend with Levi and she couldn't even remember what about work was stressing her out and why. Who cared if Scott got the VP of Marketing position? Did it really matter in the end? Wasn't life about *this*, engaging with people and enjoying their company?

They went to dinner at the stylish Miro in downtown LA where Levi's friend Isolde, who wrote for *The Atlantic* and was a regular on various political podcasts like *Pod Save America* and *VOX*, joined them.

Isolde was one of those people who had no filter and said what she wanted. "I'm so glad you got rid of that woman you were dating. She was dumb, Levi."

"She was my fiancée and she wasn't dumb," Levi protested.

"She was a vapid fashionista," Isolde said.

"Her being a fashion blogger doesn't automatically make her vapid," Levi said.

Asmi gasped. "A fashion blogger? You mean like…what's her name…Olivia Palermo? I know her because I sat next to her on a flight once."

He had been engaged to an Olivia Palermo type and now he was dating *her*, Asmi thought. There was no contest. Olivia Palermo would win every time. Some people date up and some people date down. Levi was not dating up with Asmi.

"Not as famous as her, but, yes," Levi said sheepishly. "She's a Southern Belle and has her own podcast and blog about fashion and makeup. She's passionate about fashion, there's nothing wrong with that. Not everyone has to be a liberal activist like Isolde."

Isolde made a face. "At least this one knows how to read."

"But she probably can't compete with the fashion blogger when it comes to fashion," Asmi said. "Hey, to each his own. My previous relationship was with a guy who was married to another woman, so I have no moral high ground."

"I like her," Isolde said. "So, marketing, ehh? But do you feel like you're making a difference?"

"Yes," Asmi said honestly. "I market technology that is making the world cleaner and greener. I sell enzymes that make manufacturing paper more efficient and less polluting. I sell enzymes that make bread last longer so it's nutritionally viable for people at a lower cost."

"You mean like Wonder Bread?" Isolde made a face.

"Well, not everyone can afford French baguette from Zinque. We have to feed the masses," Asmi said.

That evening, their last together, Levi and Asmi made love in the living room, a little desperate for each other because they didn't know when and if they'd see each other again.

They huddled on Asmi's couch, a blanket around them because the evenings got cool in Laguna. Asmi could feel what she'd feel once he left—she'd be lonely and not just alone. She could sense it because the past two days had been magic.

"Isolde is a snob and hardly likes anyone, but she liked you," Levi said. "I knew she would."

"Did you really date a fashion blogger?"

"Yes," Levi said. "They're not all dumb, you know."

"Hey, I'm not Isolde. I think anyone who can make money doing what they do is smart," Asmi said. "I on the other hand am not a fashionista."

"And you're old, let's not forget that," Levi added and Asmi laughed.

"It's just that you're so hot that I can't help but feel insecure," Asmi said.

"And how am I supposed to feel? You're well-traveled and you have this *air* about you, like you know what you're doing while I'm mostly feeling like I'm waiting for my next book to do a lemming off the cliff," Levi said. "We all have our insecurities, Asmi."

HE INSISTED on taking a Lyft because he had an early flight and he didn't want Asmi to deal with the traffic on her way back from LAX.

"I'd like to see you again," Levi said after he had put his suitcase in the trunk of the Lyft.

She went on tiptoe and kissed him. "Yeah, me too."

"You sure?"

"Not sure at all," Asmi said. "But let's do it anyway."

"Come see me in Memphis next month," Levi offered. "It's my birthday. Be my present."

Oh boy. A birthday? Were they doing birthdays now?

"I'll check my schedule," she said in her best corporate voice.

He could be the one, Asmi texted to Ananya that evening as she sat alone on the couch where she and Levi had made love the evening before.

Good. High time, Ananya responded.

I miss Etienne.

SNAP THE FUCK OUT OF IT!!!!

AND THEN SHE SAID...I'M LIVING MY LIFE BY DEFAULT

EXCERPT FROM THE BUSINESS WORKBOOK "AND THEN SHE SAID..."

SO, many of us, men and women, live our careers by default and not design. We don't plan enough, and the times we do, and the plan doesn't work out, we're disappointed, so we're further incentivized to not plan and continue to live by default—to fall into whatever opportunity comes our way. Some of the reasons why we do this are:

1. We don't have the guts to be ambitious, because we're afraid of failing; if we don't even try, we don't have to fail.
2. We have decided that plans never work out; and we're fine with whatever—because if we plan and we fail, then we really fail—it's so much easier to not even try.
3. We don't know what we want and we're not working hard to find out, because if we knew what we want we'd have to try to get it and then we may fail—but if we don't try, then we don't have to fail.

I'm sure you can see the common theme. We don't plan our careers because we're afraid of failing. Well, if you fail enough, it means you're trying hard and that means you're winning.

Careers don't *just* happen—you must make them happen. You must know who you are, what you want, and how you can get it. You must relentlessly pursue your dreams. You must get used to failure. You must stand up and be counted, every time, even when your legs hurt and there are blisters on your feet.

Plan your career. Dream big. No one else is going to do it for you. Even though your inner critics are going to tell you to be careful and dream small—you must silence the critics and take control of your dreams. They may or may not come true, but you won't be standing at the end of the road, looking back and thinking, *I wish I had leaped high and tried to Play Big.*

13

IT'S HARD TO BE A TWINKIE IN A DING DONG WORLD

"EXCUSE ME?" Asmi asked because she wasn't sure she'd heard Max, Cara's boss, correctly. "Are you asking me about Daniel's girlfriend?"

Asmi had been urgently summoned to Max's office that morning. She had thought that this was about her usage of the *f word* so she was more than a little surprised when he started to talk about someone's girlfriend.

Max cleared his throat. "You and Scott had a meeting for your marketing managers in Dana Point in January this year?"

"Yes."

"With spouses."

"With a plus one," Asmi corrected. She'd gone alone; there were still some single people left in marketing.

"Daniel had a girl with him," Max said.

"A girl?" Asmi said.

Max raised his hands in defeat. "A woman?"

"Yes."

"Someone from Scott's team has made a complaint that the girl…woman was underage," Max said. "Do you know how old she was?"

Asmi raised her eyebrows and shook her head. "As a rule, I don't card plus ones, Max. What's going on?"

Max sighed. "Scott fired Bob Conway, do you remember him?"

"Yes."

"Bob is over fifty and he has sued for age discrimination and for a hostile work environment. He said that at this meeting in Dana Point, Daniel, one of his peers had an underage girl with him and that he'd picked her up at the hotel bar. There's more with regards to the hostile workplace stuff but...we need to sort this one out first because this would not be he said-she said if she was *actually* underage."

Asmi stayed silent for a long moment, unsure about what to say to a *very* agitated Max.

"I have no idea how old she is...was, but she was young, and some people teased Daniel about his *Twinkie,*" Asmi said. "Max, I doubt she was underage. Daniel dates a lot since his divorce, but he's not a complete idiot."

"Let's hope so because we have to investigate now that there is this legal thing," Max said. "I hate these lawsuits. Someone underperforms, we let them go because of it and they turn around and sue us. It's *so* American." Max was German and had a healthy disdain for American tardiness, culture and norms.

"Maybe he did have a hostile work environment, have you thought about that?" Asmi asked as she got up from her chair. "Scott's boys' club exists. I doubt Bob fit into that club."

"Why do you say that?"

"Because Bob doesn't drink," she said before she left Max's office.

JIM HAD ORGANIZED the meeting at Dana Point for Scott and Asmi's senior staff where they would *align* on the year's plans. Of all the corporate jargon, Asmi hated 'align' the most. Then there was *triangulate*. Once at a previous job she'd asked her boss to help with an issue she was having with a colleague in another team and her boss had said he couldn't help because, "I don't want to *triangulate* the issue."

There was the *get on the same page,* the increase *customer intimacy* and sometimes *customer penetration* and her favorite, *the low hanging fruits,* which always made her think of balls hanging around a flaccid penis.

They hadn't known then that Jim would be retiring. Scott and Asmi had been amiable but no more. Jim had created a "competitive" culture. She didn't mind competition, but she did mind that it sometimes interfered with everyone's ability to work together. In some ways Scott was right, and for them to succeed, they needed to be aligned but thanks to Jim's *"he said this about you"* and *"she said that about you"* management style, it was difficult to align or work well together.

Scott had brought along his wife, the lovely Andrea. A stay-at-home mom who probably always has fresh homemade lemonade in the fridge and cupcakes baking in the oven. Asmi had met her a few times and liked her except when she made a fuss about how Asmi was *still single* like she had a disease. The meetings were a waste of time and most everyone was eager to get to the bar after endless death by PowerPoint presentations.

They were all having a good time at the hotel bar when Daniel walked in with someone who looked like a teenager. Her name was Cindy. She was bubbly and immature; and incongruous with Daniel, an introvert and a divorced father in his forties. He was dedicated to his children, always making time to say goodnight to them no matter which part of the world he was in.

He was known to be a *swipe left-swipe right* player who preferred Bumble to Tinder. Once, after a few drinks in Savannah during another meeting, he had confessed to Asmi that after he slept with a woman, he didn't want to see her again and wondered if he'd ever find true love.

Cindy, due to her youthful presence was nicknamed *Twinkie.* And Scott had made a big deal out of carding her, a way of ribbing Daniel about what a stud he was to have picked up such a young chick. Cindy had not shown Scott her ID.

During dinner, it had become apparent that there were those who were *in-the-Scott club* and those who were not.

"Wow," Gustav whispered to Asmi, "I'm so glad I work in our team. These guys are awful. Poor Bob. They treat him like dirt. And Daniel's girlfriend, she's over eighteen, yes?"

Bob had talked to Asmi that evening and told her that the *new times* were beyond him. He had been with GTech for nearly a decade and a half and now he felt left out.

"You have to drink at these things and hang out until the wee hours of the morning," Bob said, "I'm too old for that. But I do my job, Asmi."

"That's all you should worry about," Asmi told him.

"I don't think it's enough," Bob said sadly, "I don't *fit* in. I don't drink, I don't gamble, you see, and...I think they're trying to get rid of me."

"If you feel the way you feel, you should talk to Scott," Asmi said.

"Scott?" Bob snorted. "It's *his boys' club*, he likes it like this."

"Then I suggest you talk to Evan, he's your HR partner, isn't he?" Asmi suggested.

Bob shook his head. "HR knows. There've been complaints. No one has done anything to fix the culture here. Do you have any openings in your team?"

"Not right now," Asmi said. "I just hired a product manager. But if anything changes, I'll let you know."

"Look, I just need a job until I retire," Bob said. "My wife is... not well and I need insurance. I don't want to cause any problems."

Before Asmi had an opening in her team, Bob was fired and now he was suing GTech for 11 million dollars.

THAT AFTERNOON as Asmi was getting ready to head to the

airport, Scott marched into her office and closed the door behind him.

"Did you tell Max that there's a boys' club in my department?"

"Yes, I did," Asmi said, which she could see surprised Scott. He had obviously expected her to deny the accusation.

"Just because you're not getting Jim's job doesn't mean you have to tattle to HR about me," Scott said once he found his voice.

"You do know that *everyone* at GTech knows that there is a boys' club in your department," Asmi said, as she looked through some papers she wanted to read on the flight. "It's not a secret, Scott."

"Bob was a low performer," Scott said.

"Okay." Asmi put the papers in a folder and stuck it inside her computer bag.

"I can't believe that this is happening," Scott said and sat down. "Do you know they're investigating culture in my team? Apparently, it's hostile."

Asmi put her laptop inside her bag and smiled at Scott. "I heard. Look, Scott, the fact is that you have a cultural problem in your team."

Scott shook his head. "No, it's a cultural opportunity, Asmi. Now that I know, we'll open the circle up and include others in the club. I'll start taking people out to lunch. That will fix everything."

Asmi sighed. Was this the kind of leader they wanted as VP of Marketing?

"Your problems run deeper than lunch, Scott. Wake up and smell the guacamole, my friend. You need to kill the boys' club," Asmi said as she zipped her computer bag close.

Scott rose, shaking his head. "You know why people stay in my team?"

"*Some* people," Asmi said.

"Because it's fun. We have fun together," Scott said.

"This is a workplace, Scott, not a frat house," Asmi said.

"We have women on my team who fit in just fine," Scott said.

"Oh, I know," Asmi said. "You mean women like Stacey who get drunk and make blowjob jokes?"

"Stacey is a high performer."

"The problem is that it's not enough for Stacey to be a high performer. To succeed and get attention, she also needs to be part of your club," Asmi said. "I've heard all the stories and I'm glad, as you should be, that HR is investigating and trying to help you uncover your problems so you can solve them."

"You're just jealous because my team is tight and yours is not," Scott said.

"Your team is a frat house," Asmi said. "I'd be mortified if my team functioned like yours. You should be mortified. Look, I have a plane to catch. I have to get to Paris for a course at INSEAD, so I'll see you in Sweden for the meeting with Short Poppy. If you need to talk about your culture issues and brainstorm, feel free to call me."

"I think I'll be fine," Scott said. "But thanks for the offer."

Scott walked Asmi to her car. "Are you still against the Short Poppy acquisition?"

"I'm just making a business assessment," Asmi said, trying to control her annoyance.

"You and I need to…you know start *aligning* more."

"Of course," Asmi said in her most noncommittal corporate voice.

"Seriously, Asmi," Scott said. "I think you're very talented, smart and creative; but once I have Jim's job, you and I have to start aligning more."

Asmi stopped walking and turned to face Scott in the GTech parking lot. She looked him in the eye and said, "What does alignment mean to you?"

Scott shrugged. "Just that we need to be on the same page on certain things."

"What things?"

"For example, that seminar that flopped in Nice. If we'd

discussed it before, I'd never have given you permission to do it," he said.

Asmi nodded, her voice flat even though she wanted to scream, "You don't have Jim's job. And your definition of alignment sounds very much like *asking for permission*. I have earned my stripes, Scott, and if GTech doesn't trust me to make decisions, I can always find other employment."

Scott smiled at her. "Don't get your dander up. But of course, if you feel you can't make it work with me as your boss, then you should do what you should do."

"And what does that mean?" Asmi asked, her heart pounding.

"If you want to find another job, you should," Scott said.

Asmi let out a short laugh. "Scott, you should worry about the HR investigation into your team and not so much about aligning with me. About me finding another job, how dare you suggest that to me? We're peers and colleagues. Even if you were my boss, you'd better think long and hard before asking me to go find another job without cause. I don't think HR would like you making such a statement."

As Asmi walked away from Scott he called out, "And Daniel's girlfriend was twenty years old and not underage."

Asmi had to resist the urge to flip him the bird.

ASMI AND CARA met at Drink LA at the Tom Bradley International Airport as they always did when they were traveling together. As a rule, Asmi tried to not eat anything on the plane when she flew east to beat jet lag. Drinking was fine but not eating. Sometimes she did eat on the plane because it was an endless flight and she was bored. She always ended up paying for it with feeling like crap for the two-three days she was in Europe and by the time she started to feel better, she was on a flight back home.

They ordered burgers and Cara ordered a glass of red wine

and Asmi a Lagavulin on the rocks.

"I'm looking for a new job," Cara said.

"What?"

"It's too much," Cara said. "I've just had enough with the whole situation in marketing…not your marketing, but Scott's. It has split wide open now and there is an investigation, a freaking lawsuit and everything in between. I'm tired and even a little disgusted with how Max is handling this."

"I thought Evan was handling it," Asmi said.

Cara shrugged. "They pulled me in last week because of the workload."

"Scott accosted me today on my way out and told me I should find another job if I won't *align* with him when he's my boss," Asmi said.

"What?" Cara shook her head and drank some wine. "I can't believe they're thinking of making him a senior executive of the company."

"There are so many Scotts in Corporate America. How do they get there?" Asmi wondered.

"That's what drives me up the wall, you know. I'll find another job and go to another company and there will be an asshole like Scott there, as well, and then what?" Cara said. "I'm feeling dejected. I think you should share some sully details about your weekend with your hot stud to make me feel better."

Asmi laughed and gave her some details.

"So, you're going to work on fucking it up," Cara said.

"My sister said the exact same thing. I don't do that, do I?" Asmi asked.

"You certainly do. Remember the guy from American Express?" Cara asked.

Asmi nodded.

"He was crazy about you. It lasted what, four weeks?"

"Two weekends," Asmi said. "I'd just gotten promoted. I was busy."

Cara shook her head. "No, that wasn't it. This is what you do. You sabotage relationships. But the married man hung around for four years. He didn't even make you happy. It was on-again and off-again and on-again and off-again."

"There was a lot of drama," Asmi agreed.

"I'm glad that's over," Cara said.

"Me too," Asmi said even though she was sorely tempted to reach out to Etienne and tell him that she'd be just an hour away from him for three nights.

As they were boarding the plane, she got a text from Levi: *Wish I was coming with you. Enjoy the Scandinavian sunshine.* She hadn't told him that she'd also be in Fontainebleau because she hadn't wanted the *'are you going to meet him since you're in Paris'* question. They were hardly in a relationship and she already felt compelled to shell out half-truths. It was *never* going to work out.

THE BREAK THE BOYS' CLUB WORKBOOK

EXCERPT FROM THE BUSINESS WORKBOOK "AND THEN SHE SAID..."

I HAVE READ several articles that talk about how women can break into the boys' club, join the club, or be part of the club. I say let's break up the club instead, because there is no room for it in the contemporary corporate environment.

So, how do we break it? There's no magic foolproof formula. Dismantling a boys' club is about changing culture and change management takes time. Here are **four** steps to try to kill the cancer of a boys' club and/or find a way to gain your mental equilibrium when working in a hostile work environment:

1. **Document – reveal – repeat.** The first step towards change is to make the company accept the problem. This happens by showing leadership and your peers through proof and facts the nature of the issue and where it's present. You'll need to do this repeatedly, in one-on-one meetings, and in large meetings where the discussion is around engagement—wherever you get a chance. Warning: this step can be exhausting.
2. **Bring in the specialists**. If leadership refuses to acknowledge the problem, then you must go to HR to push them to help leadership see the problem.

3. **Let the top brass know**. Sometimes things change once HR gets involved and other times, nothing happens. Then it's time to make an official, anonymous or named, speak-up. A speak-up in most corporations will get the legal department engaged.

4. **Leave.** If nothing changes, find another job, but make sure that you vet the new organization carefully by asking the hiring team questions, checking Glassdoor, getting information from the horse's mouth by checking on LinkedIn who knows someone at the company and asking them, and interviewing your future manager as rigorously as he or she interviews you.

~

IF YOU'VE EVER SAID, "THERE IS A BOYS' CLUB IN MY COMPANY," REPEAT AFTER ME

- I will be cognizant of the existence of a boys' club and do everything I can to break it up
- I will be transparent about how exclusivity and a hostile work environment affects me and be there to support others who experience it as well
- I will not be afraid of speaking truth to power
- I will be prepared to leave if nothing changes after I've done everything I can to change it (because let's face it, no one else is going to change the environment if you don't)

14

LIFE RAFTS ARE LOCATED BELOW YOUR SEATS

"I HAVE A PHONE INTERVIEW TOMORROW," Cara said when they met for dinner at a café close to the Hôtel Victoria Fontainebleau where they were staying. "After the training. It's with DuPont."

"You can't go to the dark side," Asmi said.

"You bet I can," Cara said. "And when it comes to it, you're going to be a reference."

"Okay," Asmi said.

"I've lost faith in Max," Cara said. "The way he's handling this Scott situation is not the kind of company I want to work for. I told him that Scott should be fired, not promoted. He told me I should mind my own business and know my place. I feel like I can't fight the good fight here."

Cara and Asmi walked around the quaint village of Fontainebleau with its perky carousels, cobblestone streets and French cafés where they served the usual fare, such as *coquilles* Saint-Jacques, *blanquette de veau, soupe à l'oignon*, steak tartare and others. For dinner, Cara ordered the *magret de canard* and Asmi the *cassoulet*, which Etienne had introduced her to at a café in Lille. They both remembered the café and Lille with fondness because they'd had sex in the car outside the café in the dark parking area before dinner.

Cara and Asmi had been in INSEAD for another course three

years ago and had done the touristy bit of checking out the famous twelfth-century Château de Fontainebleau. That last time they had stayed for a weekend in Paris—where Etienne had spent one evening and half a night with Asmi before skulking off to his wife's bed. The next day Asmi had confessed her sins to Cara and they'd become best friends.

"Maybe the trick is to learn to deal with Scott, not run away from him," Asmi said.

"Oh, come on, if he becomes your boss, you'll have to run," Cara said.

"I know," Asmi said.

"Do you know why Max initiated an investigation via Mercer? His words, by California law we must investigate and that protects us from liability," Cara said. "No, oh damn, people are being treated like crap and we're not that kind of company… oh, no, it's all about covering our ass."

"Are you being too idealistic?" Asmi asked.

"No," Cara said as they entered the gardens of the hotel. "And what if I am? Why is idealism a terrible thing? And…pot calling kettle. I've seen you do some stupid shit that makes no sense from a corporate perspective because you thought it was the right thing to do. Like when you went guns blazing to save that guy in finance who was about to be fired and hired him in your team."

"He's worked out amazingly well as a business analyst. But as you yourself said, it was *stupid*," Asmi said. "I pissed off a lot of people when I did that."

"If they're pissed off, it means you're doing something right," Cara said.

Asmi shook her head. "A coach once told me that my biggest problem is that I don't appreciate the benefits of not pissing people off. If only I could be softer in the workplace, my work life would be a lot less dramatic."

"Softer equals doormat," Cara said.

~

ASMI ALWAYS BELIEVED that if she could afford it, she'd go back to school to get a PhD in something. There was such a charm about university life.

As she and Cara walked to their class the next morning, she saw a young man lying on a bench, reading a textbook and she thought, *ah, the luxury of doing nothing but educating oneself, the pleasure of it.*

Their professor was ethnically Indian and from INSEAD Singapore. Dr. Seema Verma sneaked out during breaks and lunch to smoke cigarettes and that's how Cara who smoked and Asmi, who dabbled, got to know one another.

The evening of the first day of the course, INSEAD had booked them all for a night of pizza and pool at a little bar. Asmi liked executive leadership courses because she ended up expanding her network and meeting new people.

"It's impossible in Germany to be a mother and a career woman," Bernadette Wustmann, a VP of Marketing for a pharma company's Europeans operations in Berlin, said. "There is no daycare. You have to hire a nanny and it costs as much as your salary."

Vibeke Nielsen, a director of digital marketing for an FMCG (fast moving consumer goods) company, the name of which Asmi didn't catch, said that things were different in Scandinavia, where childcare was subsidized, and women got eleven months maternity leave.

"How's it in America?" they asked.

Asmi shrugged. "I'm neither married nor a mother, but from what I hear it's somewhat the same as Germany. A lot of women feel that they need to stop working once they have children because daycare is so expensive and if their husbands make enough money then it's the better emotional and financial option."

"Ridiculous," Vibeke said. "All these women giving up their careers to be what? Housewives? And what happens when the children leave? I have two girls and they're teenagers; on their way out. If I didn't have a job, I'd have less money, yes, but I'd also have nothing that was mine."

"I don't understand what the noise is about," Liam something who was a director of something at some financial institution in New York said. "When women talk about having choice, why can't they choose to stay home? Freedom should include that."

"It does," Asmi said, grabbing her whiskey as she eyed Cara and Seema going out for a smoke. "It's just scary that it's 2019 and so many women have to stay home after they have a baby because they're not given the opportunity and incentive to join the workforce after they have a child."

She didn't wait for Liam's response but by the noise Vibeke and Bernadette made, she figured he was in for a fight. This group of women here, they were all about *leaning in*.

"My daughter keeps telling me I must quit so I must but...it's my favorite thing in the world," Seema said about the glowing Marlboro Lights cigarette she held between her fingers. "If I didn't have a daughter, I'd smoke all the time, then I won't have to worry about getting cancer and dying."

Asmi took a cigarette from Cara who smoked American Spirits because it was the *healthier* cigarette, if there ever was such a thing.

"I have no kids and no man," Asmi said, "Maybe I should pick up smoking. Being healthy is just the *longest* way to die."

"But cancer is a *horrible* way to die," Cara said, blowing out smoke.

"And with no man and no kids, you'll have no one to take care of you, so I suggest you keep it to social smoking," Seema said.

Etienne used to smoke occasionally, especially after a good meal and Asmi had started smoking with him, outside the restaurant, before they headed back to their hotel room. He'd kiss her after and there would be the taste of tobacco, never sexy before, but definitely so with Etienne. Now, as she stood outside a restaurant in small town France with a cigarette, the ache in her heart was stronger.

But what about Levi?

She didn't have an answer for that.

"WHAT IS THE PURPOSE OF WORKING?" Bernadette asked as four of the women from the course sat in the hotel's beautiful garden, sharing a Laphroig 10 after pizza and pool.

"Money," Asmi said.

"Money, yes, but I like my job," Cara said. "I *really* like it. The job. Not the company right now, but the job."

Seema shrugged. "I'm in academia, I have other sets of issues, but like Cara, I like my job, even *love* it."

"I sometimes wonder what the purpose is. The thing is that I don't care about the company stock going up by another euro-cent…I sometimes struggle with why I work so hard, what's the meaning of life," Bernadette said and then grinned, "Especially after some fine scotch."

Asmi raised her glass, "To Scotland."

They all took a sip of their whiskey and repeated, "To Scotland."

"Is academia better than the corporate world?" Cara asked Seema who laughed aloud.

"No!" Seema said. "Last year, I was getting ready to submit a paper on some leadership statistics, nothing to do with gender and this other professor I know tells me that he knows the journal where I was submitting, and I'd be better off adding his name to the paper even though he did no work for it."

"What?" Cara said.

Seema nodded. "Yeah, and he was right. One journal turned me down and another, after when I added his name, accepted. A man's name in the author credits, even if they didn't do shit to write the paper makes a difference."

"This is by far the saddest thing I've heard in a long time," Asmi said. "We're working in a male-dominated global society, no way around that fact. Instead of making money for our companies, why not make our goal helping other women rise. Don't tell anyone because it's not entirely legal, but if I have an equally good man and woman up for a position, I hire the woman."

"So, you're saying that instead of thinking about the organization, think about female employees," Bernadette said thoughtfully.

"I meet too many women leaders who pull other women down," Seema said.

"It can be a veritable bitch fest with female leaders," Cara agreed. "I've seen such horrible things in various organizations. One manager I know wouldn't let another top female who reported to her get any visibility. She kept marginalizing her until she quit and took her talent to another company."

"I have a theory," Asmi said, holding up her hand. "Women are insecure in the workplace...well, most women are. But with women, they feel they can fight, and they do. But with men, they are too insecure to fight. And this is why men get away with so much and no one calls them on it."

"Women go after women. Men go after women. No one is giving us a break here," Bernadette said. "They hired a new VP of Marketing in my company in the US and he's rude. *Really* rude. Comes with the attitude that *you Germans are fucking up* and I must fix everything. I put up with it for a while and then in one email, he asks for something and I ask him to explain and he responds that he won't explain and then says something like, *you're an experienced marketing VP and I expect you to know better.* He sends this email to me with his direct reports and mine on cc."

"What an asshole," Cara said.

"Yes," Bernadette agreed. "In the past, I'd ignore it. But this time I sent him an email directly and said this kind of email etiquette will mean we cannot work well together. And then I set up a call with him and told him that when he sends an email like this, he loses respect and ground with the marketing team in Germany as they see him as a leader who lashes out when stressed."

"It sets such a horrible tone in the company," Seema said. "What did he say?"

"I thought he'd have definitely received this type of feedback before, but he hadn't or he has and hasn't bother to learn from it," Bernadette said. "He didn't apologize. He said that I deserved it."

"I'm glad that you spoke up," Cara said, lighting up a cigarette. "You know, too many people just let it go because it's uncomfortable. And so these bullies keep doing it over and over again."

"I used to be one of those people, the one who kept silent," Bernadette said, "Not anymore. Hashtag Me Too."

"Me too! And good for you," Asmi said and they raised their glasses and finished their whiskey.

Happy and tipsy, they headed for their rooms in the hotel. Asmi's defenses were down and her room was so French that she did what she knew she was going to do, she couldn't help herself. She sent a text message to Etienne, telling him she was in Fontainebleau for the next two nights.

LEVI CALLED EARLY in the morning when Asmi was getting ready. "How was your first day?" he asked.

"Great," Asmi said. "It was *really* good."

"You seem off," Levi said.

"I'm so sorry, Levi, but I'm in a hurry to get to class," Asmi lied. "Can I call you…oh when *you* wake up in the morning? It'll be afternoon here."

Asmi felt horrible during class for two reasons. One, Etienne had not answered her text message. Two, Levi was thinking they were in a relationship and as much as Asmi wished she was in a relationship with Levi, she couldn't muster what it took to commit. She'd have to tell him if she saw Etienne. She'd have to. And then what?

The evening of the second day, INSEAD took them to A'xel, a Michelin star restaurant in Fontainebleau that Asmi and Cara had been to before with another INSEAD class.

"The many euros they take from us for this course," Cara whispered to Asmi when they were seated at a long table, "Looks like some of it is spent here."

Asmi's companion to her right was Henrik Frederiksen, a Dane who worked for a pharmaceutical company in Copenhagen and was impressed with her. "You seem to have the best questions," he said.

"Thank you," Asmi said.

"I agree with you that our job as leaders is more about coaching than about the content of the job," Henrik said. "But I disagree with you that coaching alone can change culture. What can one leader do? Especially us in middle management, if the top leadership is not on the same train."

"I think one person can make a difference," Asmi said. "Culture changes slowly but you create change agents through coaching and then you're not alone, you have culture ambassadors who can drive the agenda. It doesn't happen overnight though."

Henrik nodded. "You seem like a capable leader."

Asmi shrugged. "I'm *okay*. I learned from my mistakes and I made many."

Asmi called Levi between the main course and dessert. He sounded like he was busy and Asmi wondered if he was already distancing himself from her because he could feel her aloofness.

HE WAS SITTING under one of those white umbrellas in the garden, drinking a glass of red wine when they came back from dinner.

Asmi's heart stuttered. She didn't want Cara to know. Part of the reason was that Cara would try to talk her out of it and another was that she was embarrassed. After all the drama of breaking up and *this is really the end,* and *this is really the last time* talk, here she was once again, in the same place with Etienne.

She texted him her room number and declined everyone's offer for a nightcap, saying she was tired.

Asmi's hands shook as she opened the hotel room door when he knocked. It had been...what...four months since she'd seen him? No, six, nearly six. Last time she had seen him was in February and it was now early August. This was the longest they had gone without seeing each other in four years.

"Hi," Asmi said.

Etienne shut the door behind him and kissed her.

Oh! Asmi thought, this urgency, this *need* for her, this is what she loved about being with Etienne. This was *everything.* She didn't have this with Levi.

After they made love, he just held her and said, "I missed you very much."

"Me too," Asmi said.

"Don't tell me about anyone you saw in the past months," Etienne said. "I don't want to know. I love you and I want you and you are back with me and that's enough."

"Did you..." Asmi asked.

"No," Etienne said. "There's no one, only you."

Etienne and his wife were in a sexless marriage, it was one of their main issues. In the four years they'd been together, it was during the summer when they were on holiday that he'd have sex with his wife, maybe once or twice. *Holiday sex,* he called it, and a way to pretend that all was *okay* with their marriage.

Etienne never called his wife by her name. He always said *my wife.* They had been seeing each other for nearly eight months before Asmi had asked him to tell her his wife's name.

"Why must you know this?" he asked surprised by her question.

"I don't *have* to know...I'm just curious," Asmi said.

According to her therapist, this was how Etienne managed

his relationship with Asmi. He compartmentalized. *His wife* and *his mistress*. It was also how he operated, what was his and what wasn't his. Each one existed in its own compartment and he didn't like to mix them.

My wife can never find out.

I can't live without you.

I have children.

You are the only woman I have loved like this.

I love my wife. I really do.

You understand, don't you?

She needs me. She cannot have her life without me.

I can't stay the night in Paris.

She'd heard it all. But she still loved him. This *must* be love; it had to be because it was so strong. This addiction for each other had to be special. Asmi had come to believe that this was what probably everyone having a sordid affair, sneaking around felt— this is how those who had affairs rationalized it. *I don't want to hurt my family; but my heart is with the man/woman I'm seeing on the side.* This is how something that society defined as wrong continued to perpetuate and people continued to sleep with other people's wives and husbands.

"I'll be in Barcelona in two weeks, any chance you're there as well?" Etienne asked when he was getting ready to leave around two in the morning, so he could be home in an hour, lie about where he was and keep up the appearance of being a dedicated family man.

Asmi shrugged. She was sitting in bed, naked, a sheet spread over her thighs. Her heart was hammering in her chest. He was going to leave, like always. Nothing had changed. Nothing would change. If she wanted him, these were the terms.

"I could be. Are you asking me to be?" Asmi asked.

Etienne finished dressing and leaned to kiss her on the mouth. "Yes, my darling Asmi, I am."

"I'll try my best," Asmi said, feeling like a bomb had exploded in the room and the silence was white and she could barely hear herself.

He kissed her again and when he reached the door, he turned and said, "Say you love me."

Asmi blinked and cleared her throat. "Why is it so important for you that I say it?" He asked often when they made love, *tell me you want me, tell me you love me, tell me you're mine.*

He tilted his head and smiled. "I understand you're angry with me but I'm so happy you asked me to come see you. I want to see you again in Barcelona. Give me a chance to make it up to you. You mean more to me than you can imagine."

"I'm not angry," Asmi said, *at least not with you.*

He smiled. "Well then I'll say it. *I love you.* I love you very much. I will always love you."

"Don't make promises you can't keep," Asmi said. *Always love you? Could she be that gullible?*

His blue eyes were bright, and he looked radiantly happy.

"Do you know that since your text message I've been singing," Etienne said. "You make me happy. Now sleep well and I'll see you in a few weeks."

After he left, Asmi sat still for nearly an hour until her phone came to life. Etienne sent her a message. It was a typical Etienne message—full of flowery words that made her feel wanted, loved, and desired.

It was amazing to see you again. You're a beautiful woman and I love you very much. Don't go away again. Life is hard without you.

She didn't respond. She knew he'd not think anything of it except that was she was asleep.

At five in the morning, she gave up and went for a run. She felt like shit. She hadn't slept the whole night. She'd screwed up her life, again. She had to find a way to tell Levi. End that farce and admit that she couldn't get rid of Etienne.

There was a Polish or Dutch or some European saying: *true love never rusts.* This was true love. So, she decided to stop pretending she was over Etienne; stop working so hard to be over him and just give in.

After all, he had literally *begged* her to come back. He must love her very much. The previous night he'd made love to her with such longing that Asmi was convinced that he was the man for her. It might be morally corrupt and societally *blah blah blah*, but it was right for her, right for Etienne. They were good for each other. They made each other happy.

She replied to his text message at breakfast. *It was very nice to see you again. I'll book some meetings in Barcelona. Text me the exact dates.*

He didn't respond to that text that day or that night.

All okay? She sent him a text message after she boarded her flight to Stockholm the next day.

She saw his response when she landed.

I'm sorry. This was a mistake. Last night my wife and I made love again. I know this is not the answer you want, but it's the only one I can give.

THE KNEE HARASSMENT IN THE NUTS WORKBOOK

EXCERPT FROM THE BUSINESS WORKBOOK "AND THEN SHE SAID..."

FIRST THINGS FIRST. You are not a victim. Repeat after me: I AM NOT A VICTIM. One more time. Come on say it with conviction: I AM NOT A VICTIM.

Got it? Good.

You may be the target of bullying or harassment; but you are definitely not a victim who is going to take it lying down. Imagine you're in public and a man tries to attack you, what would you do? You'd scream for help and then you'd report the incident to the police. Do that here as well.

There is a misperception about HR that they are here to *only* protect the company, which they are. But HR also protects the company by protecting the associates who work at the company. It's not in HR's best interest to protect a bully or a harasser because that leaves the company open to legal liability.

Most of the time HR is unable to act because legally what has happened is not harassment—it's bad behavior. Most women don't even complain, because they're never sure if they're being too sensitive or there is some internal reason why they feel humiliated around their manager.

Here is an FAQ to help you:

Q: How can you make HR see that bad behavior = unaccept-able behavior when it goes on and on and on?
A: Document **everything**. Forward all emails to a private account. Save everything.

Q: How do I know I'm not being too sensitive?
A: Keep a journal. Document everything and when you start to feel there is a pattern, reach out to a colleague, mentor and HR business partner, take the proof to them and ask them what you should do. Talk to your friends. This will help you get external validation for something you already know—you're not being too sensitive, you're being harassed.

Q: What is the consequence of speaking up?
A: Most companies have a non-retaliation policy. But many companies are full of shit. There is retaliation. How can there not be? It won't be that you'll lose your job, but there might be subtle jabs from people who know you're the reason they're being investigated. If this happens, document and send the incident report to HR immediately. HR will ask them to shut up, because it's a lawsuit waiting to happen.

Q: I think it is too hard to speak up. How do I make it easy?
A: You can't. The process is hard. The investigation is hard. Speaking up is difficult. If you feel your mental health is at stake, don't do it, find another job. But if you feel you have support around you, then keep pushing for justice and better working conditions—even when the going gets tough, which it will.

Q: What if nothing changes?
A: That happens as well. Then move on. But you want to be able to look back and say, "I stood up for myself. I'm nobody's victim."

15

HOW DO YOU SAY
BASTARD IN SWEDEN

"BÅSTAD," the woman at the Hotel Riviera Beach reception said with a broad smile when Ananya asked her how to pronounce the name of the city they were in.

Ananya squinted. "I don't mean to be impolite, but that sounds like *bastard*."

The woman laughed. "A lot of non-Scandinavians call it that."

"We're staying in *Bastard*," Ananya announced to Asmi who immediately responded with, "Bo-staa-d."

"I like my pronunciation better," Ananya said.

Asmi met Ananya in Stockholm where they'd stayed a night and then had rented a car to drive six hours south to Båstad for a meeting planned between Short Poppy and GTech counterparts of R&D, marketing and sales to see points of *alignment*. It was all *hush-hush* and only the C-suite had been invited, as well as Scott and Asmi because Jim was on vacation in Malta for the fourth week that month.

"I didn't realize it was so desolate—at least they have a spa," Asmi said when they reached their room. There were two bedrooms in a stark minimalist style and a huge deck with a view of *Laholmsbukten*, the Laholms Bay. The living room had a cozy couch with a cashmere blanket and a gas fireplace.

"This is fabulous," Ananya said.

"You won't be bored?" Asmi asked.

Ananya shook her head. "Absolutely not. Are you kidding me? Peace and quiet and this beauty? My Kindle is loaded up and I can either sit here with a glass of something and read or head to the heated indoor pool or get a massage. This is like the *perfect* holiday."

They had dinner at the hotel restaurant on that first night and went back to their room to sit on the balcony. Ananya had bought a bottle of *The Peat Monster*, a blended Islay scotch at the Arlandia Stockholm International Airport. She opened the bottle and served it neat in glasses from the hotel room.

"This is heaven," Ananya said as she held a cigarette in one hand and her whiskey in the other.

It was ten in the evening and the sun was still out. It wouldn't set until three or four in the morning and then would rise again even before it had completely set. It was a warm August evening in Sweden.

"Now, will you tell me why you've been so...moody?" Ananya said.

"I'm not moody," Asmi said.

"You're off."

"I'm perfectly fine."

"*Hey*, it's me," Ananya said and held out her cigarette to Asmi.

She shook her head and sighed. She looked at her sister and realized that she had to tell someone before the acidic humiliation inside her broke down what little self-esteem she had left.

"I saw Etienne when I was in Fontainebleau," Asmi said hurriedly, not wanting to explain further because it grated on her, the embarrassment of having given Etienne another chance just to have him reject her. She downed her scotch and poured herself another glass.

"*Ooooh*," Ananya said. "And now you're back with him again? Is he coming here?'

Asmi shook her head and then burst into tears. Ananya patted Asmi on the shoulder.

Asmi told her what happened and showed her the text message from Etienne. Ananya made a sound of disgust when she read it. She continued to pat Asmi's shoulder after handing her phone back.

"He always does this. The minute I give in to the relationship, he pulls a stunt like this," Asmi said, sobbing, big gulping tears. "It's so humiliating. It's like he's comparing me to his wife and I'm failing on all fronts, you know? I don't want to compete with his wife. I don't give a shit but...he makes me feel like this. He's been begging me to come back and when I let him in, he says he's having sex with his wife again."

It took a good fifteen minutes for Asmi to stem the tears. She looked up at Ananya with red rimmed eyes. "Am I stupid?"

Ananya crushed her cigarette. "You're not stupid...well no more than any..." she paused and sighed, "Actually, *yes*, you're stupid. Asmi, the man is a jerk. You're swayed by the French accent and the manly sex."

Asmi choked out a laugh as she wiped her nose with a paper napkin. "Manly sex?"

"The dominating sex. He dominates you. He controls the relationship. I understand that you want that in your personal life because of your job. You must go to work and make decisions and drive the agenda. You have to dominate in the office, and you want to be dominated by your lover," Ananya said. "But he's using you and that's fine if you're using him as well— but he's also trying to control you and that's where the problem comes. You're not on equal footing."

"You don't think I'm in love with him?" Asmi asked.

Ananya shrugged. "Love shmove. Love is overrated. No one gives a shit. Who cares? Love or no love; this man is not your friend, not your companion, he's not with you—he's not on your team. You understand?"

"Is Venkat on your team?"

"Yes," Ananya said. "He's always on my side. *Always*.

213

Against his parents, mine, the kids...always on my team and I'm on his."

"Who's on my team?"

"I am," Ananya said. "Venkat is. Just like you're on my team and his. Do you understand?"

"Yes, I think," Asmi said. "Cara is on my team. Mila is on my team. But...Etienne is not on my team. It just stings. I'm not sure if my ego is hurt because he rejected me *after* I gave into him; or my heart is broken."

"We label things. Heartbreak and ego wounds...it doesn't matter," Ananya said. "Just accept that he made an ass out of you and move on."

"How come you're so wise?"

Ananya raised her glass to cheer Asmi and when they touched their glasses with a satisfying clink, she said, "I started therapy last month."

"No shit," Asmi said. Ananya had never believed in therapy, always saying it was a fancy person's thing and not what down-to-earth people did. She could solve her own problems. She didn't need some stinking psychologist.

"I know," Ananya said. "Venkat said I should try seven sessions; our insurance gives them for free, and it gave me a reason to get out of the house. *Doctor's appointment, Amma, I have to go.*"

"You have to tell them to not come for so long next time," Asmi said. "You know I've invited them to come and stay with me."

"They know you're never around and they want someone to torture," Ananya said and then shook her head. "They're bored, Asmi, and they're lonely. They want company."

"Then *she* should've invested in having a better relationship with us," Asmi said.

"*She* is incapable of relationships," Ananya said. "My therapist thinks she has narcissistic personality disorder. She also thinks maybe that's why you and I are so fucked up."

"You're not fucked up," Asmi said.

214

"That's sweet," Ananya said.

"You are supposed to say neither are you, Asmi," Asmi said.

"But that would be a lie."

"I HEAR you brought your sister along?" Scott asked when they were in the meeting room on the second floor of the hotel.

It was a bright summer day and impossibly beautiful. Sweden was green even in the summer because it rained so much; and there was a picture postcard quality to the view from the meeting room.

"Yes," Asmi said as she settled into a chair across from him.

"Must be boring for her," Scott said.

"No," Asmi said. "She's having some R&R." Before Scott could pursue the topic further, she added, "Have you looked at the new forecasting for Short Poppy?"

Scott shrugged. "Just stop arguing with Matthew and let him have this. He wants to build his agritech empire. Let him."

Before she could respond, Matthew entered the meeting room with Isadora and Max.

Elvira and Mats from Short Poppy were accompanied by Liselotte Olsson, their legal counsel, and the meeting meandered as such meetings usually did. They went over the same things repeatedly.

Darach McNeil, GTech's VP of R&D who had kept his Scottish accent despite moving to California two decades ago, was sitting next to Asmi and spent most of the meeting going through his phone, apparently disinterested in the proceedings. Asmi didn't know Darach well. He was known to be loud, passionate and opinionated; and his heavy Scottish accent sometimes made it hard for people to understand him, especially when he was on a rant. There were stories about Darach and Matthew going at it in the CEO office loudly enough for everyone on the floor to hear them argue. It was well known that Darach and Matthew respected each other and were colleagues as well as *close* friends who *golfed* together. And when you were invited to golf with them, it was equivalent to being a made man in a mafia movie.

During a break, Darach asked Asmi if she'd like a *proper* cup of coffee as he was going to go to the café downstairs to buy himself one. Asmi offered to join him.

"Looks like you and Scott are handling things well with your boss on extended leave," Darach said as they waited for their lattes at the café. He had left his phone in the meeting room and Asmi realized as he stood there, watching her intently, this was a job interview. Matthew had probably asked Darach to assess Asmi and Scott.

"Yes, I believe we are," Asmi said and wondered if she should add something about how Matthew's guidance through this time had been invaluable but since she'd had exactly two one-on-one meetings with Matthew in the past six months it would be insincere, so she didn't say anything.

"Is Matthew working with both of you?" Darach asked. "I know Scott is in his office all the bloody time."

Was he now? Asmi thought uncomfortably. She wished they'd just announce him as Jim's successor, so she could go underground and lick her wounds.

"Maybe he needs more help than I do," Asmi said with a smile and picked up her latte that the barista pushed across the counter.

Darach let out a loud boisterous laugh. "Well then, Isadora mentioned that underneath all that quiet professionalism, you have what it takes."

Asmi almost blurted, *is that what she said?* Instead, she kept her *quiet professionalism* and just smiled, it was hard not to. Darach was not known to give out compliments and this was *definitely* one.

"What do you think about Short Poppy?" Darach asked as they walked back to the meeting room with their lattes.

To tow the company line or to not tow the company line, that was the question. "I think it's not the right company for us," Asmi said. "They're too early in their innovation cycle for GTech. We like to acquire slightly more mature companies. We'll struggle with Short Poppy."

"Are you afraid of struggle?"

Asmi shook her head. "I think we won't get enough bang for our buck with Short Poppy."

"But Matthew is determined," Darach said. "Maybe it would be better for you to find ways to make this happen."

"I'm happy to disagree and commit," Asmi said, looking Darach in the eye as he held the door of the meeting room right before he opened it, "But while we're still discussing the subject, I feel it's important to state my opinion. Isn't that why I was asked to give my opinion?"

Darach looked at her and nodded. "I'm not for the acquisition either."

"What does Matthew say to you about your dissension?"

"That I'm too negative and I tell him that's my bloody job," Darach said and as he pushed open the door, he added genially, "I hear your sister is with you."

"Yes, we met in Stockholm," Asmi said.

"Please extend an invitation from GTech to her for dinner tonight," Darach said and then whispered, "We're all very curious to meet your sister."

"Why?" Asmi asked, surprised.

"Because meeting family is the fastest way to get to know someone," he responded.

"INSTEAD OF SENDING it just to Darach, I cc'd the entire R&D department about how pissed I was with him," Matthew was telling a story, in command of the table at Restaurant Sang as they ate an appetizer of cane-cured salmon with asparagus and grated egg yolk.

Ananya was thrilled that she was invited to dine with Asmi and the executive team, while Asmi was concerned. Usually, with peers or other colleagues it would not be a problem but with the C-suite, she worried about how Ananya spoke her mind and didn't always appreciate the benefits of a filter. She had to restrain herself from warning Ananya to behave because besides being rude, she knew it would hurt her sister's feelings.

Ananya sat in between Matthew and Darach, who was impressed that Ananya drank Scotch.

"We all drink scotch," Ananya said. "It's our family pastime."

"Mine too," Darach said. "Are you a Macallan kinda girl or..."

"Islay," Ananya said, shaking her head.

"Peaty. Only an experienced and sophisticated palate truly enjoys that," Darach said and then looked at Asmi who sat across them in between Scott and Isadora, "I must say you're full of surprises. I thought you'd be a wine sort of person."

"Why is that?" Isadora demanded as she picked up her glass of the 2013 Henri Bourgeois, Jadis Sancerre. (There had been a long discussion between Isadora and Matthew about the Sancerre, which Isadora wanted versus a 2011 Domaine Paul Blanck Riesling from Alsace, which he wanted, and in the end a bottle each was ordered so everyone would be happy.)

"Just that girls like wine," Darach said.

"Did you just say *girls*?" Asmi asked amused.

"He certainly did," Isadora said.

"We're having a nice meal; do we have to be politically correct here as well? I think we can be less PC in Sweden, what do you say, Matthew?" Darach said, raising his glass of Riesling wine with a provocative smile.

"I don't get the problem," Scott piped in, "If someone called me a boy at my age, I'd be flattered."

"Is that because you find being an immature boy flattering?" Ananya asked crisply. The table fell silent. Asmi wanted to be upset but she loved that her sister had said what she'd been thinking. Ananya was a housewife and a bona fide feminist.

Darach let out a laugh. "Atta *girl*...oops, lady."

"Men like to pass off sexist remarks as jokes," Isadora, the only female C-suite executive at GTech, said to Asmi but she was talking to the whole table. "However, it doesn't change the fact that it is sexist. Elvira, what is the status of gender equality in Scandinavia?"

Elvira, the CEO of Short Poppy shrugged, "In the public sector and politics, it's fifty-fifty. In corporate Scandinavia, the glass ceiling is made of steel. It's rare to have a woman CEO."

"But you are one," Matthew said.

Elvira smiled. "I said rare, I didn't say nonexistent."

"So, there is no *real* problem," Scott said. "We have plenty of female leaders in the US. I just think that we should hire based on talent and not gender."

"And how many female managers do you have in your management team?" Asmi asked Scott.

"Women don't want the job. I've tried, believe me. You're single with no kids. It's easy for you to travel as much as we do, but for other women they don't want to do it," Scott said. "They want to be with their families."

Asmi turned to face Scott, and asked coolly. "Why is it that you can travel as much as you can even though you have children, and women can't?"

Scott shrugged. "I don't know, you tell me why women feel like that."

"Because..." Asmi began.

"Children, children," Max interrupted her, clapping his hands. "Let's not try and solve the issue of diversity and inclusion at dinner tonight. Cara is working on that project for GTech. I think a better discussion would be if we should order..." he peered through the wine menu, "the Stag's Leap Cabernet or the Château Larmande Grand Cru Classé from Saint-Emilion to go with the veal."

Asmi felt anger radiate from Isadora. She put her hand on Asmi's forearm as if asking her to let her take this one and then in a calm voice said, "You Germans know fuck all about wine. You should leave it to the experts." She held out her hand for the wine menu, which Max handed off to her without a word of protest.

~

"CAN I just say that you were amazing the way you told him that he wasn't even good enough to pick the wine," Ananya said to Isadora in the taxi back to the hotel. Asmi, Ananya, Isadora and Elvira were in one taxi...the one Scott called the *girls' ride*.

Isadora shook her head. "I'm sick of men saying it's all fine now. Yes, yes, Isadora, it was bad years ago but now, *voila*, gender inequality is solved. It's all good now."

"I sit in too many meetings where I'm the only woman... especially as an entrepreneur and I first have to prove that I'm good enough to do what I'm doing because I'm a woman and then I can do what I have to do. Men are accepted as being good at their jobs from the start," Elvira said.

They reached the hotel and Elvira declined Isadora's invitation for a drink and went to bed. Isadora, Asmi and Ananya ordered espresso martinis and went out to the patio with their drinks to enjoy the balmy night with the sky still light at ten in the evening.

"Darach is impressed with you," Isadora said to Asmi. "As am I. You handle yourself well, and I like it that you're not scared of Matthew."

"What are you talking about? I am scared of Matthew," Asmi confessed.

Isadora laughed. "As you should be if you're smart, because he's a scary man. But Matthew is also fair...don't get me wrong, he can be an asshole, but overall, he's not a misogynist. Not like say Max is...or even Darach to some extent, though more than half of the R&D management team is women. But to have a VP of HR who thinks men are better than women and he's given the diversity and inclusion initiative to Cara because he thinks it's a waste of time."

It was peculiar that Isadora was being so open, when in Las

Vegas Asmi felt she'd been trying to warn her from pursuing the VP position.

"How do you deal with the sexism at the high table?" Asmi asked.

"I use humor," Isadora said.

"Does it work?" Asmi asked.

"Not in the day of #MeToo. I think we must deal with the issue head on and not use humor to deflect. Why is it that a Harvey Weinstein got away with doing what he did for thirty years? Because women didn't speak up. I'm from another generation and I use humor because without it I'm just an angry woman who can't control her emotions. I do lose control when I'm angry and then I feel guilty about it," Isadora confessed.

"We live our lives feeling guilty," Ananya said. "I feel guilty for not working. If I was working, I'd feel guilty for not being home enough."

"I feel guilty for not feeling bad about being single and childless," Asmi said. "I know I'm supposed to be chasing the white picket fence."

"I used to feel guilty for traveling," Isadora admitted. "My two daughters are grown up and...it's not common knowledge but I'm getting divorced."

"I'm so sorry," Asmi said.

"I'm not," Isadora said. "We had a good twenty-two years and then the gas ran out of the marriage car. We tried to refuel and couldn't, so we had to let it go. Everyone keeps saying how sorry they are, and they expect me to feel bad, but I just feel *free*."

"I'd feel *free* too if my kids were out of the house and I could get rid of my husband," Ananya said with a faraway look in her eyes. Then she turned and looked at Asmi who was gaping at her, "I think about divorce...all the time. But I also realize that I'd then be a cliché, one of those women who wasn't leaving a marriage because she was unhappy but because it left her unfulfilled."

"Marriage doesn't fulfill," Isadora remarked. "It's the greatest...*fake* news."

"Exactly," Ananya said. "Imagine my surprise at finding that out now after nearly twenty years of marriage, that there is no rainbow at the end of this storm."

Isadora held up her glass and Asmi and Ananya cheered. "To *freedom*," they said together.

～

ASMI TALKED to Levi that night because it had become awkward, her avoiding him. They were not in a relationship, but she had to be polite. That night in Fontainebleau with Etienne weighed on her, that happy weekend with Levi weighed on her, that Scott would get the job she thought she was qualified for...weighed on her. It appeared that she was not successfully piloting her life and that weighed on her.

A coach had once asked her, "Do you live your life by design or default?" Asmi used to live by default. And now, ironically, when she was trying to live by design, she felt rudderless.

Levi could hear her reluctance over the phone. He could feel her rejection. He was the bigger man, so he said, "Hey, if this has run its course for you, that's fine."

"I'll be honest," Asmi said, wondering what that word meant to her anymore. *Honest*! Such a simple word but the hardest, most difficult part of it was to be honest with oneself. Every self-help guru out there will say that the most important relationship you have is with yourself, so what are you supposed to do when you're cheating on yourself, when you aren't authentic?

"That would be good," Levi said, and she could feel his smile.

"I'm not ready for a relationship," Asmi said and the words rang true inside her. "I know, I'm nearly forty and my biological clock has run out of battery so it's not even ticking anymore, but I'm not ready to commit my life to another. I enjoyed our time together. The sex is awesome."

"The sex is pretty phenomenal," Levi agreed.

"I can keep having sex with you, but I can't...you know... how do I put this, be beholden to you," Asmi said.

"Okay," Levi said. "It feels like the reverse of a romantic movie...but I can deal."

"Really?"

"Sure," Levi said. "So, tell me, what are you wearing?"

They didn't have phone sex, but they talked about gender inequality, as it was top of her mind after the dinner. As always, their conversations left her feeling charged and excited. She promised to call again when she was back home and then they could make plans to meet soon.

After the call, she wondered if she'd committed to a relationship and if she had, did she have to tell him about that night with Etienne. She didn't have time to ponder over it because when she looked at her phone as she got into bed there were five emails from Matthew. She found her computer and went to work into the wee hours of the morning so the asshat CEO had what he needed for the meeting the following day and thought, *they don't pay me enough for this shit.*

IF YOU'VE EVER SAID... "HE DIDN'T MEAN IT, I'M JUST SENSITIVE," REPEAT AFTER ME

EXCERPT FROM THE BUSINESS WORKBOOK "AND THEN SHE SAID..."

- I am not a victim; I'm a target and targets don't lie down and take shit from anyone
- I'm not over sensitive, I'm being harassed, I don't have to carry the guilt for someone else's bad behavior
- I will document bad behavior and report the facts, keeping emotions out of it
- I will fight the good fight; but I won't die on this hill— there are other companies that would love to hire a great associate like me

16

OH ROME! CITY OF THE SOUL!

"I DON'T HAVE my speech ready. Hell, I'm not even sure what to wear," Asmi told the woman she was standing in the passport control line with at the Rome Fiumicino Airport. "This was all very last minute. I found out the day before yesterday while I was flying back home from a meeting in Miami."

Asmi met Kaylee Murphy, the Senior Vice President for Branding for a tech company on the plane. They got talking as they waited for the bathroom on the plane and realized they were both going for the same Women in Technology conference in Rome. The conference was at Hotel Adriano close to the Palazzo Montecitorio and just a three-minute walk from the Spanish steps.

Isadora had been invited to speak at the conference, but she had personal commitments and had asked Asmi to go instead. She had wanted to say, no, I can't go speak at a "Women in Tech" conference but Isadora had simply said, "This is your chance to lean in. So, lean the fuck in."

The evening in Sweden had changed their relationship and now Isadora was actively mentoring and sponsoring Asmi. This was her way of pushing Asmi to get more visibility as a woman leader, driving her agenda of getting Asmi on the executive team. But Isadora was honest about the fact that Matthew was more inclined to hire Scott because "weak leaders like to hire mirror images of themselves, it's the easier option." This was a strong statement against their boss and Isadora was reputed to be cautious, but during that warm August night in Båstad, in between espresso martinis, she had decided to trust Asmi.

"Suit," Kaylee said. "Always a pant suit. Hillary may have made it the country's female *mantra,* but we were wearing pantsuits long before that."

They got past passport control and went straight to the taxi stand. In the taxi, Asmi wondered aloud why women had to dress like men.

"The hell with authenticity, we have to dress to fit in and not stand out," Kaylee said.

"But do you really think that dressing like a woman is not the right thing—and that we must put on the *man suit* to get ahead?" Asmi asked.

"You have to dress like a *corporate* woman," Kaylee said. "I mean…sure you can get away with the odd earring, but we have to present ourselves to be heard in a boardroom of gray and black suits. We can't be the airhead wearing a Calvin Klein silk dress with some frilly shoes. Maybe works in the fashion and the media world, even advertising, but tech? Absolutely not."

Kaylee had all the right credentials. Asmi had checked out her LinkedIn profile when she connected with her on the plane. She had an MBA from Kellogg; a bachelor's in communication from NYU and was voted one of the top twenty female branding executives in *Business Week* a year ago.

Kaylee invited Asmi for drinks that evening where she said she'd introduce her to some other women leaders from tech in her network. They met at the Adriano hotel's famous bar *The Gin Corner,* the first lounge dedicated to gin in all of Italy.

"They have over one hundred kinds of gin," Kaylee said when they settled into their seats. "I love this place. It's curated by Barbara Ricci, she's from the Adriano family."

Kaylee who was familiar with the menu ordered a gin and tonic but not *just any gin and tonic,* she was specific about the tonic—she wanted a pink pepper Schweppes but left the choice of the gin to the bartender, "Surprise me."

Asmi went safe as she wasn't a fan of cocktails and preferred her liquor straight or on the rocks and ordered a Scottish gin called Rock Rose that the bartender said was "perfect on the rocks with a sprig of rosemary."

"Rome is a city that feeds the soul," Kaylee said to Asmi. "I'd love to live here but my husband has a family business in Sacramento, so Silicon Valley is as far as he can go."

"What kind of family business?" Asmi asked.

"Cattle," Kaylee said and laughed. "Who would've thought that a nice Boston girl would end up with a California Cowboy? We have an apartment in San Francisco, and he goes back and forth to the ranch. How about you?"

"Single," Asmi said and thanked the bartender who placed their drinks in front of them. She picked up her glass and said, "*Saluti.*" Kaylee touched her glass to Asmi's.

"Children?"

"None. How about you?"

"Four," Kaylee said and laughed. "They're aged between ten and twenty and yes, after the fourth one I had to have a *mummy tuck* because everything down under was coming loose."

"You're doing it all. Man, child and career," Asmi said.

"A lot of women are," Kaylee said. "Do you worry what would happen to your career if you had a family?"

"No," Asmi said. "I never felt the need to have a steady man."

"How refreshing," Kaylee said. "I meet too many women who keep saying how they've not found the right one and if they did, he's married. There is a sense of desperation in single women as they get older...not that you have it."

Asmi shrugged. "I know how it goes. I feel that I *must* want the man and child. At work, especially, too many women will judge you for being single."

"Well...there is a certain amount of...I don't know...selfishness in being single or choosing to be childless," Kaylee said and then immediately added, "I don't…let me take that back. To each her own, you know."

Asmi controlled a sigh. Kaylee was *that kind of a woman* leader who liked women like herself. Women who'd chosen to have children and were in secure marriages, she trusted this type of woman more than she trusted the Asmi type of woman.

"I just watched a Ted Talk by the writer Chimamanda Ngozi Adichi," Asmi said. "There are women in Nigeria who wear an engagement ring or a wedding ring even if they're single, so they'll have more respect at work. I'm glad we live in a country where that is not the case."

Kaylee took a sip of her drink, watching Asmi as she did so. She smiled. "Bravo. Don't take it lying down, no matter who it comes from. What do you plan to do if you don't get the VP of Marketing position? What kind of job are you looking for?" Asmi had told Kaylee about her *Corporate Hunger Games* during their flight.

Kaylee's network was a candidate's wet dream. Tech CEOs, senior executives and one Jo Shaw, an executive recruiter that Kaylee insisted talk to Asmi because she *is one of us*. An African American woman, Jo reminded Asmi of Jada Pinkett Smith: she was petite, she was in shape, and she exuded confidence while she dropped names like Sheryl (COO of Facebook), Indra (CEO of Pepsi), Virginia (CEO of IBM), Mary (CEO of GM) and Safra (CEO of Oracle).

"Matthew Baines," Jo said when Asmi told her she worked at GTech. "I don't even know why he hired Jim, a total train wreck. You're up for the job? I thought it was going to that guy from Yale…what's his name…Beauregard."

"Scott Beauregard the Third," Asmi said.

"Yes, him," Jo said. "What are you looking for?"

"Ah…well, I think I'm ready to take my next step," Asmi said and didn't sound like she thought that at all.

Jo made a face. "You have the disease. I call it the "female doubter" disease. You go with that attitude to Baines he'll eat you alive. I know him and he's a ballbuster. Are you a ballbuster?"

Asmi cleared her throat. "I was once called a Powerful Director with a Black List."

Jo raised her eyebrows appreciatively. "I like that. Why were you called that?"

"I fire low performers," Asmi said. "It's not always popular. Once, I cleaned out a team in my previous company and they'd been there for over a decade. I got into a lot of trouble because of it."

"What did you learn from that?"

"Don't try and build your team before you have your team," Asmi said. "I was trying to make it work even though I knew I'd have to get rid of four out of five of them. I did succeed but my reputation took a hit and then I left for GTech."

"Your reputation was probably fine," Jo said. "But there was probably a personal toll. I understand. Middle management is the toughest job. But you stuck to your guns and that's what matters in middle management. What do you like about GTech?"

"I like my team," Asmi said. "But then I handpicked them. When I got the job, I did what was known as the *mini marketing massacre*, but it needed to be done."

"Are you a woman leader or a woman's leader?"

Asmi had never been interviewed in a cocktail bar before and she felt exhilarated despite her surroundings with Jo's rapid-fire approach. "A woman's leader."

"You didn't have to think about it."

"No," Asmi said.

"Then why do you not say you *want the fucking VP of Marketing position*?" Jo demanded.

Asmi licked her lips and took a deep breath. "Because I don't know if I'm good enough."

"Ah," Jo said. "Do you know how often I hear women saying that? All the time. Do you know how often I hear men saying that? *Never*."

"I've just been a marketing director for three years," Asmi said defensively, "And ..."

Jo lifted a hand to silence her. "I'm going to help you tonight," she said. "Have you read the book *Playing Big* by Tara Mohr?"

Asmi shook her head.

"Read it," Jo said. "My coach, this amazing woman, Annie, who lives in Montana coaches from it. The book talks about the inner critic. We all have the inner critic. What does your inner critic look like?"

"Excuse me?"

"Is it a he or a she? When you doubt yourself, who do you hear?" Jo asked. "Close your eyes and think about the critic."

Asmi cleared her throat. The music was playing. The bar was noisy and yet here she was in a booth with a *ballbuster*, closing her eyes, thinking about her inner critic. It was hokey as hell.

"She's me," Asmi said and opened her eyes. "But she has a hooked nose."

"Ah, well," Jo said. "Let's make her different from you. What does she wear? She should wear something you'd never wear."

"Long flowing black clothes...but it's the shoes. I'd never wear those shoes...the one with the witch heel," Asmi said and then laughed, "She's like the Wicked Witch of the West."

"Fabulous," Jo said. "And how does she sound?"

"Smug."

"And what does she say to you...say when you're in a meeting with Matthew Baines and he's asking about your career plans," Jo said.

Asmi licked her lips. "She's saying that I'm not ready. Then I say, no, I'm ready and she says, so what, they'll still give the job to Scott."

Jo nodded. "Good. Now I want you to close your eyes and go back in that room with Matthew and imagine this witch is sitting across from you. She's sitting next to Matthew."

Asmi nodded with her eyes closed.

"How are you?" a woman screeched and came by to give Jo a hug. Asmi opened her eyes.

"We're working on her inner critic," Jo said.

The woman smiled and looked at Asmi. "Who's your inner critic?"

"The Wicked Witch."

"Love it," the woman said. "Mine is the Borg Queen from *Star Trek*. Enjoy."

"Who's your inner critic?" Asmi asked Jo.

"Agent Smith from *The Matrix*," Jo said and then shrugged, "I had a difficult father. But there is never just one inner critic, there are several and they come out at different times for different reasons."

"You all have much cooler inner critics than I do," Asmi said.

Jo sighed and Asmi nodded. "I get it. That was the witch speaking."

Jo smiled. "You're catching on. Now, I want you to go back to the room with Matthew and the witch. Are you there?" Asmi closed her eyes and nodded. "Good. Now imagine there is a volume knob on the witch. On her belly or her..."

"Forehead," Asmi said.

"Good. Is she talking?"

"Yes. She's saying *you're not good enough, you know that, stop pretending*," Asmi said.

"Excellent. Now turn down the volume," Jo said. "Just do it."

Asmi lifted her hand as if turning down the volume.

"Now respond to Matthew."

"I'm ready for this job," Asmi said and then opened her eyes and was about to say more when Jo hold up her hand.

"No," Jo said.

"But..."

"You said it. That's all," Jo said. "Keep turning that volume down. did you see it has already shifted? You didn't say *I am not ready*, you said that the witch said *you're not ready*. You have already distanced yourself from your inner critic."

"All I need to do is ask the Witch to shut up and I'm good to go?"

"Don't argue with the Witch. Don't ask her to be silent. Just turn the volume down. That's all you need to do. And if you must talk to her, say, *I've got this*."

Asmi smiled slowly. "What was the title of that book again?"

Jo pulled out a business card and scrawled the title of the book she'd suggested earlier and gave the card to Asmi. "Connect with me on LinkedIn and when you're *sure* about what you want, call me. I like to help women. I like women who *lean in* and I like to help them *play big*. But you must *really* want it. Fix the doubting disease, turn down the volume on your inner critic and then we can do something with you."

After that, Jo left to intimidate someone else.

Kaylee winked at Asmi from a distance and Asmi gave her a thumbs-up sign. The boys may have a boys' club but so did the women. The difference was that the women accepted all women and men wanted men just like them in their club. The women had a *huge* advantage—the advantage was diversity.

"I HEARD THAT YOU WERE FABULOUS," Isadora said on the phone the evening after Asmi's speech. She had taken Kaylee's advice and worn a dark blue pant suit with white pinstripes, but she had also worn strappy cocktail-hour blue *Nearly Nude* Stuart Weitzman sandals and long triple drop gold earrings from Tiffany's, which had been a gift from Etienne.

Kaylee sent her a message before she gave the speech, *you've got this. P.s. the shoes rock.*

She had changed her speech after meeting the women in *The Gin Room*. Her talk was going to be about helping young women enter technical jobs in the biotech industry, but she spoke about how women need to let go of their doubting disease and made them laugh with the story about how she found her inner critic. She had done it to impress Jo and she had succeeded because Jo sent her a message via LinkedIn after the speech: *You did good. Call me when you're ready.*

"I met some awesome women," Asmi said. "Thanks so much for this chance, Isadora."

"Good," Isadora said. "Who did you meet?"

Asmi told her about her conversation with Jo and the discovery of her inner critic. Isadora asked Asmi to buy two copies of the book Jo recommended because she also needed to discover and silence her inner critic.

∽

ASMI WAS on a high when her phone beeped during the conference dinner.

It was Etienne.

Valencia.

That was the entire message. They had been to Valencia two years ago. He had work there and she had taken a week off and flown in. That week had been special because they had a whole week together and not just a stolen evening or night. They had never felt closer.

I've tried to stay away but I want you. I always want you.

Her heart stuttered.

"You okay?" the woman she had just been talking to while they ate their dessert asked.

Asmi nodded blindly.

"Bad news?" she asked, looking at Asmi's phone.

"It's fine, just a...it's nothing," Asmi said.

Her phone beeped again.

I'm sorry. I'm so sorry. Let me make it up to you. Please. I can't go another day without you, no matter you're several time zones away.

Asmi muted her phone and put it face down on the table. Every time this thing between them ended and she'd stopped feeling anything for him, he'd reach out and she'd be eighteen again, a teenager in love, her hormones raging, her heart in her throat.

You're going to forgive him and you're going to go right back to being a pathetic loser, the Wicked Witch said.

Asmi didn't want to do what she always did and respond to his message. She excused herself and walked out of the hotel. The Spanish Steps were close by and Asmi followed the signs, her phone in the pocket of her dress.

There you go again, the witch said.

Asmi flicked her Tiffany earrings with her fingers as she walked the lively streets of Rome in the night.

She stood atop the Spanish Steps and thought about Keats who used to live in a house on the corner at the bottom of the steps. It was a museum now and she had been there the last time she'd been in Rome.

Touch has a memory. O say, love, say,
What can I do to kill it and be free?

She took the stairs and then sat on a stair half-way down from where she could see the Fontana della Barcaccia. Not the famous Trevi, this was the Fountain of the Old Boat, shaped like a boat and made in the opulent Baroque style. Etienne had told her its story when she'd been in Rome with him two years ago. Tiber had flooded in the late sixteenth century and Romans used boats for transportation. A boat was left in the square when the water subsided and became the inspiration for the fountain.

She hadn't noticed before, the last time when she was here with Etienne, that the boat was half sunk, below street level.

Asmi saw lovers, friends, families, locals and tourists—all milling up and down the stairs. Some just passing through, some for whom the steps were the destination. The sun had set, it was a warm September day—and she was in Rome, seated at the Spanish Steps. She'd had the privilege to speak to five hundred women from around the world. She should be happy, and she wasn't.

Feeling sorry for yourself again, the witch said.

She had traveled the world, Asmi thought. She'd been to all the places most people talked about Paris, Rome, London, Brussels, Berlin, Sydney, Mumbai, Stockholm, New York, Cape

Town…everywhere. And she had been to all these places alone. With work. She and Etienne had spent time in some of these cities, but they weren't *together*. She was *alone*. There was that cliché wasn't there, *I'm alone but not lonely,* and what garbage that was. She was alone and sometimes she was lonely. Ananya would say that it was possible to be married and be lonely. Lonely was an emotion, fleeting, in and out, not a permanent situation.

You'll never meet anyone ever who is yours. It's going to be Etienne who loves his wife more than you, the witch said.

Asmi watched a young couple, probably on their honeymoon; run up the stairs laughing and wondered if she wanted to be with someone. Yes, she did. *But* she also loved her freedom. She loved that she didn't owe anyone anything, that she could travel the world. She could do what she wanted, when she wanted and how she wanted. Being in a relationship came with a price tag, as did being alone.

Her phone vibrated, and she looked at it. *Come back. Please.*

Was this love? Or as Keats would say, *was it a vision, or a waking dream?*

There he goes again. You know you can't resist him, the witch said.

Asmi reached out in her mind's eye and turned the volume control on the witch's forehead down, all the way down to silent.

I deserve better, she whispered to herself… *in a partner, in my job, and my whole life. I deserve better.*

Leaning in, she thought was not just about leaning in at work, it was about leaning in all the way into life. By saddling herself with Etienne she had been pulling away from her life.

No, she thought, *no, she didn't want to go back.* She wanted to move on, past Etienne. She could respond to his message and say, "No, this is over" but she had said it so many times. Maybe it was time to do something else.

You know you want him, the witch whispered.

Asmi once again turned the volume down and each time she did, the witch's voice was lower than it had been before.

There is nothing stable in the world; uproar's your only music.

Etienne was now in her past. Was Etienne a mistake? Who knew? Maybe she needed Etienne to get to where she was right now. Maybe he was a mistake that had stunted her for the past several years. Maybe she had been pulling away from her life because she felt she didn't deserve any better, that Etienne was the best she could do, that Marketing Director was the best she could do in her career...that she wasn't worthy of what she wanted from life, that she didn't have permission to reach out for what she wanted. To aspire to what she wanted, she first had to accept what she didn't want. She didn't want Etienne. She didn't want his drama.

The witch was silent as Asmi opened her contact list on her phone and blocked Etienne's number. There, she thought, smiling. She didn't have to respond. She just needed to end it.

To sorrow I bade good morrow...

She stood up and took a deep breath, a smile breaking out on her face, a smile she couldn't contain.

She ran down the stairs, feeling a burst of energy inside her. She was ready, she thought; ready to take the next step. At the bottom of the stairs by the baroque fountain was a gelato stand and she stood in line behind a few people, looking at the menu of flavors.

"Chocolate or vanilla?" a man said from behind her.

Asmi turned and saw a man she didn't know. Only in Italy, were you guaranteed that a man would hit on you no matter how you looked and no matter who you were with. Ananya had been with Venkat and the kids in Verona and an Italian man had asked her out for coffee. She turned him down but now believed that Italy was the best place for a woman to find her mojo after two kids and stretch marks.

The man was wearing a suit as if he was on his way back from work. "I saw you on the stairs...it seemed like you had an epiphany and then you came running down to get a gelato."

Not Italian, Asmi thought after hearing his accent. British?

"I did have an epiphany," Asmi said. "And I was thinking rum raisin. How about you?"

The man smiled at her and shifted his backpack from one shoulder to another. "Now I feel that I have to be creative because I was going to say vanilla." Asmi ordered their gelatos and paid for them.

They took their ice creams and stood by the fountain. His name was Renato, half-Italian and half-British, working in some bank in Rome.

"What was your epiphany about?" he asked.

Asmi smiled broadly at him. "I figured out what I didn't want."

"And what was that?"

"That I didn't want to live a life where I felt I didn't deserve better," Asmi said and then grinned. "Too much information?"

He shook his head. "I was watching you and I wanted to know what flashed through your mind. You have a very expressive face. I could see the moment you...I don't know, made a decision."

"I did," Asmi said. "I decided to stop a bad habit."

"Have you eaten?"

"Yes, this is dessert," Asmi said.

"Let me pay you back for the gelato. I know this great bar..."

Asmi shook her head. "I have an early flight back to LA."

He nodded. "Thanks for the gelato," he said.

"You're welcome," Asmi said and then went up the Spanish Steps with her gelato in one hand and a smile on her face that came all the way from the inside.

GET WHAT YOU'RE WORTH WORKBOOK

EXCERPT FROM THE BUSINESS WORKBOOK "AND THEN SHE SAID..."

IF YOU'VE EVER SAID, "I DON'T KNOW IF I'M WORTH IT," REPEAT AFTER ME

- I am worth every dollar I earn and then some
- I will always fight to get what I'm worth
- I will not punish myself with a low salary just because I'm uncomfortable negotiating
- I will never say yes to the first offer; I will always ask for more
- I will show humility and be realistic (based on facts and data)

FILL OUT the following worksheet to prepare yourself for a new job negotiation. Remember, when you get a new job is the best time to negotiate—incremental raises within a position without a promotion are always minimal, so if you want to get that big pay hike, this is where you must put your energy.

- Job title:

- Job description: (Be descriptive)

- What do you bring to the table?

    1. _____

    2. _____

    3. _____

- What are you missing based on the description?

    1. _____

- Based on your research, what is a realistic paycheck you can expect?

    _____

- What is the offer? _____

- What do you think their top three arguments will be to say no to your demand? How will

    you counter each argument?

    1. Argument against: _____ Counter: _____

    2. Argument against: _____ Counter: _____

    3. Argument against: _____ Counter: _____

- What is the final pay package you will ask for? _____

- What are other items you would like to see in the overall package? _____

Fill out the following worksheet to prepare yourself to negotiate your salary during an annual performance review. During
this time of the year, there is some flexibility in giving a raise so
use it to your advantage. Negotiate your salary during a performance review (unless the review is awful).

- Job title:

- Job description: (Be descriptive)

- What are your top three exceptional achievements in this job in the past year?

    1. _____

    2. _____

    3. _____

- What are your top three biggest misses in this job in the past year?

    1. _____

    2. _____

    3. _____

- Based on your research, what realistic paycheck will prevent you from thinking when you're working on a weekend, "they don't pay me enough for this shit": _____

- What is your current salary? _____

- What do you think their top three arguments will be to say no to your demand and how will you counter them?

    1. Argument against: _____ Counter: _____

    2. Argument against: _____ Counter: _____

    3. Argument against: _____ Counter: _____

- What is the final pay package you will ask for? _____

And what do you do when you don't get what you want? Then you have a choice to make. Take the new job or don't. If you feel you're worth more, find the company that sees in you what you know is there. If you feel you're being shortchanged in your current job and there is no raise coming your way that will satisfy you, it's time to move on or fight for a promotion.

17

BRAZILIAN BLOWOUT

"THIS IS NOT MY BUSINESS," Asmi said to the VP of Sales, Gary Baker. "This is the detergent business; this is Scott's business."

"Yes, I know," Gary, a salesman from Atlanta, Georgia, said in his southern drawl. "But you understand the urgency of the situation. We need to untangle this mess in Brazil and get the distributor to pay us."

"I don't understand why you want me to go," Asmi said. "This is a sales issue plus the distributor is Scott's."

"Scott is in Asia. Matthew wants you to run point on this," Gary said and as he rose to leave Asmi's office he added, "And it's one hell of a cluster."

Asmi met Cara for lunch and complained about the urgent Brazil issue that had landed on her plate.

"I have to go to São Paulo tomorrow," Asmi said. "I don't understand why I have to go. And no one can explain this to me except that it is what Matthew wants."

"He's testing you," Cara said.

"And this is a DSO, a daily sales overdue thing...a payment thing. I'm supposed to go and collect money? What am I? A mafia bagman?" Asmi said.

"It's a test," Cara said, digging into her taco. It was Taco Tuesday and the office canteen pulled all the stops.

Asmi eyed her taco nervously. Her stomach was jangling again. "I felt so good after Rome, but since then I haven't slept for six hours straight. I'm perpetually jet lagged. This thing with the VP position is stressing me out and...this place is driving me nuts."

"Why don't you get a medical marijuana card? Smoke a little Indica in the evening after work and Zen out," Cara said. "That's what I do. By the time Oscar comes home from work, I've forgotten about the job."

"Don't you think I have enough problems without turning into a pothead?" Asmi asked.

"This is California, they want you to smoke a joint to keep up with the state," Cara said.

"I don't think a joint is going to fix our issues in Brazil."

"Say hi to Leticia for me. I like her. Luiz...he's a creep and he's incompetent."

"I know," Asmi said. "You know Leticia is actually running our office there? I don't know why we won't fire Luiz and just promote her."

"I've talked to Gary about it, but he says that we've invested so much effort into Luiz with coaching and training and all that, so we have to give him a chance again and again and again," Cara said.

"I don't get it," Asmi said. "Why do we reward shitty leadership with executive coaching and leadership training? Why don't we just fire the guy?"

"You know why. It takes balls to fire people and corporations have no balls," Cara said. "Do you think they're sending you because you know the distributor there? What's-his-name?"

"Gabriel Sousa. I know him a little and this was before they split marketing and gave me baking, wine and paper. That was four years ago," Asmi said

"Matthew wants to see how big your balls are," Cara said.

"I have no idea what I'm going to do," Asmi said. "I'm afraid Matthew is going to find out that I don't *actually* have balls."

"Oh, come on, Asmi," Cara said. "You have *big* hairy ones.

Believe in yourself, everyone else does. Just go to São Paulo and let your instincts guide you. You'll show Matthew what you're made of."

Asmi nodded and reached out for the volume knob on the Wicked Witch even before she spoke.

∾

ASMI MET Gabriel Sousa nearly six years ago when she first started to work at GTech and was responsible for setting up distributors in high growth markets.

Gabriel was who you thought when you thought Brazilian soccer player, and in fact he had played soccer when he was in the University of Miami. After graduation, he played for smaller leagues in South America but that was as good as he got, he told Asmi. "The professional soccer you see on television is a completely different game than what I was playing. I couldn't compete."

He picked Asmi up at the airport as Leticia; the Brazilian marketing manager was going to arrive in São Paulo late that evening from Mexico City where she was attending a biotechnology symposium.

"I'm glad it's you and not Scott," Gabriel said as they drove to São Paulo's business district Morumbi where Asmi was staying to be close to the GTech office.

"I'd rather Scott was here," Asmi said. "You need to explain to me what's going on."

Traffic in São Paulo was as bad as one imagined traffic could be in a big city and they inched slowly on the highway.

"Brazil is having problems...the whole world knows, yes?" Gabriel said.

"Yes," Asmi said.

"Well, Scott seems to not read the same news and he keeps pushing. I told him that it was a '*no go*' but he doesn't listen. We have a chance with our customer Brilho to sell our protease for about two hundred thousand dollars," Gabriel said.

"This is a private label detergent manufacturer?" Asmi asked.

Gabriel nodded. "They do both, branded and private label. They're big in Brazil. But they're struggling like all other companies. They're buying less and less enzymes like everyone else. *But* they are launching a new low tier detergent and they want to put cheap protease in it. They're looking at us but they're also looking at BASF, DuPont and AB Enzymes...everyone. We've done trials with them and now we wait for the decision."

"When will you know?" Asmi asked.

Gabriel shrugged. "Maybe this quarter or next or next. Brazil is...what can I say, things are bad here right now."

Asmi sighed. "But you bought the product, Gabriel so I don't understand why you haven't paid us."

Gabriel shook his head. *"No, I did not buy the product.* I told Luiz I would *not* buy the product, but he said I should take it, warehouse it, and when the Brilho deal comes through I can pay."

"What if the deal doesn't come through?" Asmi asked.

"Then Luiz said he'd take the product back," Gabriel said.

"You have this in writing from Luiz?"

"He gave me his word," Gabriel said.

"And what else did he give you his word about?"

"That he would give me a twenty percent discount when the deal came through," Gabriel said.

"I assume this is also not in writing?" Asmi asked and Gabriel nodded.

Asmi took a deep breath. Luiz had recognized revenue for the product he had given to Gabriel without receiving payment. The only time revenue was recognized was when the product was *sold*, either to the distributor or the end customer. What Luiz had done was illegal.

"Does Scott know about this?" Asmi asked carefully.

"I don't know. I think this is Luiz's scheme. Scott has been putting pressure on him and...you know I work mostly with Leticia and she told me that...look, she's not happy working for

Luiz and why should she be? She does all the work and he treats her like a secretary," Gabriel said. "Have you talked to Luiz?"

"Yes, briefly on the phone," Asmi said and then sighed. "He's at the same conference as Leticia in Mexico City. We have a meeting tomorrow."

"Luiz is pressuring me to pay for the product," Gabriel said. "I want to be upfront with you. I'm not paying for something that doesn't have a buyer. I don't have that kind of cash flow. I can't afford it."

Asmi nodded. Well this was a cluster, she thought. *Thanks for nothing, Matthew.*

~

ASMI CALLED Isadora from her hotel room.

"Looks like Luiz stuffed product with Gabriel Sousa and recognized the revenue without getting paid because he made a deal with Sousa that he only needs to pay once he has a buyer," Asmi told her.

She heard Isadora sigh. "Does Scott know about this?"

"I don't know," Asmi said. "I'm going to meet Leticia tonight for drinks, alone, and get the skinny on this."

"Well, this is a *cluster*," Isadora said.

"That's what Gary said. What am I supposed to do?"

"What do you think should be done?"

Asmi took a deep breath. "Find out what happened and let Matthew and Gary know."

"That's all?"

"Well, Luiz reports to Gary. I guess he'll deal with it," Asmi said.

"Do you think Gary will deal with it?"

Asmi sighed. "No. He's kept Luiz on even though he's pretty much useless."

"Gary won't do anything," Isadora said. "But now legal will have to be involved so something *will* need to be done."

"Right," Asmi said.

"When I first got this job, we were having trouble with quality in one of our factories. I spoke to the factory manager in Minnesota and he said that his uptime was great. Now this guy had been in the company for two decades and I just got here so I go to Matthew and say that we have a problem because this factory manager was more interested in uptime than quality and was shipping defective product out to customers," Isadora said. "I wanted Matthew to tell me what to do."

"What did he say?"

She heard Isadora laugh. "He said it was my call and he'd support my decision. I fired the factory manager and there was fallout. People loved him and my engagement survey that first year was awful. I felt like shit, like I wasn't up for the job, that it was too big for me. Matthew supported me all the way. What's the moral of the story, Asmi?"

"That I was sent here to clean up a situation and I have to *actually* clean it up," Asmi said. "*But*, Isadora, I don't feel I have the right."

You don't. You know you don't, the Wicked Witch said.

"Neither did I and I *actually* had the job," Isadora said. "You are an officer of the company. You have evidence of an illegal activity."

Asmi hesitated.

This is not your business. It really is not, the Wicked Witch said smugly.

"You were the VP of Operations then. I'm…I don't know if it's my place…but…I definitely can make recommendations for next steps and if Matthew agrees…I guess I can implement the next steps," Asmi said.

"Excellent. Call Matthew and explain the situation and what you recommend," Isadora said.

"I'll send him an email," Asmi said. She didn't want to talk to him about this. That would be much harder.

"You'll call him first and talk directly to him," Isadora said firmly. "You can and should send a written report, as well. If this is as serious as you say it is, your direct manager needs to know immediately."

"You're right," Asmi said.

"Good luck," Isadora said cheerfully.

Asmi's hands were shaking when she put her phone down. It wasn't that she didn't make decisions, she made them all the time but that was in her department, her purview. But this was something else. This was not her business. Why would anyone care what she had to say? Would Matthew think she was over-stepping her bounds? Would he tell her off?

You're going to fail, the Wicked Witch said.

Asmi leaned forward and reached for the volume dial on the witch's forehead and turned it down.

LETICIA WAS in her late thirties and had been with GTech for ten years now. She and Asmi had a good relationship but not an open one like Asmi had with some of her other marketing managers.

They met at the Canvas Bar of the Hilton Sao Paulo Morumbi Hotel for drinks that night and made small talk about the conference in Mexico, about the Brazilian economy, politics…the usual. Asmi drank scotch and Leticia nursed a glass of red wine.

"I spoke with Gabriel," Asmi said after the initial pleasantries and Leticia instantly stiffened. "Can you tell me what's going on?"

"You should talk to Luiz," Leticia said.

"I will," Asmi said. "But I want to…"

"And Scott," Leticia added. "You should talk to them. I'm just the marketing manager, you know."

"Come on, Leticia, you all but run the GTech office in Brazil. Everyone knows that."

Leticia took a sip of her wine and then faced Asmi and said carefully, "If everyone knows this, why is it that my career has been at a standstill for three years?"

Asmi wanted to say, *what do you want me to say? You know how it is.* But wasn't it Asmi's job to change the status quo? Isn't that what she was supposed to do as a leader?

"Why do you think your career is at a standstill?" Asmi asked.

"Because no one cares," Leticia said. "You want my work, but you still want to keep Luiz in as General Manager because he's a man, and everyone knows that there is a boys' club in GTech. Scott comes here, and he and Luiz go out and have fun. I'm never invited. The only time I'm invited for something by global is for your meetings like the one we did in New Orleans. I have no visibility with senior management, Luiz makes sure of that."

"What have you done to gain visibility?" Asmi asked.

"I've talked to Luiz and he keeps making excuses."

"Who else have you talked to?"

Leticia shrugged and looked uncomfortable. "No one cares, Asmi."

"I care," Asmi said. "Talk to me."

"Look, you all in headquarters take care of each other and right now it's not easy to find a job in Brazil, okay? I need my job," Leticia said.

She was angry and justifiably so, Asmi realized. Angry, bitter and tired. Just like Asmi. Why bother to fight for the VP job? Who cares? Hadn't she had this same conversation in her head? But Asmi had support. There was Cara, Isadora and her sister. Now it was her turn to be that support for Leticia.

"Luiz is incompetent, I think most people know this," Asmi said even though she knew that as a senior leader she should not be this transparent about her opinion about another leader in the company. "But who do we replace him with?"

"I'm sure it won't be difficult to find someone better," Leticia said.

"Why not you?" Asmi asked and watched Leticia. She saw the shock and then disbelief run through her.

"Do you think I could do the job?" Leticia asked uncertainly.

Asmi smiled. "If you have to ask the question, Leticia…"

Matthew's question echoed in Asmi's mind, when he'd asked her what she wanted for her next step and Asmi had dawdled instead of saying, balls out, *I want the VP of Marketing position because I'm the most qualified person for it.*

She wondered who Leticia's inner critic was.

"Scott has been pushing us to meet our numbers. I said last year when we did the budget, that these are numbers we can *never* meet," Leticia said. "But Luiz was too afraid to say anything to Scott."

"Why? This is macroeconomics, it isn't Luiz's fault that Brazil's economy is tanking," Asmi said.

Leticia took a sip of her wine and gestured to the bartender to pour her another. "It makes me *very* uncomfortable to speak out against my boss, okay?"

"It made me uncomfortable to say that Luiz is incompetent," Asmi said. "Let's deal in facts and let's be transparent. What is said here stays between you and me, okay?"

"Luiz told me that Scott told him that if he didn't meet his numbers he'd be fired."

Asmi nodded.

"Luiz was...is desperate to keep his job," Leticia said. "He made a deal with Gabriel for Brilho. We met our target for last year and no one asked how. I told Luiz that we should not record revenue like this, but he didn't listen. Mario, our finance manager, does what Luiz says, and so it happened."

"Scott didn't know about this?"

Leticia shook her head.

"Why didn't you say something to Scott or Gary or anyone?" Asmi asked.

Leticia had tears in her eyes, "Why do you think you're here? I did an anonymous Speak Up about it. I've been waiting for Luiz to find out it was me and...you don't understand what Brazil is like. The glass ceiling. It's *really* real here."

"It's *really* real everywhere," Asmi said and put her hand on Leticia's shoulder.

"I thought if I did a good job, people will notice and I will have my career," Leticia said.

"I have noticed and I'm going to fix this, Leticia. You can trust me."

"Marisol said I could," Leticia said.

Marisol was a marketing manager who reported directly to Asmi and they'd been working together for several years now. When Asmi was younger, she didn't always get along with everyone in her team, but as she'd learned more about leadership, she'd become a better leader, and if nothing else, her team trusted her implicitly because she delivered on her promises. Now, she'd made a promise to Leticia and she wasn't sure how to deliver on it, but she was going to find a way.

The volume on the Wicked Witch stayed on silent.

AFTER SPENDING A DAY WITH LUIZ, Leticia, and Mario the finance manager, and pouring through various Excel sheets and financial reports, Asmi knew exactly what had happened.

"We have a meeting with Brilho tomorrow," Luiz said to Asmi when they met in his office to discuss next steps. "You should come. We will get the contract, and everything will be fine. All solved."

"Luiz, you understand what you did is out of compliance, don't you?" Asmi asked.

Luiz shrugged. "It's…last month or this month, this year or last year, a quarter here and there. The deal is ours."

"Gabriel is not so sure. He said that Brilho has been running trials with all enzyme manufacturers so how do you know the deal is ours?" Asmi asked.

Luiz grinned. "Maybe I have better contacts than Gabriel."

Highly doubtful, Asmi thought and then hoped that he hadn't gone ahead and bribed someone at Brilho because that would just make a shitty situation unbearable.

"I think if you come for the meeting with Brilho it will give us leverage," Luiz said. "You can see how well we do our jobs here, Asmi. You will be impressed."

After talking to Luiz and concluding that he just didn't want to accept his culpability in something that was illegal, Asmi knew what needed to be done.

She called Cara first and explained the situation to her.

"I want the job to go to Leticia," Asmi said. "How do I make that happen?"

"Tell Matthew," Cara said.

"Does he even know who Leticia is?"

"Probably not," Cara said. "Let's do this. I'll talk to Max and Gary here. I'll make sure they're on board. You convince Matthew that Leticia is the right choice."

"And Scott?"

"Who cares," Cara said. "He's in Asia. And he has no access to Gary or Matthew on this topic. He doesn't even know there was a Speak Up because whomever did it, put his name as someone they didn't want to be involved in the investigation. The only ones that know are: Max, Legal, me...and Mathew."

"Would Max tell Scott?"

"Max may be a lot of things, but he's not going to do something out of compliance," Cara said.

"Okay. You do the ground work with Gary and Max...and I'll do the work with Isadora and Matthew," Asmi said. "Let's get our girl promoted."

AFTER SHE SETTLED things with Isadora who said Leticia had her support if the matter came to the leadership team, Asmi called Matthew from the meeting room she had commandeered for the duration of her stay. She waited for Celeste, Matthew's assistant to pick up the phone and put her through to him. She had *never* called Matthew before, Asmi realized. Usually, it was the other way around.

Game face on. Volume on low on the Wicked Witch.

"Hi Matthew, how are you? I hope this is a good time," Asmi said.

"I have ten minutes before my next meeting," Matthew said, and he was so curt that Asmi felt her confidence flap. But she pulled up her socks. She had to do this. She had asked Leticia to trust her and that meant she had to deliver.

"I'm afraid this may take more than ten minutes, Matthew and I don't think it can wait," Asmi said and then told Matthew what she had found out about GTech in São Paulo. "I wanted to let you know what's coming down the pike before I spoke with legal and finance at HQ."

She heard Matthew call out to Celeste and ask her to move his next meeting.

"Well this is a cluster fuck," Matthew said.

"I have recommendations on next steps," Asmi said.

"Okay."

Asmi stood up to feel taller and said calmly, "We need to push the nuclear button. Luiz will be put on immediate administrative leave along with Mario. We need to bring some finance people from HQ to clean this up. I strongly recommend we make Leticia the General Manager."

It took Matthew maybe fifteen seconds to respond, but for Asmi each second hammered through her heart like a long minute. Had she been belligerent? Had she overstepped? Did he even know who Leticia was? Should she have explained who Leticia was and how right she was for the role?

"Sounds good," Matthew said. "Just clear with Les in Legal to see if there are some Brazilian laws we need to be aware of, and get Anish in the loop and have him send you someone from his team."

Les was the GTech legal counsel for Latin America, Anish was the VP of Finance.

"Thanks, Matthew," Asmi said.

"And what about the Brilho account?"

"There's a meeting tomorrow, it'll be good for Leticia to run that as her first big project as GM," Asmi said.

"Good idea," Matthew said. "I'll see you at the town hall meeting, then."

"Yes," Asmi said but Matthew had already hung up. She would return on Thursday night and he was saying he wanted her in the office on Friday morning at eight a.m.

Inconsiderate ass, she thought, but she was smiling. She had leaned in and it hadn't been difficult at all. Matthew had said yes because he trusted her recommendation. She didn't have to convince him about Leticia. He just said go ahead and do it. There were no barriers on the outside, she realized, just those inside her. She felt sorry for the Wicked Witch.

～

"WHERE IN THE WORLD ARE YOU?" Ananya asked as soon as Asmi answered her phone. "I've been texting and calling and no response."

"São Paulo and I'm sorry, but there just hasn't been much time," Asmi said. "I'm getting on a plane in about fifteen minutes to fly back home."

"You go to the coolest places. What's it like?"

"The airport?"

"São Paulo."

"I don't know," Asmi said. "I went from airport to hotel to office; and then office to a customer site and then back to hotel and then office and then airport. Traffic sucks."

"That's it?"

"I like this mango-milk dessert they make…it's like a mango *shrikhand*," Asmi said. "Outside of that I didn't see much of the city."

"But you went so far. Can't you stay an extra day?"

"Nope," Asmi said. "I have to be at a town hall meeting tomorrow morning; and next Monday I leave for Berlin for a European sales and marketing meeting."

"Do you know what's happening with your VP position?"

"I have no idea," Asmi said. "But I did something cool in

Brazil." She told Ananya about how she had managed to get Leticia the promotion she deserved and unraveled a hairy compliance issue.

"I've not heard you this excited in a long time," Ananya said. "It's nice."

"I like my job, Ana. I just realized...no, remembered that. I like making change...making a difference for the better," Asmi said. "I don't want to lose it or give it up."

"What part of your job do you like best?"

"All of it...the business, the..." Asmi trailed of.

"I think the part of your job you like best is helping people," Ananya said. "Especially, helping women. What you really enjoyed about this whole thing in São Paulo is that you got this Leticia person a promotion."

"She deserved it," Asmi said.

"It's still what you like most about your job," Ananya said. "You like to see people grow. You've always liked that. You're always the one who'll coach and push everyone to reach for their dreams. I don't know why you don't feel you have the permission to reach for your own."

"I'm ambitious and driven, ask anyone," Asmi said defensively.

"For others," Ananya said.

"I'm fighting for this VP position, aren't I?"

"Oh, please. Half the time you want to quit your job and live in my guest room," Ananya said. "Speaking of guest room, it's your birthday at the end of the month."

"That's an odd segue," Asmi said as she started to walk toward the gate with her boarding pass in hand as the announcement was made for business class passengers to board.

The woman at the counter beeped Asmi's pass and looked at her passport before waving her on.

"I think you should come visit the parents. They're the ones staying in our guest room," Ananya explained.

"Your head works in mysterious ways," Asmi said.

She settled down in her seat on the plane. The woman sitting across the aisle from her was *very* familiar, but she couldn't place her.

"It's for your birthday, Asmi," Ananya said.

"I don't want to do anything for my birthday," Asmi said absently, trying to look at the woman in the seat across the aisle without openly staring.

"You owe me and you're going to celebrate your fortieth birthday with me," Ananya said.

Asmi thought about it for a moment. She didn't *really* want to be alone on her birthday drinking Scotch whiskey, did she?

"Sure, I'll come," Asmi said, squinting to recognize the woman with the familiar face. "On my way back home from Berlin, I can stop for D-day."

"B-day. Buy something for them, okay? To make peace," Ananya said.

"I don't want to because no matter what I buy *she* is going to complain and...*oh my God*," Asmi squealed and then dropped her voice, "You won't believe who's sitting next to me."

"Who? Oprah?"

"No. she probably has her own plane," Asmi said, "I think it's Sheryl Sandberg."

"*The* Sheryl Sandberg?"

"Yes," Asmi said.

"Don't you think she would have a private plane?"

"Maybe," Asmi said. "But it's her. I'm almost sure."

"What will you do?"

"I don't know."

"You have to say something to her," Ananya said. "Get her autograph."

"That's so gauche," Asmi said.

For the rest of the flight, Asmi tried her best to find out if the woman sitting next to her was indeed *the* Sheryl Sandberg. Barring staring at her face, there wasn't much she could do besides swift glances. At one point, she even managed to get a blurry photograph on her iPhone. She forwarded the picture to Ananya and Cara and they both texted back that they couldn't make out much except that the photograph was that of a woman.

It was when they were getting ready to land that Asmi managed to peek at the woman's boarding pass while she was filling out her custom's form. It was Sheryl Sandberg.

She texted to Cara. *It's her. I saw her boarding pass.*

Cara wrote back. *OMG!!!*

Asmi wrote, *what should I do?*

I don't know. I'd be too star struck to say anything.

Asmi managed to stay a step behind Sheryl Sandberg as they went through passport and customs quickly because they both had Global Entry. As they walked through the long walk way post customs to the exit at LAX, Asmi speeded up and caught up with the woman in the front of her. Asmi finally found her courage to say something when they were outside the airport.

"Excuse me," she said. "You are Sheryl Sandberg, aren't you?"

Sheryl Sandberg smiled. "Yes."

"I just wanted to say thank you," Asmi said. "For writing *Lean In* and for changing the lives of so many of us. You're my hero."

"That's so nice of you to say," Sheryl Sandberg said.

"I learned to *Lean In* because of you. I'm still not there, but I'm getting better," Asmi said.

"We're all getting better," Sheryl Sandberg responded. "Just keep at it."

"I will," Asmi said as they shook hands.

I'm never washing this hand again, she thought like a schoolgirl who'd met her favorite rock star.

HOW TO GET AHEAD
WHERE YOU ARE

EXCERPT FROM THE BUSINESS WORKBOOK
"AND THEN SHE SAID..."

I HEAR MANY WOMEN SAY, I'm working my ass off, but they're not promoting me. Or, I want to be in department x (example: marketing), but I don't know how to get there from department y (example: R&D).

Traditionally, women wait for good things to happen to them. The problem is that the phone never rings; no one hands you a great job or a place in a rocket ship for you to achieve all your professional dreams. You must fight for it—there is absolutely no free lunch, even when it looks like it might be.

Here are **three** things you can do when you're doing the job and no one is paying attention (Caveat: If you're working for a lousy company that doesn't know how to manage talent, the below steps may have to be repeated several times):

1. **Book a meeting with HR.** Talk to your HR partner about your next step. Run your CV by them. Ask them for help in identifying next challenges and opportunities. HR is not just there to hire and fire people; they're also there to manage talent, which is you, and help the company grow by helping you grow.

2. **Book a 1-on-1 meeting.** You want to book a "separate" meeting with your boss to discuss your career—and not your day-to-day work. Your goal with this meeting is to let your boss know you're ready to take the next step, why you think you're ready based on your accomplishments and what he thinks you need to do to get there. Ask if he thinks you're ready, and then ask what he is going to do to help you get there.

3. **Book a skip-level meeting.** Ask your boss if it's okay for you to set up a skip-level meeting with his boss. This meeting allows you to meet your boss's boss and let him or her know what you want for your next step, why you feel you're ready and what advice they have for you to get to your next challenge.

∾

CHANGING DIRECTION – IS IT POSSIBLE?

Sales people often ask me how they can get into marketing. I have had a customer service rep ask me how she can become a marketing assistant, and an inside sales rep who wants to become a field sales rep. I once hired a financial controller to become a business intelligence manager. It happens more often than you think, and is an excellent way for people to grow and thrive in a company, and a great way for a company to keep their talent.

But how do you make this move? Here are **three** tips to help you get from department x to department y to grow your career in an unknown territory:

1. **Research. Research. Research.** Find out everything you can about the type of job you want (talk to colleagues, managers, leaders, HR partners, people in your LinkedIn network, strangers you meet on a plane, et cetera) and understand what skills are

needed to succeed in the position. Match those against yours and identify gaps.

2. **Engage in projects.** I recently invited a sales associate to work on a marketing project for a quarter. I have asked a customer service rep to start writing articles for an internal magazine to get her copywriting experience. Use projects to close your skills gaps. Talk to the head of the department you want to join and find out what projects you can be part of. Remember, you will do this in addition to your current job, so make sure you have the bandwidth with the blessing of your manager.

3. **Network**. Make sure people in the company, your manager, his manager, the head of the department you want to move to, your colleagues...everyone should know that you're looking for a next step in your career. I once told a manager whose job I wanted to let me know if he was quitting. He called me a week before he turned in his notice, so I had time to prepare to audition for that job. When people know you're interested in a position and you have shown that you work hard to learn and grow, they will give you a chance.

18

ACHTUNG BITTE, THIS FLIGHT IS DOUBLE BOOKED

"I DON'T UNDERSTAND why you couldn't tell me what was going on, after all this was the detergent business," Scott asked for the third time since he'd met Asmi at Berlin Tegel Airport. They were waiting for the elevator in the lobby of the Radisson Blue Hotel, Berlin, famous for AquaDom, the world's largest freestanding aquarium with nearly 2,500 fish and one million liters of seawater. Asmi had requested a room with a water view.

"I'm repeating myself, but here I go again. This was the result of a Speak Up. You know they're confidential, so you were told when Legal decided you could be told," Asmi said as she had the first two times and was relieved when the elevator opened.

Asmi pressed the button for the tenth floor. The doors of the elevator closed, and Scott said, "I know what you're trying to do."

"What is that?" Asmi asked as she wheeled her suitcase in front of her so she could make a fast escape out of the elevator when it stopped.

"You're not getting the job, Asmi," he said. "Matthew already told me it's mine."

Asmi felt a hammering in her chest. Would Matthew do that? Yes, absolutely, he'd do that.

"Then there's nothing for you to worry about," Asmi said when the elevator dinged and stopped at the tenth floor.

They both stepped out and Scott came to stand in front her, barring her way. He was a big man and for a small moment Asmi felt intimidated by his size, but she hid it when she saw the excitement in his eyes, the knowledge that he was trying to scare her, threaten her. It wasn't the first time a man had tried to assert physical superiority, but it had been a while. Since she'd climbed up the corporate ranks, she had learned to hold her own and the men she worked with knew better. Apparently, Scott seemed to lack the maturity to understand that some women were harder to bully than others.

"If you're not doing it, you should start talking to recruiters," Scott said, smiling at her. "I don't think it's going to work out between us."

Asmi faced him and said calmly, "Scott, that's a defeatist attitude, of course we can make it work."

"I hired Luiz," he said harshly. "How dare *you* fire him and replace him with Leticia? She's not even a sales person."

"She brought that Brilho deal home. Gary thinks she's great and since she reports to him, I don't see your problem. Also, I wouldn't tell people you hired Luiz, because he's lucky there are no criminal charges against him. Looks bad for you," Asmi said. "Don't worry, Scott, I'm a *very* good coach and leader. I'll make sure you and I sort through our issues and work well together. Now, if you'll excuse me."

She walked past Scott. Instead of gritting her teeth with anger, which is what she'd normally do, she smiled. She'd handled that beautifully.

Asmi: 1, Scott: 0, Wicked Witch: 0

∼

THERE WERE ABOUT forty people at the meeting and nearly all of them were whispering about Luiz and what had happened in Brazil. It was a bit of a scandal because it wasn't commonplace to have someone in GTech make such an egregious compliance violation.

Jonathan Burges, an American, had been running the EMEA (Europe, Middle East and Africa) GTech office for three years now. He had moved with his partner and two dogs to Berlin and loved the city. He and Asmi had started working at GTech at the same time and had become friends during orientation week six years ago.

"I hear that *you* fired Luiz," Jonathan said during a break in the meeting when Asmi was getting coffee.

"Why is everyone so curious about the details?" Asmi wondered.

"First, he was Gary's direct report and second he was Scott's golden boy," Jonathan said and with his head indicated that they should go outside to prevent anyone from eavesdropping on their conversation.

"Matthew told me to get it done and I got it done," Asmi said. "I cleared it with Gary who was happy to have me deal with Brazil because he had a shit storm in India."

"What happened in India?"

"They may lose the Ujala contract and that's one of their biggest customers," Asmi said and then smiled. "We only seem to be having problems with the detergent business. The baking business is doing just fine. We just picked up a big customer in China that makes *mantou*…steamed bread."

"Let's not forget that we're doing an excellent job for baking, wine and paper in Central Western Europe," Jonathan said.

"I thank you for that."

"Look, have you thought about moving to Europe?" Jonathan asked.

Asmi narrowed her eyes. "Not really."

"I want to go home," Jonathan said. "Jerry wants to go home. I've told Gary to get me out of here by Christmas. He asked me who could replace me, and I said maybe you could. It's a lateral move but it's commercial and you'll have P&L responsibility."

But it's a lateral move and I want my next challenge, Asmi thought. What bothered her was that Jonathan didn't think she could get the VP of Marketing position. He was so sure she wouldn't get that job that he was offering her his job and he wanted her to be grateful for it.

Maybe you should see the writing on the wall, the Wicked Witch said and even though her voice was on low, Asmi could still hear her.

"Let's keep talking," Asmi said and looked at her watch. "I better go and prepare, I'm presenting next."

She went straight into the bathroom and called Cara.

"Is there something I don't know?" she asked after telling her what Scott and Jonathan had said to her.

"I *think,* and I have no proof but they're also looking outside," Cara said. "You know Max, he's the opposite of transparent. But what is Jonathan going to do here? We don't have an open position for him."

"I think he wants to swap jobs with me," Asmi said.

"He's not qualified for your job," Cara said and then sighed, "But if only qualified people got jobs, we'd have much fewer problems and far less need for HR."

"Do you think Scott's telling the truth that Matthew told him the job is his?"

"I doubt it," Cara said. "You know Scott, he likes to *hear* what he wants."

"He tried to physically block me today outside the hotel elevator," Asmi said. "I was just about ready to knee him in the nuts, but you'll be happy to know that I only did it verbally."

Cara laughed and was telling her a personal story about physical intimidation at the workplace when Asmi noticed herself in the bathroom mirror. She was wearing a black dress, her hair in a ponytail. She had on red lipstick. She smiled and saw herself, as she never had before, not *really,* a career woman who could slay dragons. How come she'd missed this about herself, she wondered? How had she not noticed that she, Asmi, was a powerhouse? When people told her she was smart, she never believed them. When they told her that she intimidated them, she decided that it was her fault and she needed to be softer. When they told her, she was a role model for many women associates, she imagined they were just being polite. But that was the Wicked Witch talking and now that she was silent, Asmi wondered what if it was true that she was smart, intelligent, tough, professional, intimidating and a role model?

"Anyway, I don't think Matthew has made any decisions yet," Cara said.

"Cara, I don't think it matters what Matthew said. What matters is that I want this job and I'm going to get it," Asmi said.

"Now you're talking. How are you going to do it?"

Asmi inhaled deep. *Chin up, shoulders squared, tits out.*

"I'm going to find out," Asmi said, feeling delirious with excitement.

THAT NIGHT AT DINNER, Asmi sat between Benedict, a sales manager from Bavaria, and Jonathan and wished she could've ordered room service instead. *But* that was not an option with a meeting such as this where you simply had to show up for dinner in the spirit of team building.

"How do you get along with Scott?" Jonathan asked as they watched Scott crack a joke at the other end of the table, making everyone around him laugh.

"Just fine," Asmi said.

"Really? I heard there was some friction and that you're probably leaving when Scott gets promoted," Jonathan said.

Why did everyone assume that Scott would get the job? Because she had not made it clear that she wanted it. That was it, wasn't it? Scott was behaving like the job was his and everyone assumed it was; and Asmi tiptoeing around the subject gave her an air of defeat.

"I don't think you should count your chickens until the fat lady sings," Asmi said.

Jonathan wrinkled his forehead. "I think you're mixing metaphors."

"I know," Asmi said. "The fact is that Matthew and the leadership team have not made a decision about the VP of Marketing position."

"Come on, Asmi, no offense but you know Matthew is going to give it to Scott. Everyone knows that," Jonathan said.

"Why? What does Scott bring to the table that is so amazing? My side of the business is doing better. My team is more engaged than his is and I'm not under investigation for a hostile work environment or have a lawsuit from a former associate," Asmi said.

Jonathan shifted uneasily. "All that may be true, but Scott is Matthew's boy. He hired him. He's been grooming him. He's not going to promote you over someone he's invested so much time and energy on."

"Jim hired Scott," Asmi said.

Jonathan shook his head. "It was Matthew...well, officially Jim but Matthew knows Scott's father very well. They're friends. Part of the same old boys' club. Don't tell me you didn't know. Everyone knows this."

So much for confidence, Asmi thought, feeling that balloon of exhilaration deflate inside her. The Wicked Witch laughed gleefully.

"I don't think that is common knowledge in HQ. How do you know this?" Asmi asked.

"Scott told me," Jonathan said, looking confused. "And...it's in the grapevine. That's why I thought you'd appreciate getting my job. You'd report to Gary and get away from Scott."

Asmi nodded. "Or find a job elsewhere. I'm told it's a candidate's market right now."

"You're not going to leave GTech, are you?" Jonathan said. "Come on, you're a lifer."

"Why would you think that?" Asmi asked surprised that this was how she was perceived, that she'd stay even if they humiliated her by giving her job to a nitwit like Scott.

"I don't know, it just...it just feels that way," Jonathan said, and then not very subtly, turned his attention to his companion on the other side to avoid any more uncomfortable conversations with Asmi.

Benedict, who wasn't much of a talker as he struggled with his English, ignored Asmi who sat through the meal, pondering her career, her life choices and not feeling good about any of it.

The Wicked Witch had found her voice...again.

AND THEN SHE SAID...WHY DO I NEED A MENTOR?

EXCERPT FROM THE BUSINESS WORKBOOK "AND THEN SHE SAID..."

WHEN I WAS A YOUNG PROFESSIONAL, a coach asked me to find myself a mentor in the organization. I didn't have the courage. I was afraid that the mentor would criticize me, and then, I feared critical feedback.

All our lives women have been told that we can do everything men can do, only better—and we want to prove it so badly that we're too afraid to be vulnerable in front of someone, allowing someone to see us and tell us what's wrong with us.

I got over it and got help and I've never looked back. Most of my career, I've had a mentor, a coach and a therapist—because I admit that I need a team to help me become the best version of myself. I'm not going to get there with mediocre managers and useless feedback, which is commonplace.

Women also struggle more than men when approaching someone to be a mentor, because we are asking someone to give us something for nothing. This makes women uncomfortable.

Mentor-mentee relationships may appear to be one-sided, but they're not. The mentor gets as much from the relationship as the mentee. The mentor is able to see things from a new perspective because of this relationship, the mentor (especially if within the company) discovers new talent that he or she can promote; and the mentor learns more about his or her own management style.

In addition, a mentor becomes your coach but can also grow into your sponsor. When there are new opportunities in the company or if a recruiter calls them about a position, they can help you get to your next step.

People ask me if women should have women as mentors and it simply depends upon what you're trying to achieve. Focus on what you want to achieve with a mentor and then find the best person who fits that profile regardless of their gender. However, it's easier to find male mentors than female ones in senior positions, because there just aren't enough of us in high enough positions.

~

How to get a mentor?

Here is a **five**-step approach that has never failed me:

1. **Know what you want.** This is the hardest part of the process. Before you even approach a potential mentor, you need to be clear about what you want to achieve. Example: I am low on self-confidence and I want to work with a mentor to improve how I handle myself in meetings and with superiors. Or, I'm perceived as being aggressive and intimidating; I need help in being perceived as softer. Or, I'm ready to take my next step but I don't know what it should be or how to get there.
2. **Find your mentor.** You can ask HR or the leaders in your organization to help you find a mentor. Say, if you want to get a role in branding, then it would be a good idea to find a mentor in the branding department if you don't work there. If you want to get leadership mentoring, it would be good to have a mentor who is

at least two levels above you and is from a completely different department. You can also find mentors outside the office, someone you met at a party who impressed you professionally, or someone in your network. Once you know what you want out of mentoring, you can identify the right person to help you.

3. **Approach your mentor**. If you've done step 1, then this is easy. Tell your mentor what you want to achieve and ask if they're interested. If they say yes (and most of them do), decide how often you'll meet and then invest time in getting to know each other.

4. **Use your mentor**. Go with a specific point to discuss at every meeting you have with a mentor. This is not a cup of coffee and a chat session. Be specific. Example: I have to coach an associate tomorrow whose performance has been dropping for the last few months. How do I do this? Or, I have a performance review with my manager tomorrow and I want to negotiate my salary. What is your advice on how to approach this?

5. **Pay it forward**. A good mentor can help you soar to great heights; and being a mentee is training you to become a mentor yourself. Officially, invite women to approach you if they want help. Unofficially, see your role as a mentor for colleagues and peers; this can be symbiotic, sometimes you will mentor them and sometimes they will mentor you.

19

THIS IS THE FINAL
BOARDING CALL FOR ALL
PASSENGERS

ASMI READ the email twice in the Lufthansa Senator's Lounge at the airport in Berlin. She and Scott had received an email the night before asking them to fly to Copenhagen from Berlin for a meeting about Short Poppy. Matthew wanted Scott and Asmi to present their case for how to manage the acquisition of Short Poppy, if he made the decision to acquire them. After the GTech meeting there would be a final meeting with Short Poppy where Matthew would reveal his decision. But Asmi felt that it was a done deal. Matthew wasn't listening to Asmi, Isadora or Darach, all of whom had who had spoken out against the acquisition.

The email had been crisp and from Celeste.

Dear Asmi and Scott,

Matthew apologizes for the short notice, but he requests you to attend a meeting with the GTech leadership team in Copenhagen the day after tomorrow. Since you're both in Berlin, please fly directly from there to Copenhagen. I can help you with airline tickets, so please get in touch with me.

For this meeting, please put together a strategy and implementation plan for how to merge Short Poppy commercial operations into GTech (see attached white paper and Short Poppy

organization presentation). Your presentation should be for thirty
minutes with another thirty minutes for Q&A.

The email went on to ask them about dietary requirements as
Celeste was making dinner reservations; and requested that they
send their presentations to Celeste the night before the meeting
so Matthew would have time to review them.

It wasn't the first time that something like this had popped
up on short notice and every time, Asmi would pack her bags
like a good soldier and show up.

She now had a great excuse to not attend her birthday party
at Ananya's house with their parents. But she was loathe to call
her sister who had been texting about what kind of cake Asmi
wanted and she had indicated that there was a big birthday
present surprise awaiting her, as well.

Her job was important to her and this was an important
meeting. Obviously, the last of the *Hunger Games* contests that
Scott and she would compete directly in. But Ananya was also
important. Asmi's birthday was important. She didn't want to
give up her life and for what? If not attending this meeting
meant she wouldn't get the VP position, then so be it. She was
turning forty. She wanted to be with her family.

Hi Matthew,

*I'm afraid that I'm unable to change my plans to come to
Copenhagen. I have made plans with my family in Milpitas, which I
cannot cancel. I apologize for any inconvenience this causes.*

*Attached, please find my presentation. I will be happy to call into
the meeting and present via Skype and take questions from the team. I
hope this will be possible.*

Best regards,

Asmi

She didn't hear back from Matthew until after she landed.
The response was brief.

No to Skype. Presentation is okay. We will use it without you.
  Matthew

∞

"Forty," Asmi said, looking at the chocolate cake Ananya had ordered from Bijan Bakery on Market Street, her favorite place to binge on pastries. Ananya had somehow managed to get forty candles on the cake and had lit all of them without setting off any of the smoke alarms.

"Happy Birthday to you," Anjali and Arjun sang while Ananya and Venkat watched Asmi and Ananya's parents warily.

Madhuri was evidently not happy. Her daughter was now forty years old and *still* single, Asmi knew her mother was disappointed.

"You'll never have children now," she had said to Asmi while Ananya had lit the candles.

"I don't want children," Asmi said. *Did I really ditch Copenhagen for this?*

"How can you talk like this?" Madhuri cried out. "You're a strange woman, I'll tell you that."

"Okay," Asmi said and then looked at Ananya angrily, her look saying clearly: *Is this what you made me come here for?*

Ananya and Venkat had bought Asmi *Hamilton* tickets for December in New York. As Ananya focused on lighting the candles, Venkat handed the envelope to Asmi.

"Two for you and two for us," Ananya said excited. "The kids won't be coming."

"I need to bring a plus one?"

"It's in December, you have two months," Ananya said. "Plenty of time."

"Time for what?" Madhuri said, wiping her face with the *pallu* of her sari. "She's like a wilted flower."

Asmi raised her eyebrows at that. "Say what?"

"Well, you are," Madhuri said. "You're forty years old."

"Yes, *Amma*, I get it," Asmi said, losing her patience. "I know

272

I'm forty. I know that I'm *never* finding a man or getting married, because the only man who seems to be interested in me is married to another woman. To top it all, I just ditched an important meeting to come here and, in any case, it doesn't matter because my CEO is probably going to give that VP position to his friend's son. So yeah, I'm forty and a failure. If I can learn to live with it, so can you."

Her mother pursed her lips then and walked out of the living room. No one chased after her to bring her back. There was no point. She wouldn't be happy if someone went after her and she wouldn't be happy if someone didn't go after her; and both Asmi and Ananya had had enough practice in this area to know that not dealing with their mother when she was in such a mood was the better option.

Asmi blew out the candles and then hugged her niece and nephew who whisked themselves away to their rooms with their slices of cake.

"Your mother says these things because she's worried about you," Asmi's father said to her as he stuck a fork into the red velvet cake.

"There's no need for anyone to worry about me," Asmi said, licking cream cheese off a finger. "Things may not be looking up right now, but I at least have my health."

"I CAN'T BREATHE," Asmi said as she woke Ananya up at four in the morning. "I mean...I think I'm getting enough oxygen, but I feel like I'm not. I just can't seem to get..." She struggled to breathe again. "It's been going on since I went to bed and my ribs are hurting now." There were tears in her eyes.

"Okay," Ananya said, sitting up. Despite the commotion, Venkat hadn't even moved in his sleep. Ananya pushed him. "Venky, wake up."

Asmi struggled to breathe. She felt like the oxygen was not going into her lungs and she could only take shallow breaths.

But with every breath, she struggled to drag in air and every time she *just* couldn't. It was exhausting.

It had begun when she went to bed and checked her email on her phone. Since she had blocked Etienne's number he couldn't call or text her, but he could send emails to her because she hadn't blocked that and he had, to wish her a happy birthday. That email was followed by a text message from Levi who also wished her a happy birthday.

She deleted Etienne's email and responded to Levi's with a simple: *Thank you.*

Etienne had sent her a few emails since Rome—first asking her to come back and then saying he understood and promised to stay away from her. He had kept his promise for a good two weeks at least. Asmi deleted all his emails and didn't respond to them. Something inside her had clicked and she didn't care one way or the other about Etienne. Sometimes, when a door closes, you want to get a hammer and nails to make sure that bitch stays shut. This was one of those doors.

How did you celebrate your birthday? Levi wanted to know.

With my parents and sister's family. My mother is distressed that I'm never getting married or giving birth.

She didn't say that to you, did she?

Yes, directly.

That's harsh. Well, I think you're a wonderful, capable, beautiful and sexy woman and now an official cougar.

It's been a dream I had since I was a little girl.

He called her then.

"How are you?" he asked.

"I'm good," Asmi said.

"I've missed you," Levi said. "I didn't think I would, but I did. I...wanted to reach out but I felt maybe you didn't want it."

"I don't know what I want," Asmi said.

"Are you seeing someone else?" Levi asked.

"No," Asmi said.

"Well...I just wanted to say Happy Birthday."

They stayed on the line silent and as Asmi felt he was about to say something to end the call, she asked, on impulse, without thinking, "Hey, Levi. Are you free on December sixteenth?"

"Specifically?"

"Yes," Asmi said. "My sister got me two *Hamilton* tickets in New York and I'm inviting you…officially."

"You do know that December is like two months away?"

And that's when the breathing problem had started, mildly at first.

"Yes, I know."

She heard Levi whistle. "That's some commitment."

"It's just a musical," Asmi said, trying to sound casual.

"Okay, December sixteenth in New York. It's a date," Levi said.

The breathing problem got worse after she ended the phone call and when she still couldn't sleep or breathe at four in the morning, she was half hysterical with frustration and aching ribs.

"You get the kids out of the house in the morning," Ananya said to Venkat as she got out of bed. "I'm taking her to the ER. Don't tell the parents anything."

Ananya drove Asmi to the ER at Good Samaritan Hospital. They'd been there a few times before, usually with Arjun or Anjali when they were little.

"Do you think something is *really* wrong with me?" Asmi asked tearfully as they walked in.

"No," Ananya said and put her arm around her sister. "You're going to be just fine. It's probably allergies or mold or something."

It wasn't a long wait in the ER because at five in the morning the peak hours had passed. A nurse checked Asmi's vitals as she asked her what was going on. She went through her checklist while Ananya stroked Asmi's back, worried but stoic.

The nurse asked Asmi to lie down on a bed and asked them to wait until a doctor could come by to check on her. Asmi couldn't lie down so she sat up on the bed.

"You poor thing," Ananya said as she watched Asmi struggle to drag air in. "Has this ever happened before?"

"No," Asmi said. "Well...never like this. Occasionally, I'll feel I'm not getting enough oxygen and then after a short while I'm fine. But not like this...for hours...until my ribs hurt."

The doctor was a young intern who asked the nurse to run several blood tests, an EKG, lung x-rays, and a few other tests. Ananya wanted to know details, which the doctor patiently gave.

"What do you think could be wrong?" Ananya asked.

"We'll find out," the doctor said.

"Am I going to die?" Asmi asked.

"Oh, you're such a drama queen," Ananya said and then looked at the doctor, "Is she?"

The doctor laughed. "I doubt it," she said. "Let's do the tests and then we'll see. Okay?"

Two hours, several blood tests, a urine test, a lung x-ray, an EKG, a CPAP mask, which was an antihistamine mask later, Asmi still couldn't get enough oxygen into her lungs. Ananya stood next to her, looking very concerned, texting furiously with Venkat to keep him abreast of Asmi's health.

They were separated from the other patients by one of those shower curtain type things. The doctor came back, secured the curtain and looked through the results of Asmi's tests.

"Good news, everything looks good," she said cheerfully.

"Then why isn't she *feeling* good?" Ananya asked.

"Are you on any anti-depressants?" the doctor asked.

"No," Asmi said. "My therapist and I have talked about it in the past, but not lately."

The doctor put the file with Asmi's tests on the foot of the bed and pulled up a chair.

"You should sit as well," she gestured to the other chair.

Ananya sat down very tentatively. "What's wrong? Just tell us."

The doctor only smiled and looked at Asmi. "I see that it was your birthday yesterday. Happy Birthday."

Asmi nodded, slowly gulping in air.

"And you're a marketing director," the doctor continued. "Is your job stressful?"

"No more than any other job," Asmi said.

"What?" Ananya scowled. "Her job is *very stressful*. She works all the time. She travels all the time. She was in Brazil and then Berlin and then she's here and next week somewhere else. She's always jets lagged."

"I don't do jet lag," Asmi said.

"How's your sleep?" the doctor asked.

Asmi sighed as understanding dawned. "This is a panic attack, isn't it?"

"Yes, it looks like it," the doctor said. "Why do you think you're so anxious?"

Ananya looked confused. "Are you saying there's nothing physically wrong with her?"

The doctor grinned. "I don't believe so."

Ananya slumped in her chair in relief. "Panic attack I can handle. Lung cancer...now that would be a whole other thing." She texted Venkat, presumably to tell him that Asmi was fine.

"I think I...turned forty and..." Asmi shrugged as she drew a long breath, which she could take all the way into her chest. One out of about ten or fifteen breaths would bring relief instead of frustration. Her eyes filled with tears at her stupidity. This was the dumbest reason ever to have a panic attack.

"I think you should talk to your therapist and see if your doctor thinks you should have anti-depressants," the doctor suggested. "For now, I'm going to give you a Benzodiazepine. That should take the edge off. I would recommend psychotherapy, but you already have a therapist."

Asmi nodded. "I'm so embarrassed."

"That you had a panic attack because you turned forty?" Ananya asked and when Asmi nodded, she said, "As you should be. Worrying us for nothing."

∿

ASMI'S MOTHER blamed herself for Asmi's "breathing problems." But once she was reassured that Asmi was alright, she blamed Asmi for it because she worked too hard and traveled too much and didn't have a man.

"If you were married, you'd have someone else earning, as well, and then you wouldn't have to work so hard," Madhuri said while Ananya handed Asmi her third cup of *calming* chamomile tea.

"It's talk like this that is stressing her out," Ananya told Madhuri. "You can stay here with her if you say nice things. Otherwise, you have to leave her alone."

"I'm her mother and I can say what I want to her," Madhuri said.

But Ananya was in lion mother mode and no one was going to cross her, not even her own mother.

"Leave her alone," Ananya repeated. "She already has a tough life with a tough career, and we need to be supportive."

"I'm supportive," Madhuri said. "I'm trying to find her a husband."

"She doesn't want to get married, *Amma*," Ananya said. "She doesn't think it's necessary."

"Everyone has to get married and…"

"No," Ananya interrupted her mother. "Not everyone. Asmi will do what she wants to do. Look at her, Amma! She's beautiful. She makes a shit ton of money. She has a great apartment in Laguna Beach. You really think that she'd be single if she didn't want to be? If she wanted to get married, she could get married tomorrow."

"I could?" Asmi asked.

"Drink your tea," Ananya said. "*Amma*, she doesn't want to get married and have children. And what does one get from marriage? Is it really that great?"

"I can hear you," Venkat called out from the adjoining dining room where he was working on his computer.

"Good," Ananya said. "Marriage isn't all that terrific so if you want me to stay, Venky, you should put some effort into it... you know-put your back into it."

"Look at how you talk to your husband," Madhuri said.

"*Amma*, our marriage is different than your marriage. Asmi's life is different from my life and your life," Ananya said. "It's not for you to judge."

Madhuri stood up angrily. "I don't need to be treated with such disrespect. We will see if we can change our tickets and leave early."

Both Ananya and Asmi could see that their mother was waiting for a long moment for one of them to say, *no, no, you should stay* but when neither of them spoke up, she stomped out of the living room.

Ananya slowly lifted her shoulders and let them drop. "Wow."

"No kidding," Asmi said. "I should go to the emergency room more often if you're going to turn into such a firebrand."

"Do you think they'll change their tickets?" Ananya asked.

"Don't get your hopes up," Asmi said. "She doesn't want to go to India when she can stay here and make your life miserable. And then there is that wedding, they want to attend. I know Daddy doesn't want to go home because then he'll be alone with her. She'll find a way to save face about changing the tickets."

"I bet she's going to say it's too expensive to change the tickets...but then I can say I'll just give her the money," Ananya said.

"You won't do that," Asmi said and pulled her sister down next to her on the couch. She hugged her. "Thank you for being such an awesome big sister."

Ananya pulled away and kissed Asmi on her forehead. "You have to take better care of yourself. I got scared, Asmi. I mean, I'd prefer if it was something physical, you know? Something we could fix with a pill or an injection. But you've driven yourself so hard with this VP position nonsense that it's hurting you physically. You have to get this under control."

"You're right," Asmi said. "And after all this, I don't even get the job."

"The hell with that job, there are plenty others," Ananya said.

Asmi put her head on her sister's shoulder. "I know."

THAT NIGHT when they sat outside with their glasses of scotch and Asmi's breathing was under control, Venkat toasted to Asmi's better health.

"You need to not let the job become your life," Venkat said. "Work-life balance isn't just about having time to go to the gym and seeing friends, it's about keeping your life in perspective."

"I like my job, Venky," Asmi said. "And I'm going to be devastated when they officially give Scott the job."

"Who cares?" Venkat said. "This gives you time to…travel… wait, you do that all the time, so…maybe now you have time to sit at home doing nothing. Walk on the beach. Take a month off."

"What nonsense," Ananya said. "Why shouldn't she be ambitious?"

"It's giving her panic attacks," Venkat said.

"I think that's more because she hit the big four O," Ananya said. "You *should* take a month off. I fully agree. Just to catch up on sleep, if nothing else. But I think it's fair that you feel bad about losing the job to that asshole. You worked hard for it."

"But I'm still not getting the job," Asmi said.

"You don't know that," Ananya said.

"Yes, I do. I ditched that Short Poppy meeting in Copenhagen. Matthew pretty much told me to not worry about presenting there…so…I'm not keeping my hopes up," Asmi said.

"Work isn't everything," Venkat said.

"To you," Ananya said. "And that's fine, babe. But for Asmi, her job makes her happy."

"Does it?" Venkat asked. "Really? Does she look happy?"

"She's excited when she talks about work," Ananya said angrily. "She's *my* sister so butt out."

"I think she needs to find a less stressful job and..."

"No way," Ananya said. "She needs to find her next challenge. If she finds a less stressful job, she'll die of boredom."

"But she'll at least be able to breathe," Venkat said. "Let's face it, that's a basic necessity for life."

"Guys, I think this discussion is moot right now," Asmi said and raised her glass. "I'll probably take a month off and find a new job. But it's going to take a while to find the *right* new job. I'm going to start reaching out to headhunters."

"Smart move," Ananya said.

"I'm glad you'll get some time off to rest and recuperate," Venkat said.

They touched their glasses together and chorused, "Cheers... to better living through whiskey."

AND THEN SHE SAID...WHY SHOULD THEY GIVE ME THAT JOB?

EXCERPT FROM THE BUSINESS WORKBOOK "AND THEN SHE SAID..."

LET'S CHANGE THAT TO, "why should I take this job?"

Men apply for a job when they meet only 60% of the qualifications, but women apply only if they meet 100% of them[1]. So, if you made it to the interview, you're already qualified for the job. Interviews are not just about them interviewing you; it's about you vetting them and making sure it's the right place to be. You could be in the worst job possible, but your situation isn't going to get any better just because you end up in another bad place. Of course, if you're desperate (we all have bills to pay), make sure you get the best package you can to be able to stand the not-so-great place...for a while at least.

Here are **five** tips to nail any interview and ensure that you know what you're getting into (I'm not going to include the basics: take a shower, wear clothes with no stains, don't wear a pair of shorts or a blouse out of which your tits are hanging out, be on time and other interview hygiene points):

1. **Prepare. Prepare. Prepare.** An HR director once asked me to reject a candidate because she couldn't talk about our company's products cohesively. She had not done her basic online research. Do all the research that

you can about the company. Read the job description 10 times or more and make sure you are prepared to answer all the questions you can imagine being asked. Talk to people who have similar jobs in other companies (use your LinkedIn network) and talk to people who work at the new company. If you're interviewing for an in-house position, talk to the person who had/has the job or a similar one. Get all the skinny on the job, the interviewer (I even do FB and Twitter searches) and the company.

2. **Storytelling to win.** People forget what you say and remember how you made them feel. Stories have that power. When they ask, "Tell me about the last time you failed at a project at work," you better have a good and juicy story to tell them. A story has a beginning, a middle and an end—and you must **prepare** the stories in advance. Write them down so you become familiar with them and practice them with a friend to make sure you tell them well. Make a mind map and connect each required experience and personality point on the job description to a story that extolls your professional virtues and shows them who you truly are.

3. **Dress to...be comfortable.** I have a gray sheath dress that I love but every time I wear it, I feel the need to suck my stomach in. I have a pair of black pants that I love, but I fidget with my jacket because I'm afraid everyone can see how I lost the battle of the bulge. Dressing for an interview is an art. Your company research will tell you how conservative the company is —because you don't want to go for an interview to a company, where the hiring manager is wearing a pair of jeans and you showed up in your new gray Tahari suit. Balance comfort with confidence. You are comfortable in a pair of yoga pants, but you are not professionally confident in them. Vanity be damned,

try on the clothes before the interview so you know what you're wearing and how you feel in them. Shoes should make you feel good about yourself—not pinch in all the wrong places.

4. **Be authentic**. If you pretend to be someone else to get a job, they will eventually find out who you are. I recommend that you be more you at an interview than anywhere else. You don't want to get the job and then have them say, "I thought she was a shy person; and now I see she's the aggressive type." If the company doesn't want to hire your type of person, give them a pass and move on. This means no lying. It doesn't get you anywhere. No fabricating. Why bother to do that? You be you. If the job is right, you'll get it. If the job is wrong, you may still get it, but I hope you'll turn it down.

5. **They interview you. You interview them.** Most interviews end with the interviewer asking if you have any questions for them. Have at least four good ones. Focus on the most important things: leadership style, manager personality, development, diversity, and culture. Here are some examples:

1. How many women are in leadership positions in the organization and the team?
2. What is your leadership philosophy?
3. How do you deal with conflict amongst associates?
4. What does diversity and inclusion mean to you?
5. How do you handle it when an associate challenges you?
6. What kind of career path would someone in this role have?

20

THE NEAREST EXIT MAY BE
BEHIND YOU

ASMI FELT good as she got off her flight at SNA (John Wayne International Airport). She'd sent a message to Jo Shaw, the recruiter she'd met in Rome via LinkedIn when she had boarded her flight at SJC (San Jose International Airport).

Her message had been short:

I have the Wicked Witch on permanently low volume. I'm cured of the self-doubt disease and am ready for the next step. If you have any VP Marketing positions in the biotech or life sciences space, let's talk.

Jo responded by the time she landed:

Send me current CV and career profile...how about a chat on Friday at 9 a.m. EST?

Asmi set up an appointment with Jo and felt a burden lift off her shoulders. She now had a plan B. She had a plan C (sell apartment and travel around until money runs out). She even had a plan D—Ananya's guest room.

CARA CALLED while Asmi was unpacking. "Are you home?'

"Yes."

"I'm bringing greasy Chinese takeout. I need to vent."

"I'll get a bottle of red wine breathing. I think I have a Barolo."

They sat in the living room on Asmi's sole couch with the Chinese takeout spread on the coffee table.

"You have no furniture," Cara said, looking around Asmi's apartment.

It was a small one-bedroom apartment *with a view*. The kitchen, dining area and living space were all one large space. Asmi had never bought a dining table and instead put two bar stools against the counter. They were *nice* barstools that she had paid handsomely for. The couch was perfect for snuggling down and watching the Pacific from and she could fall asleep on it without any neck-aches in the morning. The scuffed coffee table had come from an antique store and was at the right height for Asmi to put her feet up on while she worked on her laptop.

She had bought a television, finally, the past summer when she had come down with the flu and realized that there was something immensely cozy about lying on the couch, binge-watching *Scandal* as she came in and out of fever and delirium.

As a rule, Asmi *always* bought flowers on Saturday if she was at home from the flower shop down the street. Usually lilies or roses and put them in a tall vase (her only) that stood by the television. She had invested in comfortable wooden furniture with thick cushions for her balcony, as well as an infrared heater for the evenings when it was cooling, which was most of fall, winter and spring.

She had no nicks and knacks, except for a metal bowl on the kitchen counter that held her keys. She had bought the bowl in South Africa, made by some local designer and was shaped like a woman holding up her hands.

The kitchen was functional and Asmi could cook a meal. Her bedroom was functional. She had a comfortable mattress atop a minimalist Japanese-style wooden bed. She didn't have a bedside table because the bed was so close to the floor. This meant that she had to store her vibrator in her closet, which was a walk-in. Her pride and joy was the bathroom. It had a wall of glass, a shower that kicked ass *and* the best part…heated floors for cold mornings.

Asmi loved her apartment and loved how she had made it hers—even if it was too much wood and not on track with Master Dingbat's Feng Shui aesthetic. Maybe too much wood was good for her. It made her aggressive, made her fight a little harder. The male-dominated world she lived and worked in required women to have sharp elbows or they'd be smothered.

When she bought the apartment, it had been a sign of her success. She had bought one of those *elegant* apartments that wealthy guys in movies have, like those hedge fund guys in *Sex and the City*.

"I have the furniture I need," Asmi said to Cara. "I love this apartment, but I wonder if it's now a noose around my neck. If I didn't have this place, I could just quit my job and maybe travel for a while and then go live with Ananya for a few months. Slowly find a new job until the money runs out."

"Try having a husband on minimum wage, two dogs and one horse," Cara said. "I'm stuck. And I hate what's going on at GTech."

"What happened?"

Cara sucked a noodle and wiped her mouth. "They closed the investigation against Scott and his team. The concluded there is *no* harassment. There are issues with behavior in the leadership team, they're going to get written up, and they're going to have to do trust exercises, 360-degree assessments, coaching *blah blah* but…"

Asmi set down her chopsticks and took a sip of her Barolo.

"I thought they'd fire Scott," Cara said.

"That was never going to happen," Asmi said. "I had thought there would be some warning letters, some team building exercise and some sensitivity training and that's what's happening."

Cara shrugged. "This is entirely unsatisfactory."

"Why? You know the drill," Asmi said.

Cara shook her head. "I'm drained, Asmi. I'm tired of the corporate nonsense. I feel that it's impossible to be a woman in the workplace. Even if I move jobs and it would be the same shit. Same gender inequality."

"Yep...I think GTech is quite normal. This is how companies are around the country...some may have more inequality than others, but it's there and it's up to us to bring change," Asmi said. "That's why I make it my job to help grow women. I mean, people like you, me and Isadora, ...you know...director level and above, we're okay. I can get an executive coach and have someone help me grow. But regular women like...Meena who's a middle manager...she doesn't get much coaching. All the books and podcasts are all about how to become an entrepreneur and how to break the glass ceiling. But Meena doesn't want to break the ceiling. Leanne in Customer Service doesn't want to break the ceiling; she just wants to go from customer service representative to marketing specialist. Who's going to coach her?"

Cara tucked her feet under her thighs and leaned against the pillows.

"Her manager should coach her," Cara said and then sighed. "But most managers are awful leaders and worse coaches."

"That's why we have to invest time in women across the organization regardless of the level they're at," Asmi said.

Cara nodded. "You helped Leticia."

"I feel there needs to be a way for everyday women to get affordable career coaching," Asmi said. "How many people can afford thousands of dollars for an executive coach?"

"Women like you and me and Isadora," Cara said. "And only because our companies pay for it."

"But what about the women like Leanne? The company is not going to pay for a customer service rep to have an executive coach."

Cara picked up her bag and pulled out a small purse. "I think this needs some extra help."

She pulled out her weed vape device PAX and dug around for her personal phone. "I keep the PAX app on my personal phone."

"You need an app?"

"To turn it on," Cara nodded and then pulled out small capsules that attached to the device. "Hmm...what should we have?"

Asmi leaned over to read the letters on the capsules. One read *Back Ache*, one read *Sleep*, and another read *Sex*.

"Does this work?"

"Oh yes," Cara said and picked up one that said *Creativity*. She loaded up the PAX and used her phone to light it up. She took two puffs and handed it to Asmi who tentatively took the device.

"How does this thing work?"

"Just puff," Cara said. "Twice. No more. The temperature is at 640 so it's hot enough."

"I have no idea what any of that means," Asmi said and took two puffs. She inhaled and exhaled. "Wow. This is so neat. No smell. You can smoke it at home without stinking the place up."

Cara nodded.

"Should we clear up the food?" Asmi asked.

Cara shook her head and pointed to the PAX. "I think we'll get our second wind."

AFTER A WHILE, they went outside and got cozy under the infrared with a blanket on one of Asmi's comfortable outdoor couches. Their feet touched underneath the blanket as they leaned against the cushions on either side of the couch. They had now lit a hybrid Indica-Sativa joint and were passing it back-and-forth.

"I feel *soooo* relaxed," Asmi said.

"Yeah, me too," Cara said.

"Hey, what happened to the DuPont job?"

"I turned them down," Cara said. "I like the hiring manager even less than I like Max."

"Known devil versus unknown devil?"

"It's too much like this job," Cara said.

Asmi took a puff and handed the joint to Cara. They sat in silence, listening to the waves against the beach and smelling the distinct mustiness of cannabis.

"You're a good coach, Cara, I wish we could bottle that up and give it to others," Asmi said.

"There are some good coaches at GTech. You, Isadora, Gary... there are many middle managers," Cara said. "It's not all bad. I just wish we could help those who don't have good leaders to guide them."

"You know, I've always wanted to write a career coaching workbook for women," Asmi said. "How to negotiate? How to not say you're sorry all day long? How to deal with a boss like Scott? How to stand up for yourself? How to get a seat at the table? How to get the next step?"

"How is this different from books like *Lean In* or *Corner Office blah blah* or what have you?" Cara asked, holding on to the joint as she tried to speculate on Asmi's idea.

"It's...affordable career coaching for the everyday woman," Asmi said. "Not about becoming VP or making CEO but just... you know, taking that small next step. Negotiating an extra thousand dollars. Dealing with an asshole boss without blowing your career. Stuff that all women need to know regardless of position but maybe someone at our level is better equipped to deal with than someone who's at the bottom of the corporate ladder."

Cara sat up, joint in hand. "Add affordable career coaching to the workbook," she said excitedly.

"Give women a chance," Asmi said, taking the joint from Cara's hand before it fell down. She tapped it out on the ashtray.

"We can start our own business—affordable coaching for women. We can offer online coaching, workbook-style coaching, face to face coaching," Cara said. She sat still for a moment and then smiled. "I even have a name for the company. *And Then She Said....*"

"Said what?"

"All the things we say. And then she said, *I'm sorry,* and then she said, *I can't do this,* and then she said, *I'm not enough.*"

Asmi considered it for a moment and nodded. "I like it."

"How do we get started?"

"We need a business plan," Asmi said. "We need to write the workbook...maybe find a way to publish it and...start small. Start with a handful of clients while we work for GTech."

"How much money would we need to fund this?"

Asmi shrugged. "I don't know. Depends upon what we want to do...we need to research the market, as well. How does one become a coach? Do you need a particular education or certification? A business case can guide us through that."

"I'm certified up the wazoo for leadership coaching. But I don't know how to write a book," Cara said. "I don't even know how to write a business case."

"Business case I can do. Book...I have no idea," Asmi said and then added, "Between us we've read a lot of business books. We can figure it out and maybe Levi can help us. He's a writer."

"Are you still seeing him?" Cara asked.

"I have a date with him on December 16th in New York. *And* this would be an excellent excuse to reach out to him," Asmi said. "Maybe it's a good thing they'll give that job to Scott. Maybe the universe is saying we need to start *And Then She Said....* There is this Sanskrit saying, *Om Tat Sat.* It means the absolute truth, that you're exactly where you're supposed to be. Maybe all this is happening for a reason."

"You know what they say, what doesn't kill you, gives you unhealthy coping mechanisms," Cara said.

ASMI WASN'T sure if it was the weed or their discussion but she had a spring in her step when she got to work the following day. Cara admitted it was the same for her. They decided to work on the business case for *And Then She Said…* the following weekend. A project they could nurse for the next several months to see if it held merit.

"There's fall in the air," Cara said with a smile.

Asmi grinned. "Two weeks ago, we had 100-degree days."

"That was September. It's October now and I'm ready to put on my boots and Cashmere sweaters," Cara said. "To feel cozy."

"While we hang out on my balcony," Asmi suggested. "And work on our new business idea."

"We're going to do this, yes?"

"Of course," Asmi said. "I can't remember being this excited about anything in a long time."

Asmi found Gustav waiting in her office. There was a crisis and Asmi was happy for the diversion because what she hadn't told Cara was that she had been invited for a meeting with Matthew Baines for the following day and the subject line on the meeting request was: *1-on-1 Meeting/Career Development Discussion.*

This was it. *Hunger Games* was over, and she was about to lose her life so to speak, the odds were not in her favor. A part of her had thought that the HR investigation would find something determinedly awful about Scott, but realistically she knew that nothing came out of HR investigations, ever.

She'd also heard from the grapevine that the acquisition of *Short Poppy* would be going through. She expected Matthew to chastise her again for her negative attitude. She wanted to call Isadora for coaching but didn't feel she'd get much out of a conversation right now. She had to prepare for this meeting with Matthew—just her, from within.

But what if Matthew offered her the job?

Highly doubtful, the Wicked Witch said.

Asmi managed to get home at a decent hour so she had time to get her hair fixed and her nails done. Fire engine red!

That evening while lying on her couch on the balcony

admiring her red toes, she called Ananya to tell her about the meeting with Matthew.

"What are you going to wear?" Ananya asked.

"Something feminine but professional," Asmi said.

"Good."

"What if he offers me the job?" Asmi asked.

"Not what but when. And when he does, you make sure you get a good solid bump in your salary," Ananya said.

"When I told you that *And Then She Said* excited me in a way nothing else has in a long time, I was serious. It excites me more than a VP position," Asmi said.

"Does it, or is it a defense mechanism to prepare yourself for not getting the job?

Asmi sighed. "You think that I want to like this other thing so that the disappointment of not getting the VP position won't hurt too much."

"There's nothing wrong in having a plan B."

"What if I get the job?"

"Then you do the *And Then She Said* thing and the hotshot VP job. Can't you do both?" Ananya asked.

"I don't know," Asmi said. "I've always wanted to write a business book."

"I've always wanted you to write a business book," Ananya said. "You'll be great at it."

"But a new VP position will be so much work," Asmi said. "It'll be intense, as it should be."

"Then you'll figure out how to write this book while working intensely," Ananya said. "Asmi, I believe this more than you do but I believe it with all my heart: there is absolutely *nothing* you can't do."

"You're always on my team, Ana," Asmi said. "Thank you."

"Oh, don't get all sappy, and get some sleep," Ananya said. "You don't want to be groggy tomorrow. I know you're stressed out right now but find a way to calm yourself down so you can sleep."

Asmi looked at the half-smoked joint in the ashtray from the previous night. "I think I have something to relax me."

She followed the joint with a call to Levi and FaceTime Video sex.

IF YOU'VE EVER SAID, "WHY SHOULD THEY HIRE ME?" REPEAT AFTER ME

EXCERPT FROM THE BUSINESS WORKBOOK "AND THEN SHE SAID..."

- Why should I say yes to this job?
- This job is mine to win or lose—I'm in control
- I'm not afraid of not getting a job; there will be others
- I will prepare my ass off for this interview and impress the socks off the interviewers
- I will get this job if I want this job

21

BOARDING PASS AND PASSPORT, PLEASE

ASMI HEARD MATTHEW SAY, *come in* and her Chanel Gold Edinburgh Charm Leather Bracelet made a tinkling sound as she opened the door to his office and stepped in. She felt the blue suede fringes of her shoes against her feet. She felt her green dress scrape gently over the skin of her stomach. Her pearl earrings caressed her cheek.

"Hi, Matthew, how are you doing?" Asmi said ebulliently.

Matthew smiled and nodded and gestured for Asmi to take a seat.

The corner office was imposing with a glass wall. It had the money shot of Orange County and on a clear day, you could see all the way to Catalina.

The day was a bright and cloudless one. Catalina was all beautiful shadows in the distance.

"How are you doing?" he asked conversationally.

"Good."

Matthew looked around his desk for something and then found a notebook that he opened.

"What do you think this conversation is about?"

"It said career development discussion so I'm assuming we're talking about my career development," Asmi said, feeling more relaxed than she expected. If this didn't work out, she had a call booked with Jo Shaw for the end of the week. There would be something on the horizon. She wasn't worried.

"What do you think should be your next move?" Matthew asked.

Asmi didn't take a deep breath. She didn't shuffle her feet or sit up straight. She didn't fumble. She didn't even have to reduce the volume on the Wicked Witch.

"I believe I should be the next Vice President of Marketing for GTech," she said.

"Why?" Matthew asked.

"Because I'm not only the most qualified person for the position, I believe I'm also the right fit with the leadership team," Asmi said. "I'm an associate's leader. I develop my people and I hire good talent. I work well across departments. I know marketing, I know GTech, and I understand the vision for the company. I know how to strategize for maximum impact, and I know how to deliver on that strategy by building a high-performance team."

Matthew watched Asmi intently as she spoke, and she didn't break eye contact until she was done even though it was disconcerting.

"What keeps you up at night, Asmi?"

"My people."

Matthew furrowed his forehead. "I expect leaders to say numbers."

"I believe that if people are engaged then the numbers will happen."

Matthew nodded.

"Oh, before I forget, I wanted to check in with you about *Short Poppy*," he said.

"I'm sorry I couldn't make the meeting," Asmi said.

Matthew waved his hand. "I liked your presentation. But *now* that we've gone through a due diligence and vetting process, what do you think?"

"I still think that they're not ready for us and if we want to get into aggrotech, we should acquire a more mature company," Asmi said.

"You won't change your mind about it?"

"Even though I don't agree with you I'll do everything I can to make it work...once the decision is made," Asmi said. "But you're asking for my opinion right now and that's what you're getting."

Matthew nodded and then seemed distracted as he looked through his desk again and then called Celeste on the phone. "I can't find that *damn* envelope."

Celeste came into the room and walked straight up to Matthew's desk and pulled out an envelope from under a sheet of paper.

"You should get glasses. You're getting old," Celeste quipped and walked out of there.

"Stop barking at me," Matthew said jovially as she closed the door shut.

Asmi had to close her mouth before it dropped open. No one, but no one talked to Matthew like this. She'd never expected the soft-spoken Celeste to speak to Matthew like this. But she was his assistant and seeing this interaction made Matthew more human.

"Ah," Matthew said as he peeked into the envelope. He smiled at Asmi. "Welcome to the leadership team. Here is your contract."

Move your hand, Asmi or say something, anything and don't babble. Don't say what. Don't say wow or something equally banal. Say something smart.

"Wow," Asmi said as she took the envelope from Matthew.

"Look at it after you get to your office and negotiate with Max. I stay out of the negotiations for the leadership team," Matthew said.

Asmi stared at the envelope and then at Matthew.

"Once you accept and sign on the dotted line, I'll make an announcement that you are our new Global Vice President of Marketing for GTech," Matthew said. "You have to decide how to handle Scott because he's going to be in your management team. What will you do with your team? Is Gustav ready?"

Asmi shook her head. "Not yet. In a couple of years."

"What's your plan?"

"I was thinking of bringing Shruti to the US," Asmi said.

Matthew nodded. "Good idea. She's high potential. What will you do about Scott?"

"I'll find out if he's coachable," Asmi said.

"Excellent answer," Matthew said.

Asmi was about to say thank you and stand up when she put the envelope back down on the table. "I need some time off before I start."

"How much?"

"Two months...I have enough vacation saved up," Asmi said. "I'll set up Shruti to take over for me and then I can start on the first of January."

Matthew leaned back on the chair. "That's a ballsy request. Most people I know would jump in, head first."

"I need some R&R. Health first. And I have these Hamilton tickets for December that I want to use." *Sometimes, a woman needed to just take care of herself.*

Neither of them spoke for a long moment.

"Okay," Matthew said. "Jim officially retires in December, so it should be fine."

Asmi picked up the envelope and then because she couldn't resist it, asked, "Why me?"

Matthew grinned as if he was waiting for that question.

"Because as you said, you're the most qualified person at GTech for the job. We all knew that. But we didn't know if you had what it takes to make the leadership team. I tested you. You handled yourself in Las Vegas. You stuck to your guns with *Short Poppy* no matter how much I said I wanted to do it. You handled yourself in Sweden with Darach and Max. You handled yourself with Scott...good luck managing him and that dysfunctional team of his. You handled yourself in Brazil. People grow under pressure and I think I applied just the right pressure to move you from Director to Vice President."

Asmi nodded. "So, this is your leadership style?"

"Oh, it gets a *lot* worse," Matthew said. "Are you ready for it?"

Asmi smiled and said, "Bring it on."

THE DREAM BIG
WORKBOOK

EXCERPT FROM THE BUSINESS WORKBOOK
"AND THEN SHE SAID..."

USE the following template to create your career plan; you can create a career plan across any number of years, and you can be as detailed or as high level as you wish. Your career plan is a work in progress, and it will change as you grow, and your dreams for the future change. Think of this as a working document that is not set in stone and evolve it as you evolve.

	Year 1–4	Year 5–10	Year 10–15	Year 15–20	Year 20–25
Age					
Title					
Level (IC or L)					
Salary					
Skills to gain	1. Skills 2. Skills 3. Skills	1. Skills 2. Skills 3. Skills	1. Skills 2. Skills 3. Skills	1. Skills 2. Skills 3. Skills	1. Skills 2. Skills 3. Skills
Personal achievements	1. PA 2. PA 3. PA	1. PA 2. PA 3. PA	1. PA 2. PA 3. PA	1. PA 2. PA 3. PA	1. PA 2. PA 3. PA

IC = Individual contributor; L = Leader

AND THEN SHE SAID...10
Coaching Lessons To Help The Everyday Woman Take Her Next Step

BY ASMI VEMULA AND CARA CAPAMAGI

"If you want to get a quick coaching lesson, this is the book. Every woman should read this." **Jo Shaw, Executive Coach**

"In a world where good coaching is hard to find; here is a book that helps with instant lessons and stories that inspire. I'm in awe of Asmi and Cara. When's the sequel coming?" **Kaylee Murphy, CEO, A Big Brand**

ABOUT THE AUTHORS

Before **Asmi Vemula** was a bestselling author and Chief Marketing Officer at GTech, she used to have the "I don't think I'm ready" disease, which she had to overcome to take her next step. In the process, she had to grow thickened skin around her heart to be able to manage the onslaught of demands that comes with being an executive. She had to learn to engage herself even when the chips were *way* down and go from "I don't think I'm ready" to "Hell, yeah, that job is mine."

Before **Cara Capamagi** was a bestselling author and the VP of HR at GTech, she used to have the "Who gives a shit, I'm outta here" disease. When the going got tough, she got going until she decided enough was enough and she was going to stay and fight to make the world a better place. And that's how she took her next step.

Notes

EXCERPT FROM THE BUSINESS WORKBOOK

1. Women in the Workplace 2017 report by McKinsey & Company and LeanIn.Org
2. Bowler, R.H., Babcock, L, Lai, L. Organizational Behavior and Human Decision Processes. Science Direct, Volume 103, Issue 1, May 2007, Pages 84-103

AND THEN SHE SAID...I'M NOT ENOUGH

1. Victoria Budson, founder and executive director of the Women and Public Policy program at the Harvard Kennedy School of Government, told Bloomberg Law Oct. 13, 2017.

CAREER VS. FAMILY...WHO'S WINNING?

1. https://www.washingtonpost.com/news/wonk/wp/2014/10/30/study-women-with-more-children-are-more-productive-at-work, April 2018

AND THEN SHE SAID...HE DIDN'T MEAN IT, I'M JUST BEING SENSITIVE

1. Werber, C. (2016, September 14). Women at the White House have started using a simple, clever trick to get heard, https://qz.com/781404/women-at-the-white-house-have-started-using-the-simple-trick-of-amplification-to-get-heard-not-interrupted/
2. Darren C. Treadway, Brooke A. Shaughnessy, Jacob W. Breland, Jun Yang, Maiyuwai Reeves, (2013) "Political skill and the job performance of bullies", Journal of Managerial Psychology, Vol. 28 Iss: 3, pp.273 - 289

HOW DO I KNOW WHAT I WANT?

1. The Wheel was originally created by Paul J. Meyer, founder of Success Motivation® Institute, Inc.

AND THEN SHE SAID...WHY SHOULD THEY GIVE ME THAT JOB?

1. Hewlett Packard Internal Report, 2014

About the Author

Amulya Malladi is the bestselling author of seven novels, including *The Copenhagen Affair* and *A House for Happy Mothers*. She knows her airports well because she works as a marketing and communication professional for a large global company. After fourteen years of mostly bad weather in Denmark, she moved to Southern California where she now lives with her husband and two sons. *The Nearest Exit May Be Behind You* is her eighth novel.

facebook.com/authoramulya

instagram.com/amulyamalladi

Also by Amulya Malladi

Made in the USA
Lexington, KY
30 August 2019